LYGIA DAY PEÑAFLOR

creep

A LOVE STORY

Clarion Books
An Imprint of HarperCollinsPublishers

Clarion Books is an imprint of HarperCollins Publishers.

Creep: A Love Story
Copyright © 2022 by Lygia Day Szelwach
All rights reserved. Printed in the United States of America.
No part of this book may be used or reproduced in any manner
whatsoever without written permission except in the case of
brief quotations embodied in critical articles and reviews. For
information address HarperCollins Children's Books, a division of
HarperCollins Publishers, 195 Broadway, New York, NY 10007.
www.epicreads.com

ISBN 978-0-35-869292-8

Typography by Julia Feingold
22 23 24 25 26   PC/LSCC   10 9 8 7 6 5 4 3 2 1
First Edition

When I was a high school senior,
a starry-eyed freshman crept up to me
at my locker and said,
"You have the cutest boyfriend."

Thank you, starry-eyed freshman.
This is for you.

A thing that you see in my pictures is that
I was not afraid to fall in love with these people.

— Annie Leibovitz

Laney Villanueva and Nico Fiore are here. They're walking toward me. She's holding books. Physics. Spanish. A tablet. He's carrying a black Jansport and wearing his purple sweatshirt that's ratty at the cuffs, the one he wears on cool mornings and carries home on warm afternoons. His eyes. Her smile. Their hands, tightly clasped, announce, *Here we are!*

The decals on the glass doors say, HOLY FAMILY HIGH SCHOOL: BE THE LIGHT! Every day I see those words. I stand behind this counter and stare at the letters backwards, and today is the day they finally make sense. BE THE LIGHT! Laney Villanueva and Nico Fiore shine.

Laney's in front of me wearing her Leadership Club polo shirt. This is the closest I've been to her since last spring when she stood behind me in line for confession. I listened to her and Anna Largo as they whispered. I wanted to hear what Laney was going to confess. I needed to know, had to know, couldn't live until I knew about her and Nico and the things they'd done together. Laney's sins must have been beautiful. But the whispers were about Anna's brother and his drinking. Anna's parents were running out of options. It was nothing important. It wasn't about Laney and Nico, their private selves, their vices, their secrets.

Laney Villanueva is happy and tan, even under this fluorescent lighting. "Hi," she says. There's a dimple in her left cheek because she's trying to kill me. "We're just getting in." She peeks at the principal's office. Through vertical blinds, we can see Father Philip on the telephone. Laney leans forward and says softly, "We were at the DMV." The scent of coconut shampoo clings to her wet black hair. I'm lightheaded from breathing her in.

Nico Fiore is rubbing her back. I can feel the even pressure of his fingers circling, I mean I can almost feel it, warm, comforting, tingly. I wonder if Laney is used to his touch or if it's distracting her at this very moment, even after ten months of being his girlfriend. She takes the quickest, slightest breath beneath his palm, only a flash of a response, but I see it, and I know what it means. Nico Fiore's touch will bring shivers until the end of time.

"We took the driver's test," Nico says. His sandy-colored hair is wet, too, and it smells the same as Laney's, of coconut and . . . what is it . . . something else . . . almond.

Laney has touched his hair. I've seen her touch it. She knows how soft and how thick it is. Just yesterday they were hugging out by the soccer field. I watched her squeeze the back of his head and curl her fingers into his scalp as he lifted her loafers off the grass. The wind blew, Laney's hair covered them both, and suddenly they were faceless, in their own separate world. I thought: this is autumn—it's the beginning of everything, not the end.

"You *both* took the driving test?" I ask. "I thought it was impossible to book an appointment." Seniors complain all the time, how they have to wait weeks for a test.

"I guess we just got lucky." Laney shrugs.

I squint at them. I've already seen them in and out of Nico's car. He already has a license. "Don't you drive a black Jeep?" I ask.

"Me? Uh. No," Nico says. "You must be thinking of someone else." He blinks. Even his eyelashes look wet. I picture him emerging from a swimming pool in slow motion, like in a commercial, his skin golden, his face upturned toward the sun.

"Oh," I say. "Probably. Sorry." They're lying about the DMV, and now so am I. We're in this together, the three of us, Laney and Nico and me.

I check on Father Philip, who's searching though his file cabinet. May he never find what he's looking for.

"Well," I tell Laney and Nico, "Mrs. Bardot stepped out for her coffee. But I can give you late passes."

Father Philip looks up at me for a split second.

"I just need to see the DMV papers," I say, in case Father Philip can hear.

"Okay . . ." Laney rifles through her tote bag, a puffy, quilted pouch with gold buckles and multiple compartments.

Item by item, she unpacks her life onto my counter. I want to run my fingers over Laney Villanueva's things: her fat yellow hair tie, a Ziploc bag of baby carrots, earbuds, her makeup pouch, index cards bound with a rubber band, highlighters in green and pink, a paperback *Othello* tabbed with multicolored Post-its, a handful of Luden's that click softly as they hit the surface, her fuzzy socks with pastel stripes. *Her ballet slippers.* Satin pointe shoes scuffed at the toes with lamb's wool bursting out from the insides. I can smell the leather soles and Laney's dried sweat. I want to bend them in my hands, feel the stiffness and the give. I have to—I can't help it—I reach out with my right hand and touch a ribbon with my pinky, its frayed end like a feather against my knuckle. I want to *be* her.

"I guess I must've lost the papers," Laney says.

I slide my hand away.

"I probably dropped them somewhere between the DMV and here." She sighs and begins to repack, tucking her pointe shoes away as she shakes her head.

"Darn." I want to keep Laney and Nico here with me for longer, for as long as I can. "Well . . . um . . ." I stall.

Their eyes—hers, dark dark brown, and his, shiny bright hazel—hang on my answer. "Did you guys pass the test?" I say finally. "Because I can copy your temp licenses to put on file."

Nico has a zit on his chin, a small pink bump that's higher and pinker in the center. It will break through tomorrow. Whenever I see Nico Fiore from across the cafeteria, it's as if I'm watching him on television. He grows taller and broader every season, and his hair goes from neat to shaggy and then neat again. His friends revolve around him. They move in and out of his storyline. Here, at arm's length, Nico Fiore is better than a TV character. He's real. I could reach out and feel his chest. He's flesh and blood and flaws. A real boy with a pimple.

"No. Neither of us passed," the real boy says, avoiding eye contact. The real boy isn't used to lying; he isn't good at it.

"I'm sorry." I stand as still as can be. I don't want to let Laney Villanueva and Nico Fiore go.

"We're terrible drivers," Nico says, looking sweetly at Laney, as if he's proud of how terrible they are.

"It was the parallel parking." Laney unfolds her hands to place them parallel. Her nails are trim and manicured with clear polish. "I didn't know what I was doing." Nico watches as Laney skews her hands perpendicular.

"That's okay. Neither did I." Nico and Laney lock eyes— dark and dark to hazel and hazel.

Suddenly, I disappear—I'm invisible to them.

"I hear that's always the killer. . . ." I say, although I no longer exist. "The, uh, parallel parking."

It's just him and her now, and the flyaway hairs that Nico is tucking behind Laney's ear. He's savoring the task, as if each strand is a reason he loves her. "It's all right, though," he says softly. "It was only our first time."

Laney leans on her elbows and tilts her head to look up at him. She's gone now, she's lost in him.

He gazes back at her. "We'll get it right. Don't worry."

She closes her eyes slowly, she inhales, her body rises.

Nico traces the outline of Laney's face with his thumb. It's over for him. He's gone, too. He's lost in her.

"We just have to retake it, right?" he's whispering to her now. As I watch them, I slip deep inside the folds of a secret. "We'll have to do it a bunch of times."

They've done it.

They slept together.

They did it just this morning for the very first time. An hour ago they were in bed, under the covers and wrapped up in each other. And then they were in the shower together, flushed and sore in tender places, laughing over what they'd just done. Then they came straight here. To me. Now I smell coconut and almond shampoo on her and on him. On them. The scent fills me to the brim. This is the biggest morning of their lives, and I'm the very first person to see them. It's a miracle to witness falling.

Love.

Laney blushes two shades redder. She drops her head and lets out a long breath. Her hair cascades onto my counter. Nico lowers his face and kisses her earlobe.

I'm done.

I'm gone.

I could watch them together all day, maybe forever. They're that beautiful.

I wish I could . . . I wish . . . I could reach my hand out. "I guess it's okay . . . this time," I say, finding my voice.

Laney lifts her head lazily and stretches. Nico shifts forward. I've broken their spell. It's my deepest regret.

"Just don't forget the test papers, next time you . . . retake it." I clear my throat.

Laney smiles dreamily at me. I stop breathing. "We won't forget next time," she says. "We promise."

We.

Laney Villanueva and Nico Fiore are a *we.* They wake every morning and fall asleep every night un-alone in the world. How does it feel? What is it like to have someone and to be someone in return?

"So, you'll stamp our late passes?" Nico asks.

It's the most ridiculous question that's ever been asked. I would stamp their passes to Emerald City, to Narnia, Terabithia, Disneyland, anywhere they want. Ask me to stamp anything, Nico Fiore, and I'll stamp it.

I lean back and peer at Father Philip again. He's looking out his window this time, gesturing as he talks on the phone.

"No problem." There's no other answer.

"Yay!" Laney springs up and down on her ballerina toes. "You're the best."

I am the best.

"Thank you so much, uh . . ." She scrunches her brow, trying to think of my name.

She feels bad for not knowing it. Don't feel bad, Laney. You are so sweet to care. I'm relieved she doesn't know me, she doesn't know the things I've done. I feel free. The past is in the past.

"Rafi," I tell her. "Rafaela. But it's Rafi. I'm a sophomore."

I went to your parents' dance studio when I was little, Laney, you wouldn't remember, there were so many of us. Your mom taught me jazz. I had a pink shoe bag with Tinker Bell on it. My hair was a short bob. I hated feeling like a tomboy. What I wanted was to be like you with your silky hair that fanned out as you spun during your solo to "The Climb." Your lyrical class was after mine. I used to watch you while I waited for Gran to pick me up. I prayed for her to be late.

All of us younger girls used to watch you. You must've known. You probably heard us scurrying across the dressing room, the zippers on our bags scraping against the wall as we elbowed each other for a better view. We would peer through the one-way glass as the opening chords of your music played. The tiniest girls, sweaty and sour-necked, tiptoed and hooked their fingers over the ledge. We knew, even then, that someday a gorgeous boy like Nico Fiore would love you.

You held your opening pose, your neck lengthened with

the lift of your chin. The lean muscles in your arms and back stretched as you reached up with open palms, fingers spread. There was so much joy on your face. I remember that the most. You would've smiled whether we were watching you or not.

"Thank you, Rafi."

Laney Villanueva from Allegro Dance School knows my name. Now, in the hallways, if I say, "Hi, Laney," she can say, "Hi, Rafi," and she'll remember that *I am the best.*

"Seriously. Thanks for helping us out." Nico's face brightens. Slight creases form in the corners of his eyes as he breaks into a grin, this grin that Laney gets to see every day. No girl is luckier. "We owe you, okay?" Nico says.

My cheeks are hot. I can't look him in the eyes. His pupils are reeling me in. I have to turn away. He shouldn't be this kind—it's too much—it isn't fair.

"It's nothing." I write Nico's name and reason for lateness on a late pass: *Nico Fiore / DMV TEST.* I roll the rubber stamp on the ink pad. "You're welcome. Not a problem," I say, even though it's a big problem. I stamp Nico's card.

EXCUSED

I take my time writing Laney's late pass. I write her name in cursive, in loops and swirls, because even her name is pretty, like a vacation destination in the Philippines. *Welcome to paradise: Laney Villanueva Island.* I roll the stamp on the pad again, although it's still loaded with ink.

EXCUSED

I write the time on each card, giving them ten extra minutes for Nico to lean against the lockers like a sitcom boyfriend and wait for Laney to swap her books out.

"I gave you ten minutes," I tell them.

"Perfect," Nico says.

They'll have extra time to say whatever they need to say before wandering into class with thirty seconds left till the bell. When you're in love, ten minutes can mean the world. Isn't that what people always say? *If we could only have ten more minutes together, I'd say everything.* These ten minutes are a gift from me to them. Each word and each glance exchanged will be because of me. Say it all, Laney and Nico. Say everything.

Laney is waiting. I scan the counter, the mailboxes, the bulletin board. There must be something that will buy me another second with them. Here: the invitations I've been stuffing for Senior Banquet.

"Hang on." I lift the box. "You might want these, too," I tell them. "Family invitations to your ring night. They won't go out until the end of the week, but you can take some early so they don't run out on you."

"Great." Laney takes enough invitations for the both of them. *We.*

Nico smiles. "Cool."

I'm out of ideas, I have nothing left to keep them here, so I hold out their late passes, one in each hand. Laney and Nico give the papers a tug. I tighten my grip for a split second. *Stay with me, Laney Villanueva and Nico Fiore. Stay.* There's something in Nico's eyes and in the way he wrinkles his forehead, a tinge of something. What is it? I need to let go.

Back off, back off.

I let go. I'm flooded with emptiness.

"Have a good day," Laney says.

I bite my lip, watching them turn away. "You too."

You two.

Don't go.

I feel the same loss as when Laney hit her final pose during "The Climb"—how I wished that song would play forever. "Have a good one." There's defeat in my voice that neither of them notices.

They walk away through the double doors: BE THE LIGHT!

I whisper, "Please, come back," as Nico lowers his arm over Laney's shoulders, where it belongs.

My eyes follow through the glass wall of the main office. Laney and Nico turn left toward the senior hallway, farther and farther from me.

Don't go.

Father Philip ends his phone call. He hangs up. He adjusts the receiver in the cradle. Silence. Coconut and almond lingers faintly. The minute hand on the clock clicks. Laney and Nico have nine minutes.

Say everything.

I hope you have a great Tuesday, Laney and Nico. In a couple hours, your hair will dry. In every class, you'll take notes and raise your hands. You'll submit homework papers and move through the halls, you'll laugh with friends, eat, drink. You'll attend Mass. It will seem like you're having an ordinary day. But all the while, you'll be thinking about your morning together. All week long. All month. All year. All *life* long . . . you will think about this morning.

I unwrap a single Luden's cough drop, one that I tucked up my sleeve after they tumbled from Laney's purse. I slide it into my mouth and roll my tongue over and around the increasing sweetness. Cherry.

We owe you, Nico said. But the truth is, the simple truth, is that there's nothing else you can give me, Laney Villanueva and Nico Fiore. I've never been part of anything purer.

It's over for me.

Over and out.

I'm lost in the autumn of them.

2

We're herded into final-period Mass in the auditorium. They've rolled the mobile crucifix and communion table onto the stage. Poof! A chapel! Last Wednesday we had an active shooter assembly in the same space. Before Thanksgiving, *Our Town* will play here. Come winter, the auditorium will host Senior Awards Night.

I pass Jenna's row, where she's standing beside Sydney Bergen, her new best friend. I know that Jenna sees me. She keeps her head low, but her eyes follow me through her hair. If she's growing her bangs out, she should at least clip them back. It's not flattering. A real friend would tell her so. *I* would have told her.

Sydney Bergen belongs on the Disney channel. She wrings her hands when she's excited, and she only talks about one thing: horse camp. She goes on and on about blue ribbons, monster-size flies, horses named Warhol and Van Gogh whose tails are dyed with hot-pink and purple food coloring. There's one cute counselor who's a Junior Olympics bronze medalist. Every summer the challenge is, who will catch his eye this year? Cue Sydney's Disney show theme song, with a *neighhhh* at the end.

My class is getting ushered into row K, house left. "Step all the way in," Mr. Needham says. Holy Family is overcrowded. They need to raise enrollment standards, because this is a fire hazard. In the hallways, the cafeteria, the parking lot, and especially in Mass, we're smashed together, feeling someone's hot breath on our necks and smelling someone's body odor beneath their Axe body spray. Right now I'm stuck shoulder to shoulder with mousey, dough-cheeked Greta Novak, who's singing "Here I Am, Lord" through her chapped lips.

The choir. How could I have forgotten about the choir? I stretch up on my toes, balancing my fingertips on the seat in front of me. I know she's in the soprano section, usually in the middle, slightly to the left. There: Laney Villanueva, between her friends Kendra Darling and Aisha Moore. Laney's mouth forms perfectly rounded O's and softly widening Ah's. *Looord.* Her jawline sharpens when she lifts her head. *Heaaahhrt.*

There's Nico. Tenor, back row, peering diagonally through his section. His hair is dry now and blonder under the lights. He's watching the side of Laney's face, admiring her vowels, too. He's turning red in front of the student body and faculty, thinking of Laney's oh's and ah's from this morning. Remembering rumpled sheets, Laney's hot, dewy skin. Reliving every touch, every taste, every sound of her. Remembering in front of Jesus.

I want to know how they first met, if they knew right away that they would end up like this—together even when they're several rows apart. I want to hear the story, the way they each lived it.

I wish I could sing. If I could, I'd be in chorus with them on A-days, seventh period, choir room 500 with Mrs. Ling. I looked up their class schedules in the office after they left me this morning. All the desktop computers are synched. I didn't break into the system; I wouldn't do that. I wouldn't even know how. You can just type a name, any student, and they appear.

Laney's name isn't short for anything. It says so on her profile. It isn't Elaine or Eleanor or Alana. It's just Laney, and that's perfect because she's exactly as you see her. She's perfectly uncomplicated. Nico's middle name is Giovanni. Nico Giovanni Fiore, the name of a fashion designer or a race car driver. Either way, he belongs on a yacht off Monaco wearing a fedora. Or is it Morocco? Whichever is the one with the rich people and the race cars.

I turn to find Jenna, and then I stop myself. This happens sometimes. I want to tell her my latest findings, forgetting for a second that I don't speak to her anymore. *You'll never believe this,* I used to say. Whatever we were doing, she would stop and scoot closer, I'd feel her drawing near. *What is it? I'm dying to hear.* She'd stare; her eyelid would twitch. *You always know the juiciest things.* Jenna used to inhale the details, every morsel. *Tell me what you know.* She would beg me.

I would tell her, only her, about Laney and Nico, if we were still friends. Jenna thinks Nico Fiore is cute, too. *Let's go around,* she used to say, and so we would walk the long way to the cafeteria in order to pass him at his locker. *Nico Fiore is so adorable,* she'd say. *I love how Nico Fiore looks happy all the time. Nico Fiore in workout sweats is the hottest.*

Jenna acts as if our friendship doesn't go that far back. But I know and she knows that we were in the same third-grade class. We sat together on the bus to the aquarium and shared leftover Easter Peeps. She knows we went to Allegro Dance together. She was there in a bright blue leotard and pink tights, thinking that they matched. She stood bowlegged beside me, our noses pressed up against the glass, watching Laney do turn leaps across the floor. Laney's were the tightest and quickest turn leaps we'd ever seen.

We tried to copy those leaps in Jenna's backyard. We used to drink red Gatorade to give us "dance power." That's literally what we called it. She remembers. We'd gulp it in shots from mini juice glasses and then wipe our stained mouths on our forearms. The juice on the folding table attracted bees. We would flex our biceps and say, "Dance power!" We couldn't turn or leap half as well as Laney, not even close. It didn't matter, though, because Laney made us believe that it wasn't what was waiting on the other side that mattered. It was the climb.

My row rises for Holy Communion. A guitar strums "Behold the Lamb of God." I follow Greta, noticing the rumples in her uniform shirt. Jenna's eyes track me as I walk up the aisle.

For Jenna, this morning was nothing special, the same old routine. She lugged herself and her Frappuccino into her homeroom, watched the morning announcements, and sang praises to the Lord, alleluia. Jenna gave her bio notes a final once-over before turning the barrel of her mechanical pencil and taking her quiz. This morning was ordinary for her, empty in that everyday way, and that's why she's listening to the choir but not *hearing* them as they join the guitar in song.

Without me, Jenna is missing the details she used to love, little things that make Holy Family alive, like Nico squinting at the clock as he adds the minutes since he's been with Laney and subtracts the minutes until they'll be together again.

I step up to receive communion. The wafer dissolves on my tongue. I turn, giving the sign of the cross, just as Jenna's row stands. We'll pass each other in the aisle. There's no way to avoid her.

I try to focus on the choir as I walk. The clear, high harmonies sound pretty and light. One of those voices is Laney's. Jenna and I are walking closer. I reach into my purse and feel for my hair clip at the bottom. I pull it out and hold it at my side, turning it over in my fingers.

She's a few steps away. I hold the hair clip out to her. Our eyes meet. She reaches for my fist, but I change my mind. I can't do it. I can't forgive her for betraying me. I slap the hair clip against my thigh and rush back to my seat.

This is the way it has to be. Because for every action, there's an equal and opposite reaction. That's basic physics, Newton's third law of motion. Holy Family is overcrowded, but that doesn't stop us from getting a decent education.

3

There's a card from Mom in the mailbox when I get home. Pink glitter with turquoise lettering: TO A REALLY COOL GIRL!

> Hi Rafi,
> I hope the school year is off to a good start. I'm starting a new job this week in an actual doctor's office! Very profesh. No more retail for me! I finally get a chair. Hi to Gran and Poppy. Here's some fun money for whatever you like. Send me a selfie when you get this!
> Love,
> Mom

Ten dollars. Not bad. I'll put the card and the money with the rest, inside my old middle school knapsack that's still hanging on my closet door. If you need to hide something, leave it someplace in the open that no one would suspect to be special. Never keep secret things in your jewelry box (lesson learned).

"Hi, Gran. I'm home." I leave my penny loafers by the door and hang up my jacket. Every day I intend to put actual pennies in my shoes, but as soon as I take them off I forget. I should also look up the whole penny loafer history, because where did the concept of coins in shoes come from in the first place?

"It's always the husband or the boyfriend!" Gran is yelling at Captain Benson through the TV.

I cross through the living room to the kitchen and push coffee cake crumbs into the sink. Coffee cake is a portal to old age.

"How was your day?" I ask over my shoulder.

"This is a rare episode." Gran's eyes are fixed on *Law & Order: SVU*. "I've never seen this one."

"That's good, Gran," I say, although she's seen every episode a dozen times. This one aired over summer vacation. Gran and I watched it together while I put her blood pressure medications in her Monday–Friday/day–night pillboxes. It's the episode where a student accuses her volleyball coach of sexual abuse, but it's a misdirected cry for help. It isn't the coach. It's her mother's boyfriend who's been abusing her.

"Here's your potassium." I bring Gran a banana. It's good for her blood pressure.

"Thank you, Bianca," she says, confusing me for Mom.

"I'm Rafi, Gran," I correct her for the hundredth time. "Bianca doesn't live here." Maybe it's the school uniform that's been messing her up. It hasn't changed much over the years.

Gran shakes the banana at the television as Captain Benson interrogates the wrong man. "Stupid, stupid!" she says.

Gran is easily satisfied by television. I can't decide whether this is lucky or sad.

"Bianca's starting a new job in an office," I say, at the commercial break. There's no use trying to talk to Gran during the program. "She sent me a note. No more retail." I'm glad for

Mom. It's hard to stand all day long. Why can't they give employees a stool? Why should salespeople have to stand to fold clothes, or when there aren't any customers? I'll never understand. I show Gran the corny card. She glances at it for a second and peels her banana. Glitter clings to my fingers. Glitter is deceivingly girly and innocent. If you rub that stuff in your eyes it can blind you. "She says hi."

"I give your mother six months at that job. Six months," Gran says with her mouth full. She doesn't want me to get my hopes up. But Gran doesn't know. Things could be different this time. Things are already different. This school year actually is "off to a good start."

"Where's Poppy?" I ask.

"Polishing. Where else?" Gran gestures to the garage. The banana peel draped over her fist always reminds me of a dashboard hula girl.

I peek into the garage, propping the door open with my toe. "Hi, Poppy. I'm home."

"Rafi! Bring me that box over there." He points to a cardboard box at the far end. "I'm taking these into the shop tomorrow."

I step onto the cold cement floor in my socks and fetch the box.

"Hello, MacGraw," I say, patting Poppy's prized 1971 Plymouth Road Runner that's hidden under a sheet.

Poppy buffs a shiny car part with a rag one last time before placing it into the box. "Gotta be worth something."

"Good luck, Poppy." I wipe my dusty hands on my uniform skirt and watch as he starts to polish a grungy piece. "I talked to this cool couple today at school. They're so nice," I tell him. "And they're gorgeous. You wouldn't believe—they look like they stepped out of a magazine."

Poppy scratches his head, searching for something or other behind him. His eyeglasses slide down his nose.

"They're seniors," I add.

He picks through another box of metal whatchamacallits.

"They sing in the choir"—I raise my voice over the clanging—"during Mass."

"Here it is," Poppy says, lifting the elbow-shaped part under the light.

"I think I might become friends with them," I say. It's true. I might. I was with them this morning, wasn't I? *The morning of.* We've bonded.

Right now, Laney Villanueva is at dance rehearsal, and Nico Fiore is at soccer practice. They'll meet up afterward at the edge of the soccer field. They'll hug. She'll be sweatier than him, but he'll smell worse. Neither will mind.

Poppy's fingers slip. He drops the car part. It clangs and bounces. "Goddamn it!" He picks the thing up and inspects it. His eyeglasses balance on the end of his nose. Moaning, he straightens his back. "It's dented, for cryin' out loud." He rubs at the chrome with his thumb.

I sigh. "I'm sorry, Poppy. I'll go make dinner."

He curses at the metal as I turn my back.

In the kitchen, I stare into the open refrigerator. Laney Villanueva and Nico Fiore and everyone else go to Astro Diner after practices and club meetings. Astro's milkshakes are thick if you ask for them thick. You have to start them with a spoon because you can't suck it up through a straw until it melts a little. That's a thick shake. Some nights, parents (the involved parents) join their kids there for dinner. Holy Family calls involved parents Community Parents. I think it means we're all supposed to share them, but they've never invited me to Astro Diner.

Jenna and I saw Angela Fortunato and the rest of the theater crowd there. They kept bursting into songs from Broadway musicals that I didn't know. It was annoying and geeky, but it made me feel uncultured, so I promised myself I'd try to learn some musicals. I guess I got distracted and forgot.

Nico Fiore and his friends and Laney Villanueva and her cousins sit at the long tables and order baskets of onion rings and fries for the group. Community fries. They talk about who scored goals, who twisted an ankle, who finished the physics homework so that others can copy, which teachers are secretly dating (Mr. Ford and Ms. Isaacs, Mr. Vinson and Mr. Morley), and which students are applying to what schools.

I imagine that's where they sit. And what they eat. And what they talk about.

Laney's cousins are ultra cool, the Filipino boys who dance hip-hop at Allegro, b-boys who call themselves the V-Boys (for Villanueva). They're the real deal, the next Jabbawockeez. They have satin jackets. The last time I checked, the contest they won was up to a million views online. It's the routine that mimics the inner workings of a deranged clock—every movement ticks and rotates in perfect synchronization. They speed up until the springs break and the clock explodes. They really are *"sick mofos,"* as the comments say. The V-Boys must take up three tables at Astro Diner. One big Holy Family.

I can make turkey meatloaf again tonight. That's easy enough, and we have the ingredients. Ground turkey always looks a little pale, but Poppy isn't supposed to eat red meat. It doesn't matter that I made it only five days ago. Nobody complains.

Here's the mixing bowl and the loaf pan that's burnt in the corners. There's no use scraping at it anymore. It is what it is, the new normal.

Ground turkey. Mushrooms. Breadcrumbs. Ranch dressing mix. Barbecue sauce. Ketchup. One egg. 375° for fifty minutes.

Nobody raves, but nobody complains.

I pose, holding the package of ground turkey against my cheek. I raise my phone in front of my face for a picture.

Click.

Send.

4

Club Day in the gym is set up exactly the same as last year. The Yearbook Club table is against the same wall. The banner is the same. The poster of yearbook covers is the same. It's as though I've been standing in this very spot for twelve months. The one difference is that Mr. Tosh is standing beside the table instead of Mr. Bryant.

Seventy-year-old Tosh, in his argyle sweater vest, is no Mr. Bryant. Last year Mr. Bryant was wearing dark jeans and a light gray blazer. He stood right there drinking coffee from a thermos. *A thermos.* Like a wilderness camp counselor. Mr. Bryant didn't believe in Styrofoam. He cared about important things like the environment. I don't, but I admired him for caring about them. He was such a good role model. The second I saw him, I wanted to follow him into the woods, crawl into his tent, and fall asleep beside him in the dark.

I step up to the table and open last year's yearbook, which is out on display.

"Back again?" asks Mariah Rourke, the yearbook editor. Mariah Rourke was named after the singer Mariah Carey. She thinks this gives her greater potential for success than the average person who wasn't named after one of the best-selling musical artists of all time. This is called nominative determinism. Additionally, the name Mariah, by association to Mariah Carey, gives the impression of achievement. The reason I know this junk is because this is how Mariah Rourke likes to introduce herself to people.

"Yup, back for more," I say. Yearbook is the one thing I've put effort into. I can get stuff done sometimes, even if I'm only named after the grandfather I never see. At first it was to impress Mr. Bryant. Later, it was because of . . . reasons.

Mr. Bryant is smiling on page 16 (faculty photo) and page 66 (with his homeroom class). I remember the page numbers. On page 82, he's writing on the whiteboard with his plaid-shirted back to the camera. His hurried handwriting slants upward across the board: *How does a revolution begin?*

Page 102 is the Yearbook Club photo. I'm standing next to Mr. Bryant in that one. When we posed, I thought, *I'm standing next to Mr. Bryant. I'm standing next to Mr. Bryant.* That night, I printed the photo out, stared at it for a thousand hours, and remembered all the things he'd said to me: *you have a sharp eye, Ms. Wickham . . . you're my go-to field photographer . . . hey, you actually made me look good in this one!* We had the exact same hair color and the very same skin tone. I hadn't noticed that before. Mariah had told us to scooch closer. His arm had pressed against mine. We had been *this* close.

I'd been wandering around in here last year, not knowing what to join, if anything, probably nothing. I couldn't find Jenna. I was about to leave to eat chocolate chip cookies in the courtyard (they'd just stocked the soft-baked brand in the vending machine). Then I saw Mr. Bryant and his environmentally friendly coffee, and he spoke to me with his warm, mellow voice. "Interested in working on the yearbook?" he asked. *Yes.* Of course I was. There was nothing I wanted more.

Mariah twirls a pen as she looks me up and down. "Not to be rude, Rafi, but are you even allowed to sign up again? I mean, didn't Mr. Bryant kick you out?"

How dare she bring that up? It's none of her business, not then, not ever. How dare she say Mr. Bryant's name at all? Mr. Bryant was mine.

"It had nothing to do with the yearbook," I tell Mariah Not-Carey. "It was just . . ." I can't describe something so intense. I shouldn't have to, either, not to anyone. That was a personal, private incident between Mr. Bryant and me. And my disciplinary records are confidential. "It was a personality conflict, that's all."

Why is she being so judgmental when she doesn't even know what happened? Mariah has no right or reason to doubt my commitment to the yearbook.

Back off, back off, Mr. Bryant had said to me. I was *too involved, too close, too much.* How much is too much? Find the line, balance, balance, balance.

Mariah clutches the clipboard with the sign-up sheet against her chest, holding my happiness in her power. I want to scream. I could jump across the table and grab that clipboard from her clawed fingers, I swear.

"Come on, Mariah." I say it calmly, so calmly, although I'm balling my hands into fists. "Look. I came up with this title." I lift the yearbook. *Holy Family High School: Smiles of the Times.* It's a play on "sign of the times." I can be clever if I try. "This was my idea." I point to the year running vertically down the left side. "I take great photos. And no one else can figure out the Piktura software."

"I had to finish the layout when you left," says Miss High and Mighty with her blouse buttoned to the top. Open one button, just one, Mariah Rourke, I dare you. "I don't want to pick up your slack again."

"I didn't slack," I say. "I would have finished, if it were up to me. I didn't quit." Mr. Bryant told me to stop taking pictures. I didn't want to stop. He *made* me. "The other photographers graduated, and everybody else is signing up for Young Activists. You need me." I point to the growing line at the Young Activists' table. Can't she see? Everybody else wants to change the world. I only want to change mine. "And anyway, Mr. Bryant isn't here anymore."

It hurts to say that out loud. He's gone. Took his thermos and left. But that wasn't my fault. Was it my fault?

Mariah looks behind me at no one else scrambling to join. There is nobody else, Mariah, there is only me offering this. *Take it, take it, take it.*

"Okay, fine," she huffs.

Yes.

She sets the clipboard on the table and slides it toward me, giving in, giving up, shoulders slumped. I'm her last resort, which is good enough for me.

Isn't this year better already? I feel it in my bones. Yesterday in the main office was a turning point. You have to recognize turning points. Take them and grab them and make something happen. Like this, exactly like this, like I tried to do last year. But this time I'll learn from those mistakes. I won't be too much. I'll be just enough. I'll be controlled and careful. I'm easy-breezy, they'll see. I'm everything they could want in a friend.

I pick the pen up, and I sign my name neatly and boldly—I own it. My mouth curls into a smile. My words slant upward as I write. I list exactly what I want so that I will not be misunderstood. This is how a revolution begins.

Name: Rafi Wickham
Position(s): photography and layout
Events: Senior Ring Banquet, Senior Superlatives, Senior
Awards Brunch, Senior Prom, Graduation, any and all
senior events

Laney Villanueva and Nico Fiore, where you will be, I will be.

5

At Senior Banquet, the rings are always displayed on a white linen table. If you hold the camera at a diagonal, letting the light hit them in just the right way, the gems sparkle. The result is a winning photo. This photograph I shot is a classic. I've seen it in many yearbooks before. I don't mind being unoriginal if I'm imitating something that works well for a reason.

I took several angles so that I have options, but the first one is obviously the best, with the rings sharp in the foreground and fading out of focus toward the back. This is the best these rings will ever look, before they're worn and scuffed and lose their luster.

I look up from my camera as the last few students walk across the stage. "Zing!" Father Philip, lover of nicknames, announces. Johnny Zingale, track star, reaches for his ring box.

There's no sense photographing everybody. It's enough to take shots of students from different social groups or those wearing interesting outfits (Sirus Gregory in a sparkly suit).

Here's a photo of Laney shaking hands with Father Philip at the handoff. "Ms. Laney Villanueva," Father Philip called her, because he appreciates the sound of her real name, as I do. Listen to the way it rolls off the tongue. *Vill-a-nue-va.*

The picture I took of Nico isn't publishable because he coughed into his arm at the last second. But it's Nico being Nico, so I like it. I'll keep it for myself. I'll start a private file for photos of just Nico and Laney. They'll be safer that way, separate from yearbook photos. It's what I should have done last year.

"Sea Bass!" Father Philip says. Last and limping, Sebastian Zweigart struggles toward him on crutches (unfortunate indoor waterslide incident). Applause erupts as Father Philip drops the ring box into Sebastian's breast pocket.

I'm basking in the secret I found out yesterday. The rings arrived in seven boxes when Father Philip was in the lobby feeding the parrots. The packages were labeled 1/7, 2/7, 3/7, 4/7, 5/7, 6/7, 7/7. I took the alphabetical senior class list and divided it into seven sections to figure out that Nico Fiore's ring was in package 2. I found his box and opened it, and there it was. Nico had their initials engraved inside of it.

L.V. & N.F.

I bet he'll give her the ring tonight. She'll probably wear it on a chain. They're like a couple from the nineteen-fifties who "neck" at the drive-in.

The ring spun heavy and loose around my finger. It was okay to try it on. I didn't scratch it, and I wiped it with my sweater before I put it back. The green stone sparkled under the light when I moved it around. I ran my index finger over the initials to feel the ridges and pressed my thumb down hard against the engraving. Again, again, again, I pressed into it. I wanted the letters embedded into my skin. But no matter how hard I pushed, the letters wouldn't stick. The best I could do was take a picture of the initials on the inside.

"The rings came!" I said when Father Philip returned. I had repacked the ring only two seconds before.

"Ah! Should we take a peek?" he asked. "I can never resist taking a peek." Father Philip is all right.

I'm going to share my photos with him, not the picture of the initials, of course not, that one will go in the private file, but this one of the rings on the table, for sure, and the others from tonight. He may want some for Holy Family's social media. He's concerned about me joining yearbook again. Every Wednesday when I help him clean the parrot cages, he says something about the dangers of me "falling back into an unhealthy space." But if he sees me taking my position seriously, he'll know that I'm not doing any harm. He'll like this ring picture; it's very profesh, as Mom would say.

Father Philip is onstage now with one hand over his forehead as the lights flicker red, violet, white. "Who's ready for a bit of entertainment? I know I am! Because what would Senior Banquet be without the V-Boys causing me to question Holy Family's liability insurance, am I right?"

My classmates hoot, "V-Boys! V-Boys!" I lift the camera. Hello, Nikon, my old friend. Check me out, the one with the Yearbook Club's Nikon D4. I am Rafi Wickham: *official*.

The V-Boys rush to claim the stage. Their music pounds through surround speakers: *"Showin' you what's real, get it, get it, get it . . ."* Quicker than I can press the shutter, they're flipping off of each other's shoulders and sliding across the floor on their heads. They're jackhammers trembling. They're diving, spinning, falling, catching, being caught. One day, when the

V-Boys are superstars, I can say that I saw them perform at our high school. I took pictures that prove it. *I know them.*

I can't photograph them while they're in motion. Although the reviews of the Nikon D4 say that it's "perfect for wildlife and sports photographers," none mention how it stands up against the V-Boys. All I can manage to capture are blurry streams of light, circular whips of hands, bent knees, flashes of stark white sneakers, and one, two, three smudged bodies propelling through midair. I swap the Nikon for my iPhone to shoot a video. I can watch the footage later, moment for moment, and freeze it into still pictures.

The V-Boys aren't fireflies you can trap in a bottle. You have to watch them from afar, this far, from behind tables ten and twelve, where Villanuevas young and old, big and small, are cheering, up and out of their seats. As Fernando Villanueva torpedoes from one end of the stage into his cousins' arms, the Villanuevas pump their fists. They holler, showing who they are to each other: their own biggest fans. A Wholly Family.

Laney's table of Filipino moms and dads and aunts and uncles are on their feet. Littler Villanuevas, who are nine and ten and eleven, pop to the beat at all the right moments. They've seen the routine a million times from behind the studio window, in the backyard, the basement. They've even practiced it with their big brothers in the living room. In a few years they'll be on this stage at their own Senior Banquet. Some of these kids are probably even more talented than their older brothers, more natural, with better rhythm, and they know it. They'll be ready. They're ready now.

I gave Laney the invitations to this banquet, extra invitations, more than other students got. Now her family is sharing this moment because of me. They'll want to remember it, and they will, because of my photographs.

Angela Fortunato and her theater crowd are over there against the wall, cheering through their cupped hands. They're losing their minds with every move because their Broadway shows can't compare. I've seen commercials for their beloved musicals with the pasty green face makeup and mechanical props that lower from the ceilings. Where's the thrill? Where's the danger in that?

The V-Boys pull the bandanas off their heads and twirl them on the tips of their index fingers. The senior class jumps to its feet. There's a sound now, a low drumming that's growing into thunder by the second. What is that noise? I don't know until it reaches table eight, where I can see the seniors tapping the blunt ends of their silverware against the white tablecloths. A single *tap* has escalated a hundred times over, pounding as the V-Boys bound off the stage.

Nico Fiore is the first to jump onto Fernando Villanueva. He rubs Fernando's head and hugs him so hard that he lifts Fernando off his feet. I feel a pang of sadness. Will they ever be happier than this? I try to push the feeling aside, but I can't. This is it. This is peak joy.

"Hey, Rafi? Can you help us serve dinner?" It's Greta No-vak. She is a gnat—why is she always in my face? "Two volunteers didn't show up for Leadership Club. We're missing people on potatoes and meatballs. Can you do one?"

"Shhh! Go away, Greta," I tell her. The overhead lights are dimming. The stage is turning halo purple, bending the room into a cool calmness. There's a snare drum, a *swish, swish, swish.*

In front of the stage, a quartet begins to play, their bows rising and dipping against their strings. I lift my camera. I recognize the song, "This Year's Love." I heard it in a movie about a girl and boy who choose immortality but then spend eternity trying to find each other again. Laney is about to appear. I know it. I feel my limbs melt a little. Dancers stride onto the stage in light gray leotards and long gossamer skirts. One girl, followed by another and then another, and then . . . Laney.

I'm eight years old again, admiring her through the one-way glass, wishing I could balance as steadily and look as pretty and be both delicate and strong at the same time.

She lifts her hand now and turns it up toward the light. Such a simple movement should be nothing at all, and yet, it is something so lovely, it makes everyone stare. What does that feel like?

I shift my gaze toward the only thing worth shifting my gaze for: Nico Fiore is watching his girlfriend dance. Beneath a flicker of orange light, Laney fans her leg up and around, painting one fluid circle in the air with her toe. Nico's face shows what's in his heart, an expression that makes my chest hurt. I'm happy for Laney and sad for the rest of us who will never be looked at this way. Nico Fiore, can you believe she's dancing for you?

I gasp when Laney does them—four turn leaps across the stage of pale blue light. Her jumps are even higher and lighter than they were years ago. With each leap, she's suspended for a breath, the way I feel watching Nico watch her.

"We really need your help," Greta, the gnat, says. "There's an apron for you."

"I'm working, Greta!" I nudge her away so that I can

photograph Laney's lean, steady arabesque.

I am still eight, but Laney has grown. Time goes and goes whether we join it or not.

Stay, Laney, I pray, as the string quartet fades and the lights soften into white. Laney bows, stretching a pointed toe behind her. It comes again, this sinking feeling. Why does every song have to end? "Last and last and last," I whisper to myself. I swipe through my camera roll—I have her here, still twirling and sweeping beneath the lights. I press the camera against my chest. I've captured her.

A red-faced Nico Fiore nods as his friends pat him on the back, as if he performed the dance himself. They know that he and Laney are a *we*. Everybody knows.

"Rafi? Will you?" Greta will not quit.

"Shit, Greta! Fine!" I yell, as the crowd applauds. "Christ. Give me the stupid apron."

●　●　●

No matter what kind of food you serve, it starts to look disgusting after you've slopped it onto twenty plates or so. At least mashed potatoes are plain and relatively odorless. If I had to serve the meatballs I would've thrown up already.

I got this down to a rhythm. Take the plate with my left hand and plop a spoonful of potatoes with my right. The thwack is strangely satisfying. *Thwack!*

"I'll have some potatoes, please. Hey." It's Nico Fiore, so handsome in a jacket and tie that aren't the school uniform jacket and tie. His zit has healed. A perfect face on a real boy. Nico Fiore makes my palms sweat. I have to wipe them on my apron. "Thanks for helping the Leadership Club tonight. Laney was worried they wouldn't have enough hands. Most of the members are in the banquet."

"Sure! I love volunteering." I scoop his mashed potatoes like no one has ever scooped mashed potatoes before. "And I loved her dance. She's incredible. She's always been so talented."

"Thanks," he beams, taking the compliment for her. *We.* "Whoa! That's enough!" Nico laughs.

I look down. His plate is one huge mound of mashed potatoes. "I'm sorry," I laugh too. "I . . . it's a big spoon." I lift the big spoon that's covered in mash.

"That's okay." He takes the plate happily. "I like potatoes."

Nico Fiore is so nice I could cry. I watch him move up in line and add green beans and carrots on top. His collar is twisted in the back. When he returns to his table, Laney will raise her hands over his neck and straighten it for him.

"Hello, Rafi."

I turn my head. Blood rushes to my face. I blink once. I blink twice. Somehow, I formulate words. "Mr. Bryant?"

Mr. Bryant is here.

"It's been a long time. How are you?" he asks. His face is fuller, but his calm, bright eyes are the same. Mr. Bryant's face.

He's here.

"Fine," I lie. My voice sounds funny, as if I'm hearing myself underwater. I might be drowning.

I've envisioned seeing him again. I've dreamed of it and fixated on it happening in so many different ways, but I never thought it would be like this, not today when I'm wearing an apron with a pinkish stain on the left boob. It should have been me finding him, me approaching him with my shoulders back and a speech ready, a speech that I prepared and rehearsed in my head dozens of times. There is nothing in my head now except for the words he said to me last spring.

Your behavior has been highly inappropriate.

You've put my family and me in a very uncomfortable situation and are causing problems for me on a professional level.

I think it's best if you drop the Yearbook Club.

"What are you doing here?" I ask, looking into those same eyes that once stared at me in that awful way.

Back off, back off.

"The senior class invited me," he says.

Of course they invited him. He's beloved, him and his blue whiteboard marker that used to stain his right cuff, him and his alt rock playlist in the yearbook office, him with his daughter's hair ties in his shirt pocket, him and his dog fetching sticks at the freshman orientation barbecue. Him.

I should have known he was coming. I handled the invitations for tonight. I stuffed them into envelopes and addressed them. But Mrs. Bardot had taken A–L and left me with M–Z. How can one seemingly meaningless detail completely change the course of this moment for me?

"You've joined Leadership Club, I see." He gestures to my big spoon. Damn you, big spoon.

"Yes." A white lie won't hurt anybody. He's the one who left Holy Family without a word, so he shouldn't expect the plain truth from me.

I want to ask where he's teaching now, how he likes it, does he miss it here, does he miss us? But I know he won't answer.

Does he miss . . . me?

Too personal. Not appropriate. Let's stick to the yearbook, shall we?
I want to ask, I need to ask, *Did you leave because of me?*

"That's great," Mr. Bryant says, lifting the plate from my hand. "It's good to see you doing so well."

Am I well? Am I doing *so* well?

Mr. Bryant's food is getting heavy. The line is impatient behind him. I have to hand his plate back. *Too clingy. Back off, back off.* Look at how I'm handing you the plate, Mr. Bryant, I am letting go. I smile at his daughter, Beatrice, who's clinging onto his leg. I'd like to say hello to her and comment on how much she's grown, but Mr. Bryant wouldn't like that.

I'd like you to leave me and my family alone.

"Thank you. It's good to see you too, Mr. Bryant," I say, even though it isn't. It was supposed to be, but this isn't how I wanted it to go at all. I can barely breathe. I'm shaky and unbalanced.

His phone is sticking out of his pocket. *Password: BossMan.*

How do you know his password? Jenna found me in the girls' room. I had swiped Mr. Bryant's phone from his desk during a yearbook meeting. From the way she looked at me, in that same horrible way, I should have known she would stab me in the back. *You're reading his texts? Don't you think that's stepping over the line?* The line. What is this line? No one ever tells you what the line is.

"Keep the line moving, Bea," Mr. Bryant says to his daughter. "Do you want any chicken?"

Mr. Bryant is here. He's here in a blue Ralph Lauren sweater over a button-down shirt. He's taking a piece of chicken from the next tray. He's asking if there's butter on the broccoli. He's lifting the broccoli. Mr. Bryant is back. But . . . he's pointing to the dessert table and . . . his wedding ring . . . is gone.

No ring. Tonight is Ring Night, but Mr. Bryant's wedding band (plain gold with a beveled edge) isn't on his finger.

"Is Mr. Bryant's wife here?" I ask Carter McKinley, who's beside me with the vegetables. Carter McKinley knows everything. He leads the academic decathlon that's been on the local TV channel. His team is still undefeated after four rounds, according to the morning announcements.

"He got divorced over the summer," Carter says.

"What?" My gut lurches. I watch Mr. Bryant's back as he and Bea head to their table.

"Bummer, right? His wife seemed real nice, didn't she? She was always at our events and stuff. Not that she can't still be nice, maybe she is. I mean, what do we know?" Carter says.

I shake my head. "They can't be divorced," I say. At Holy Family, the family is holy.

"Oh, they are. He just kept it really quiet." Carter scratches his nose on his arm. "That's probably why he left. Maybe he wanted a fresh start."

So, he didn't leave because of me. I hadn't meant that much to him. But the real reason is ten times worse.

"I know because my mom's his Realtor," Carter says. "Two bedrooms, two baths, backyard space, move-in ready. Those were his only asks."

"May I have some potatoes?" Someone is speaking, but I can barely hear.

All I can think about is the Bryants: Mr. Joshua Bryant, Mrs. Nina Bryant, Noah Bryant, Bea Bryant, Boss Man the Scottish Terrier Bryant. I used to watch them. They looked so happy.

When Mr. Bryant forced me to delete the pictures I'd taken, I told him he would regret it someday, but he made me hit Delete one by one.

Delete them right now, Ms. Wickham. All of them. I said now!

"Can I have a little more, please?" a voice asks. "Like, half a scoop?"

The Bryants are divorced, and these people are still asking for potatoes? How can they be so insensitive?

I took a picture of the Bryants at a football game last winter. The kids had hot chocolates, and Mr. Bryant and Mrs. Bryant were wearing matching Holy Family woolen hats, the green ones with the white pom-pom on top that are $14.99 in the school store. How can a couple get divorced six months after wearing matching hats? It doesn't make any sense.

Inappropriate on a professional level. Back off, back off.

I drop the big spoon and balance myself against the buffet table. I'm drowning for real now; there is no air.

"Potatoes, please?" someone asks.

"Hey, are you okay?" Carter asks. He picks up my spoon and serves a dollop for me. *Thwack!* That sound is the one comfort left in the world. Everything else has vanished.

Mr. Bryant once mentioned that he likes to make Mickey Mouse pancakes for his family every Sunday morning. Now what? It's not fair for children to go from having Mickey Mouse pancakes to not having Mickey Mouse pancakes. I want to walk right up to him at table twenty-two and tell him so.

Back off, back off.

"Go take a break," Carter McKinley tells me. He's manning both the potatoes and the vegetables now, two big spoons at a time, while I struggle to catch my breath. Carter will be on

Jeopardy! one day. *I'll take mashed potatoes for two hundred.* He'll answer the Daily Double without pausing to think.

Why is it so hot in here? It's as hot as those final days of school last June, when Mr. Bryant brought fans from home into his classroom. How could a woman divorce a man who brings his own fans for his students? I need to know, I need air, I need something.

Over there, at table twelve, Nico's father is showing off his golf swing. Laney's father is following along, eyeing an imaginary golf course in the distance. Nico is taking Laney by the hand and whisking her out to the courtyard. They pick a spot beneath the oak tree where the kid with the black nail polish on his thumbs usually strums his guitar. I know just what Nico is saying as he pulls the ring box from his suit jacket. This is the oxygen I need.

Laney, I want you to have this. I had it engraved. I can practically hear his voice.

She's looking at the very same ring that I had around my finger yesterday. I know the feeling in her heart. I felt it myself as the stone sparkled.

You did this for me? she must be saying.

She's hugging him now; she loves the ring so much. Laney should be wearing a poodle skirt and a matching hair ribbon.

L.V. & N.F.

I'm breathing again, full deep breaths, as if I'm standing beneath that tree with them.

"Why is Carter serving at your station?" Greta asks. Gnat. Gnat. Gnat. I want to smash her over the head with a giant fly swatter. "Is everything okay?"

"Everything is fine," I answer, because everything *is* fine. The Bryant family doesn't exist for me anymore, but there is still something good here. "There's nothing to worry about," I tell her, lowering the Nikon. "I caught it on camera. I caught the whole thing."

6

Gran is asleep, curled up on the sofa. Her mug is empty. I feel terrible. I should've been here to refill it. I've been serving food to other people while she's been out of tea.

"I'm sorry, Gran. Good night." I tuck the blanket under her chin and lower the volume on her rerun. "Good night, Captain Benson," I say to the television.

"The garage clicker is dead," Poppy says, shuffling his way inside. He rifles through the kitchen drawer. "Whenever you need batteries, you can't find 'em. Whenever you don't need 'em, they're rolling around everywhere."

"That's true, Poppy. The world is full of inequity." I sit at the table and scroll through my camera roll. "Thank you for picking me up so late."

"That's what I do," he says. "I drop you off, I pick you up."

"Do you want to see the pictures I took? My friend Laney danced. And her cousins did a routine."

"Here's some. No tellin' if they're dead or alive, though. There should be some kind of indicator," Poppy says, rolling two or three AAA batteries in front of his eyes. "Hold on. Let me fix the clicker first."

I won't show Poppy these pictures of Nico and Laney in the

courtyard. He doesn't need to see them. That was a private moment.

"All right. Let's see those photos," Poppy says, pulling his jacket off.

I swipe through, stopping at the good ones. "Here's one of Laney and the other dancers. Her parents are the ones who own Allegro. Her boyfriend gave her his ring. He had their initials engraved into it."

"Friends of yours, you said?" Poppy asks.

"Yes," I say, flipping through more.

I don't tell him that I saw Mr. Bryant. It would only upset him. There's no need to mention it, and I didn't do anything wrong—Mr. Bryant came to *me*. It doesn't matter anyway. I'm doing so much better.

I find the best picture of the rings. "This is one of the display."

"That's a winner." Poppy has a pretty good eye for aesthetics, with all his knowledge of classic car design.

"This one's a video of the V-Boys," I say. "They're pretty much professionals." I press Play but keep the sound low so I won't wake Gran with their music.

"Well, you see that?" Poppy yawns. "So many interesting things to take pictures of other than the nonsense from last time."

Mr. Bryant wasn't nonsense to me. Nonsense was nearly getting expelled for taking photos, which was, in fact, the job he'd assigned to me.

"I know, Poppy."

◆ ◆ ◆

I can't sleep. I have a lot to think about and so much to do. Serving the mashed potatoes gave me six volunteer points. Donating clothes to the Holy Family clothing drive will give me three more. If I keep doing good deeds I can actually become a member of Leadership Club and attend Laney's meetings. Also, Laney will probably be at the donation table.

I play the song "This Year's Love" on loop. Then I pull piles of clothes out of my closet, my dresser, and from under my bed. I sit, surrounded by mounds of old things. Soft, faded jeans in kids' sizes: ten, fourteen, twelve, eight. Scuffed sandals, size five. Black flats that tore the skin off my heels. I should've tossed them out right after I wore them. An itchy robe with a lace collar, unworn. Do all grandmas buy these for their granddaughters? Yellow hoodie with purple hearts, size extra small. A Christmas sweater with reindeer antlers. A blue and green plaid dress with gold buttons. Black pants with a snap that doesn't close.

I hated this silver dress Mom bought. I still hate it. It's still tagged: *Razzle-Dazzle Juniors*. This shimmery material is awful; it's trying too hard. But even so, how difficult would it have been for me to say thank you? I could have sent her a picture of me wearing it. That's all she's ever wanted, one nice picture. She might have been proud of me, showed the picture off a little bit, said, *Look. This is my daughter at her seventh-grade dance.* She might have wanted me. In this dress, I might've seemed more like her—with all the beautiful friends, with one true, handsome boyfriend, with admiring classmates. *A really cool girl.*

What does it matter now? This is the task at hand: gather donations and make a good impression on Laney. Focus. She'll be in her Leadership Club polo shirt, collecting and organizing and being so thankful to everyone who donates. I definitely need to gather more. That way, if for some reason she isn't manning the collection table tomorrow, I can try the next day, and then the next.

Hi, Rafi!

Hey, Laney. How's the driving going?

Hahaha! It's going okay.

Good. Well, I hope you get that license soon.

You'll be the first to know!

That's exactly how it will go when I see her.

I check Laney's social media for anything from the banquet. There's Nico's ring in her palm, tilted to show their initials inside. I widen the photo to life size and pretend to put the ring on my finger, and then I look in the mirror and hold it up to my chest, pretending to wear it on a necklace.

My phone buzzes.

It's a text from Mom. *I still don't understand why you sent me a selfie with turkey meat. Was it supposed to be funny? Can't you at least smile?*

Tonight is the night I get rid of Mom's clothes that have been stuffed in the back of her closet, I mean, *my* closet, all these years. It's my room now. It's been my room since I was three, but it still feels like hers, maybe because of her ratty clothes. They've been like ghosts hanging in here, moaning about the old days.

Mom's old clothes are a mess of faded denim, plaid miniskirts, studded belts, newsboy caps, textured tights, velour warm-up suits, and lots of black-and-white checkered patterns.

Lots. She dressed like the girls in music videos from back then, like tomboys but sexy with their belly buttons showing. I think of her sometimes, the way Dad must've seen her, prancing around all week in her school uniform, and then shedding it for these extra-low jeans, and this thing—a barely-there red tube top, the fabric so thin and so stretchy, it could easily be a headband. There was no resisting her. How could I expect this girl to be a mother to me? It's been my mistake, really. There are ticket stubs still in her pocket from the St. Brigid's Carnival. There's no date on them. They're still valid. This girl can still ride the rides.

These cotton minidresses are dusty on the shoulders from too many years on hangers. I think this is the black-and-white one from her birthday pictures. Eighteen. She's standing behind her ice cream cake; HAPPY BIRTHDAY BIANCA! She's smiling, holding a new cell phone that's still in the box.

I wonder what she wished for as she blew those candles out. Certainly not for me, although I was just around the corner.

These clothes that are closer to the front of the closet are a little more mature. Why did she have so many dress pants? Black and gray and navy, one in red and another in brown. For jobs, maybe, her earliest ones that didn't pan out.

I carry out an armful of flannel shirts. Some still have the sleeves rolled up, as if she'd worn them just last night. I pull the blue and white one off its hanger and put it on over my sleep tee. Is this the shirt? The one she wore the night she and Carlo Tedoro did the deed and created me? I have no reason to believe it's the one, but in my head, it is. I'm convinced that this is the flannel shirt, and these were the black ripped jeans, and this

gray tank top with the star on the chest is what she wore underneath. This is the outfit she chose before she got knocked up.

The star tank top is so narrow. How small had she been before I came along? I hold the tank top up against my torso. So
small. Add her expanded waistline to the list of reasons she re-
sents me.

I think these clothes are enough to donate. I can't even see
my carpet anymore. It looks like pop princesses exploded in
here. I'm sure the purses and the jackets and coats will go to
good use. I could keep this black wool coat with the red lining.
It's not bad. I can replace the buttons. Some of these things I'll
throw away, like the long underwear with the rip in the crotch,
the drawstring bottoms with paint stains, and the sweatpants.
No one wants holey sweatpants. Better yet, I'll cut them up
for Poppy so that he can use them as polishing rags. When did
Mom wear long underwear? I don't think she's ever been skiing.

I can maybe fill five Hefty bags to donate. That's five chances
to talk to Laney.

Thank you for your donation, Rafi!

You're welcome. I think I can scrounge up some more.

That would be great. You're so thoughtful.

Will you be here tomorrow?

Yes, I will.

Cool. I'll be back then! Tell Nico I said hello.

I will. Thanks!

That's the way it'll be. It's almost midnight now. I'm tired
but accomplished. Look at that mountain I have created! I lean
back against my bed, legs splayed, covered by cropped tees and
nubbly sweaters.

It's just me in Mom's still-rolled flannel shirt, surrounded by her pilled American Eagle Outfitters, her old Old Navys, and her stretched-out Forever 21s. Forever 21. Ha. That's Bianca. For twelve years I've lived with her things but not with her.

Here I am, Looord. Is it I, Looord? I blink at myself in the tilty mirror, Bianca's mirror in Bianca's childhood bedroom. I lift my phone and aim at my reflection.

Here we are, Lord—all the things Bianca left behind.

Click.

Send.

7

I knew it! Laney is working at the donation table with Lionel Rush. Her hair is in a high ponytail secured by that fat yellow hair tie. This is her casual, busy-day ponytail. I'll say hello, I'll ask her how her driving practice is going. I'll tell her to say hi to Nico for me. I'll say that I can—

"Next!" Lionel calls. He tosses a bag of donations into a deep bin behind him labeled OUTERWEAR.

I tell the girl behind me to go ahead while I pretend to check my phone. I don't want to drop off with Lionel.

"Whoever's next!" Laney says. She throws a bag into the bin labeled ADULT.

I give her my shiniest smile. "Hi, Laney!"

"Hi." She looks over my shoulder and yells at Steve and Henry Volpe, who are waiting in line. "No lamps! No, you guys. It's just clothes."

The Volpe twins stand dumbly, *dimly,* with a matching set of acrylic lamps sticking out of a box.

"We can't take those. Please don't dump them here," Laney says, exasperated.

Steve nudges me aside. "People need household items!"

"She said no lamps! Now get lost!" I push Steve out of the

way and plop my bag on the table. "*I* brought clothes. Girls, fourteen to eighteen."

Laney laughs as the Volpe boys grumble away. "Thank you, Rafi."

Bingo! She knows my name.

Laney lifts my bag with one hand and supports the bottom with the other. "You wouldn't believe what people have been dragging in." She hurls the bag into the KIDS bin. "A toaster, pool noodles, a freakin' fish tank with pebbles and coral and everything. Clothes, on the other hand? Not so much."

"I can bring more," I say. "I love purging. It's so freeing. Will you be here tomorrow?"

"I should be," she says. "That'd be great."

I'm on a roll. "How's the driving going?"

"The what? Oh, it's going well." She's blushing. "We're getting the hang of it."

"Good." I smile. "Tell Nico I say hello."

"I will. Thanks for donating. Sign the list, okay?" Laney points to the paper at the end of the table. "Next!"

RAFI WICKHAM, I sign the list, along with my email, phone, homeroom. When she sees my name, she'll appreciate me all over again. If I do something for Nico, too, they'll talk about what a great girl I am, and they'll fold me into their circle, for sure.

The school parrots, Cain and Abel, are squawking in the lobby for their breakfast. Father Philip will be on his way to feed them any second. I'll hurry back to the main office so that I can be there alone. There's that smell again, BO and Axe in this jam-packed hallway. Get out of my way.

I was right. There's Father Philip, headed in the opposite direction with the birdseed container. The biblical Cain and Abel were a farmer and a shepherd who gave sacrifices to God. In an oil painting in our religion textbook, Cain gave crops and Abel gave sheep. God liked Abel's sheep better, so then Cain murdered Abel. Today, Steve and Henry Volpe are Cain, and I am Abel, minus the murdering.

Are you cleaning your bedroom? Are those my clothes? What are you doing with them? Can you make sure you don't throw away anything valuable? Mom texted back last night.

She had been young and happy and so thin in those clothes. But it was worth the sacrifice. It couldn't have gone better for Laney and me.

I sidestep through backpacks and reach the office. Mrs. Bardot's green sweater is here, but she and her coffee mug aren't, so I can log into the computer system. This isn't wrong. Again, I'm not breaking into the system. There's no ID required. There's no password. Just click the dropdown menu and choose SCHEDULE. This isn't deviant behavior. It's all right here.

If there was anything valuable, you would have taken it already, I reply to Mom.

8

This is Nico Fiore's after-the-final-bell look: shirttail hanging, tie loose around his neck, hair messy. He's just dropped Laney off at the dance studio in the north wing. I missed the dropping off because of the crowded hallways. This has become a big problem. I don't want to miss any other encounters. This is supposed to be my year.

"Nico!" I call.

He turns. His eyes land on mine in a perfect TV over-the-shoulder moment where he looks straight into the camera. "Oh, hey, Rafi."

Rafi, Rafi, Rafi . . . Nico Fiore knows who I am.

"Hi," I say, panting. "Do you have a second?"

"Yeah, but only a second. I have soccer," he says. I already know this. The team warms up every day at 2:45.

"I have a surprise for you," I say, but not too excitedly. This is a medium I-have-a-surprise-for-you level of excitement.

"For *me?*" he asks. He seems taller and broader now that he's so close. *He's right here.*

"I gave you and Laney both a ninth-period study block for next term," I say. He could easily swing his arm around me. I'm only fantasizing, obviously. Anyone would fantasize about him. I would never do that to Laney. I understand loyalty.

"Huh?" He has three small birthmarks on his neck. I imagine Laney tracing them with her finger to form a triangle that points to his heart. *This is yours, my heart belongs to you.*

"I did it on the office computer," I say. "I brought up your schedules and compared them side by side. Laney was supposed to have AP Enviro and you were supposed to have Business. But there were two other sections of each, so I swapped them and put you both in study halls."

He looks at me sideways. "You did what?"

"There wasn't room in the same study hall," I explain. "I'm sorry about that. I had to put you in the cafeteria and her in the band room. But you can meet up after attendance."

He shakes his head. "Why would you do that?"

He thinks this is strange. People aren't used to kindness in this coldhearted world. He thinks *I'm* strange. This can't happen, not again.

Back off, back off.

"Oh. It was nothing," I backpedal. "I was bored, that's all. I did it for some of my friends, and then I realized I had to do it for people in random grades so it wouldn't be suspicious."

I hope this sounds believable, that I would tamper with schedules out of boredom, and that I have friends.

"No one will know," I say. "Once changes are made, they're made. Plus, there's no way to track it."

"O-kaaay," he says, but I can see that he's tense.

I want to tell him that Laney really appreciated my clothing donation. She likes me. She doesn't think I'm strange. All I want to do is make them happy.

"You really should have asked me first." Nico walks toward the locker room.

I follow. I can't let him blow me off. "Teachers haven't gotten the schedules yet, so they won't even know where you were originally," I say.

"Fine, whatever," he says.

Whatever? He's walking faster.

You're reading Mr. Bryant's texts? Don't you think you're crossing the line? Jenna had said.

My pulse quickens. I notice a crack in the ceiling that runs down the wall to the corner of the exit door. Is that the line? I see the dirty slab of marble at the threshold of the boys' locker room. Is that the line? How am I supposed to know where the line is?

"I'm sorry," I say. My stomach is sinking. "I—I didn't think it was a big deal."

We stop in front of the locker room.

"Heeey," Nico says. His eyes soften. "No worries, all right? Just don't go changing my grades or anything." He lets out a sweet, soothing chuckle.

We're sharing a laugh together now—Nico Fiore and me—so everything must be okay.

"I won't! I promise," I say. Nico and I are cool. I did a good thing.

This study hall will be perfect for him and Laney. They can spend last period of the day together. It's extra time. The gift of time. I want to say this, but he has to get to practice. He has an away game this Thursday at 4:00 p.m. against St. Paul's.

"Hiii, Nico." Cat Lorrey, a senior with long legs and a rolled-up uniform skirt, is walking toward us. Cat Lorrey has been flirting with Nico Fiore ever since she broke up with

DeShaun Faust. Cat always manages to talk to Nico at lunch whenever Laney sits with her dance friends. And she always seems to have something to suck on—a lollipop or Popsicle or licorice. She wants Nico to focus on her mouth, which is sugary sweet and talented at suction. Cat Lorrey must be eliminated.

"How's it going, Nine?" She names his team number and squeezes his forearm as she passes.

Don't touch him.

"What's up, Cat?" Nico answers, unfazed by her hand on his arm or the lilt in her voice. Such a good boyfriend.

Cat bites her lower lip and spins on her loafers. "I'll see you outside," she says, turning into the girls' locker room. The girls' soccer team practices at the same time as the guys. She's going to run past him in short shorts and bounce the soccer ball on her knee. She'll sweat through her jersey, and then, right in front of him, she'll tie it into a knot over her belly button.

"I'll let Laney know about study hall," he says. I stare up at his light brown eyelashes. He pushes through the door. The smell of sweaty gym socks wafts toward me.

It's all working. They're going to talk about me fondly. "Okay." I wave as the door closes. "Have a good practice!"

I'm buzzing with energy, I don't even know what to do with myself, so I enter the girls' locker room. The walls have been repainted in here, thank goodness. They used to be a gross putty color that made me look like a corpse in the mirror. This powder-puff pink is probably sexist, but it's an improvement.

I hear Cat Lorrey talking to a friend in the bathroom. Catherine Harper Lorrey. I looked her up in the system the other day after I saw her flirting with Nico. I wanted to switch her into a different lunch period, but I couldn't make her schedule work without messing with her classes.

Cat Lorrey has senioritis. She took honors classes in grades nine through eleven. But this year, not a single higher-level course. She takes electives instead: Film Classics, Fashion Illustration, TV Broadcasting. You have to admire her a little. She knows how to enjoy life.

It's possible that Cat isn't slacking. Those are respectable fields. She could be serious about these courses. She would actually make a perfect TV broadcaster with her straight teeth and her sultry enunciation. ESPN would eat that up.

This is Cat Lorrey, reporting live from Holy Family, where we're waiting for Nico Fiore to walk off the soccer field so that I can say, 'Hiii, Nico,' while sucking a Blow Pop.

Cat is still in the bathroom while her team exits the back door. That's her duffel on the second bench, the one with the yellow handles. Sometimes people forget things at home like running shorts or a tank top or deodorant. It happens. Other times, people forget more important things, like cleats. It's a real shame when that happens, because then they can't go out and practice with the team. They can't hit on another girl's boyfriend out on the field, either. Yeah, it's a real shame.

My chest pounds as I unzip the duffel. It's a rush, this fear of getting caught, doing a good deed for Laney and Nico, and the high from paint fumes. I grab Cat's cleats and hurry out with them under my jacket. They're grass-stained, heavy and big, at least a size eight. She's so tall. She's perfect for television. I don't know what to do with these shoes. I haven't thought that far ahead.

I veer toward the main office, only because it's someplace familiar. No one in this wing is even paying attention to me. I look straight at them—Owen Ivers, Hillary Poplar, Mrs. Harding—but they don't suspect a thing. They barely see me, they rarely ever do. It's okay to be invisible. People are always so hungry for attention, but attention is overrated. They forget that invisibility is a superpower. Look what I can do!

In the office, I put the sneakers in the lost and found bin. It'll be as if someone found them and dropped them off. How thoughtful!

"Rafi!" Father Philip calls from his office.

I jump.

"I'm updating the school website," he says. "Can I use some of your photos to jazz it up a bit?"

I let out my breath. "Sure! Cool."

"Great. Come in," he says, "I'll show you what I'm working on."

I glance back at Cat's sneakers at the top of the lost and found pile. I haven't been caught. Everything's fine. I'm not in trouble. Not this time.

Cat had to be taken care of. Even though the school uniform rules are strict, the girls' PE shorts are skimpy. Nico doesn't need Cat prancing her long legs around him, and neither does Laney. Sometimes, when nobody notices you but you notice everybody, it makes you the smartest person in the room. This is all for the best, even for Cat. It's important to be a girls' girl. We should look out for each other this way. Cat shouldn't get so hung up on a guy who's taken. I'm saving her from heartache so that she can focus on her broadcasting career.

Nico Fiore, congrats on scoring today's winning goal. Is there any-thing you'd like to say to ESPN viewers?

There sure is, Cat. I just want to thank my good friend Rafi Wick-ham for all her support. Rafi, you always have my back. I couldn't have done it without you.

At Holy Family, sitting on the front steps with our homework open is the thing to do while we wait for buses or rides. This is a prime seat, where I can lean back against the pedestal. As soon as I saw Colin Hennessey putting his pens away, I got ready to pounce and snagged his spot.

It's been four days since I've seen Laney and Nico because of Senior Retreat. Four whole days! The retreat is supposedly for prayer, reflection, and bonding activities. They've been classmates for four years. How much more bonding do they need? Meanwhile, my bonding activities have fallen behind. And Laney hasn't had the chance to thank me for the study hall.

They were back today, but I didn't see Laney and Nico at all because I missed lunch. Mariah Rourke had asked me to ID about a zillion students in a random band photo. Mariah doesn't know anyone's name but her own. It's so annoying.

This is a skill, pretending to do homework. I wonder how many hours I've spent faking it and what kind of student I'd be if I actually studied. But each of us has fallen into our roles at Holy Family. If I suddenly became a scholar, it would upset the delicate balance of our community. Besides, it's hard to concentrate when I have this excess energy bouncing inside my body.

But isn't it a good thing to see life in bright, boosted Technicolor, like one of Gran's remastered old movies?

Look at Valerie Setton at the bottom of the stairs. Her name is on the honorable list in the lobby every single semester, but see how she's sulking? What good is a near-perfect SAT score when she can't appreciate what's happening around her? Any moment now, Laney Villanueva and Nico Fiore will exit through those doors. Wake up, Valerie Setton! He'll be in his shorts, even though it's chilly, and she'll be in Holy Family sweats thrown over her leotard. They'll be hungry and tired in a good way. They'll hold hands. He'll reach into his backpack for his keys, and—

There they are.

I hop to my feet and zip my backpack. It feels like I haven't seen them in so long. Nico's cheeks are red. He's downing the last drop from his water bottle. Laney is unwinding her scrunchie. With eight steps left to the bottom of the staircase, he leans in to tell her something. She tilts her head back and laughs. He watches her face, pleased to be the one who makes her laugh that way. She takes a breath and laughs again, which makes Nico laugh, too. Do you hear that? Can you see it? Valerie Setton, you are missing out. This scene is worth far more than test scores.

They're walking through the parking lot now, and so am I. Her arm is hooked around his. He's clicking the doors open. I'm following quicker. They're tossing their bags onto the back seat. They're getting in.

I can't let them leave. I've missed that feeling—of being near them, of seeing them up close, of knowing what they know, like on that morning, *the morning of.*

In a blink, they'll drive away. *Don't go.*

Nico is pulling out of his parking spot. *Please don't leave.* It will be another day lost, another day of watching them from afar, when what I'm meant to be is with them. They have to see me so they'll remember. *It's me, Rafi.*

Nico lifts his arm over Laney's headrest and backs the Jeep out slowly. He looks over the right side. He looks over the left. Laney checks her phone. I run toward them, fast, fast, faster. My heart, my head, every part of me is pounding. I need them. I have to, have to, have to—I hurl myself at Nico's Jeep, shoulder first against the back corner of his passenger side. My body makes one solid *thud.* I imagine my organs crushed behind my skin as I spin. My backpack hurls into the street. I'm on the gravel, running my palms over my chest, my ribs, my stomach, my pelvis. The Jeep screeches to a stop. The doors fly open.

"Oh my god!" Laney helps me up. "Are you all right? Rafi?"

She knows me. *I am the best.*

"I'm so sorry! Shit! Shit!" Nico's face is ghostly white. See how much he cares? "Fuck! I didn't see you. I swear, I looked over both sides. I'm sorry!"

He did check both sides. He's a good driver. He passed his test—EXCUSED.

"No, no. I'm an idiot," I sputter. "I wasn't paying attention. I was looking through my backpack. I thought I'd forgotten a book. I didn't see you pulling out."

I stand on wobbly legs. This is the stupidest stunt I've ever pulled. What if Nico had freaked out and hit the gas?

"Are you okay? Does anything hurt?" He's mortified. He should be, he could have killed me, for god's sake.

"Should I get the nurse? You need ice. Did you hit your

head? You might need an ambulance." Laney touches my elbow lightly with her small, warm hand. She looks as though she's about to cry.

Laney Villanueva cares about me.

"No," I say, "I didn't hit my head. I'm fine." I could have cracked my skull open. What the hell was I thinking?

"You're sure?" Nico leans his face so close to mine.

"Positive. I'm all in one piece, see?" I hold my palms up. I'll be black and blue tomorrow, but I really am fine.

Relieved, Nico rubs his face with both hands.

"But we're definitely giving you a ride home, right, Nico?" Laney says. She is such a sweetheart. She's picking my backpack off the ground and placing it in the back seat.

"Of course. Absolutely," Nico says. "It's the least we can do."

We.

It's happening. They're escorting me into their life. He's leading me to the door. His hand is on my lower back. I feel all the tingles I dreamed I would feel. Nico Fiore is touching me. This is our very first touch. This is the smartest stunt I've ever pulled. It's the ultimate bonding activity.

I'm pinching myself, literally pinching my thigh, as if the other aches and pains aren't enough to prove that this is real. Do you see me in Nico Fiore's Jeep? Here I am with the windows open and the wind in my hair. We're driving down the school exit.

Check me out. This is what it feels like to be invited. My whole life is turning around. Didn't I say it would? I made it happen. Believe it.

Laney Villanueva and Nico Fiore and I are turning on

Grenadine Lane to Turnbow Drive. Dru Howard and his sister Odetta are stopped to our right. Dru glances at us. I've been seen.

The light turns green. Nico turns the radio up, playing a rap song that I look up on my phone so I can learn it tonight. I will memorize "Crash! Damn! Boom!" by EXO feat. Matt King Kole if it's the last thing I do. I will also search for an interview to find out if it's pronounced "ex-oh" or "E-X-O" because I can't think of a worse way to embarrass myself.

One of my assignments from Mariah Rourke is to take photos of the cars in the student parking lot, a traditional spread in our yearbook. As Poppy's granddaughter, I have a special appreciation for this. If he has taught me anything at all, it's that people like to look back at their first car and reminisce about the places they went and the friends they drove around. In the future, when Nico looks back at the photo of his Jeep, he might remember me.

Laney Villanueva and Nico Fiore are rapping while I'm in the back seat. They're better than a reality show couple because there aren't any cameras. They're not performing; they're actually this upbeat.

Laney turns to me, her eyes bright in the afternoon light and her fingers curled around her seatbelt, as she raps the second stanza. I nod along wordlessly. She'll think I'm just shy, that's all, that I need time to warm up to new people before I feel comfortable enough to rap with them.

This can only be to my advantage. People don't like when you're too eager too soon, I know this now. You can't just walk up to a person and say *take me in.* Mr. Bryant may not think I understood him, but I did. Nodding wordlessly makes me look reserved. See, Mr. Bryant? I get it.

Laney rhymes the crazy-fast bit that ends with *"No way, not ever, not me, not you,"* and then she points at me.

I point back.

This is our song now, Laney's and mine. Next time I'll know the words and I'll join in. She'll feel that we've built trust over time, which is a natural way to grow a friendship. We'll pump this song up while getting ready to go out, and every time that line plays we'll point at each other with a lip gloss applicator or a curling wand.

I'm memorizing the smell of this pleather upholstery, the way Nico rests his left hand on top of the steering wheel, and the way he scratches his neck, leaving red marks below his nape. His hair has grown even shaggier and curlier at the ends. He's like a displaced California boy in New York. He belongs on the beach with his wetsuit peeled down to his hips, showing his flat abs. He should live there someday, in San Diego or Malibu or Santa Monica; he'd fit in, and so would Laney. I could find them there, sitting pretty under the sun. I could touch the back of his hair right now, so easily. But this is just my active imagination. I wouldn't do that. *"No way, not ever, not me, not you!"*

He'll get his hair cut soon. Why does this make me sad? I shoo the feeling away by listening to the sound of his voice and Laney's voice rapping. I want to remember everything, even the pistachio shells (he's a healthy snacker!) in the cup holder, the precious, fragile little shells.

Nico revs the engine once, twice, because he can. This is living. He's a real boy with his hands on the wheel, and we're zooming. Laney Villanueva and Nico Fiore are the modern-day "Brenda and Eddie," the popular steadies who ride with the car top down in Poppy's favorite Billy Joel song.

Laney rubs her boyfriend's arm as they shout the chorus, *"Fuck this shit, the doom, the gloom. Here comes the sun, my son. Roll the stone from the tomb. We're back to the livin' now. Crash! Damn! Boom!"* When she swears (EXO sure loves the F-bomb), Nico laughs because the cursing is the opposite of her. I wonder again how Laney and Nico, the couple, began. I wish I'd been there to see it: his first sight of her, her first words to him, how it felt for them to *know*. I'm certain it happened loudly and instantly.

I'm smiling, remembering that morning, *the* morning, post-shower, pre-Mass. Nico knew that I knew about his car and his license. Now I'm his passenger. We're deeper into the lie. Nico Fiore and I are thick as thieves. We've been through so much together; these experiences bind us for life.

Back at school, there are stamped late passes on file in the main office, but Nico knows and Laney knows and I know that there are no DMV papers to match. Partners in crime is what we are. My joints are starting to ache. My body is stiffening up, and my palms are skinned raw. It means that this is really happening—we collided. I don't care that it hurts. Remember how this feels.

We stop at the light on Kent Street. There's a girl on a bicycle at the curb. I recognize the bright blue backpack. It's Jenna. She turns her head and looks me directly in the eyes. Her face asks a million questions that all boil down to, *What the hell are you doing in Nico Fiore's Jeep with him and Laney Villanueva?* I'm high on this moment. This is payback from the universe for the way Jenna shit on our friendship.

Laney turns so that I can see her phone. "Which one do you like better?" The pictures show two long-sleeved leotards. One is a rich wine color with crisscross straps. The other is emerald green with a plunging back. She wants my opinion!

"The wine. Definitely," I answer, aware that Jenna is still watching through the window. "It's a classic color, but modern with the crisscrosses." *Look at me! I am not sad. I do not miss you. I am not lonely!*

"See?" Laney says to Nico. "She likes that one, too!"

"Okay! So wear that one," he says.

I face Jenna and flash a bitchy smile that I didn't know I had in me. She's gobsmacked by me and by them in this vehicle that's throbbing to the beat. That's a new term for me, gobsmacked, but I'm into rap now and open to all kinds of words and the ways they can be manipulated and interpreted. I bet Jenna has never even heard of EXO. I look ahead as Nico presses the gas pedal.

Eat our dust, Jenna. I. Do. Not. Need. You.

Crash! Damn! Boom!

Eat. It.

We're picking up speed. Laney squirms out of her sweatshirt and throws it over her headrest. The sleeve whips my cheek, smelling of studio sweat, coconut, and almond—Laney Villanueva.

"Did I just whack you in the face?" Laney asks. She's so sweet. "I'm so sorry! That was the last thing you needed."

"It's okay," I laugh. "I'm already black and blue everywhere else. My face might as well match."

"Don't say that! I feel bad." She puts her hand over her heart.

"That's it. Rafi will never hang out with us again," Nico jokes.

We're hanging out! "No. That's not true," I say. This is just the start of the three of us.

Nico peers over his shoulder at me. "You'd better wear elbow pads next time, then, and a helmet."

Next time! I might explode from happiness.

"Which house?" Nico asks, turning onto my block.

"Fourteen. On the right with the red shutters."

Nico slows in front of my house and then comes to a stop. "Whoa . . . sick car. What is that, a Road Runner?"

"Yup, a '71," I say.

How lucky can I be? Nico is into cars, and Poppy has picked today to uncover the Road Runner in the driveway and let her sparkle. Poppy says that sometimes there's no harm in showing off a little. *Thank you, Poppy, thank you.*

"Man, she's gorgeous." I tuck that word into my memory, the way Nico says *gorgeous,* emphasis on the *gor.* "And that color. Wow."

"Thanks." I'm so proud, as if I painted the car myself. I wish I had, so that I could impress him even more. "It's called Petty blue. My grandfather had a '71 Plymouth Road Runner when he was a teenager, and so he bought the same model again, same color. He says it keeps him young."

"I love that." Nico says. He's so sentimental.

Laney touches Nico's hand. She's not thinking about how lame it is that I live with my grandparents. She's not wondering where my mom and dad are at all. She's thinking that she wants to be the woman who'll make Nico feel young when he is old, the girl who'll make him feel like this boy forever. I know that she is that person for him. If it isn't Laney Villanueva, then it's nobody.

"My grandfather named her MacGraw, after the actress Ali MacGraw," I tell them. "Both Road Runners. Both times. He says the two cars share the same soul."

Laney is googling Ali MacGraw. "Oh, *Love Story,* I've heard of that movie. She was so beautiful," she says, and I realize that beautiful girls calling other girls beautiful is beautiful.

"She still is. *Love Story* was filmed here on Long Island," I say. "Did you know that? At Old Westbury Mansion."

"Really? I love that place," Laney says. "My family took my dog Panda there a few years ago. They have special days for dogs."

I ask if they want to step out and look at MacGraw. They do. We open our doors. Their sneakers hit the driveway, *my* driveway, in front of *my* house. Nico squints as he inspects the car. Laney leans forward, cupping her hands around her eyes to look through the window. I would run inside for the key so that they can see the interior, but I'm afraid that if I leave, they won't be here when I get back.

Laney calls the matching blue leather "plush." It's my new favorite word.

"It's all original," I tell her, "the upholstery and everything."

"Can I take pictures?" Nico asks. So polite. This is what he meant by asking first.

Anything, Nico, anything you want. Everything.

He takes pictures of MacGraw's black racing stripe and front emblem. "One tough car," he says. "Man, I would love to drive a car like this someday." He takes pictures of Laney posing against the hood like she's Natalie Wood and he's James Dean. She says she wishes she had a headscarf and sunglasses. I agree. Wouldn't that be adorable?

I want a picture with them so bad. I want to have it as my lock screen. I want it in a frame beside my bed. I want it in my locker, on my laptop, in a locket around my neck. I grip my phone and I hold it up, about to ask. I open my mouth—

Back off, back off.

"Let me take one of the both of you," I say instead, because I'm learning. I don't want to ruin this. I'm being likable. I'm doing so good, I can't believe how good. I use my own phone first, sneaking in one shot, and then Laney hands me hers.

I can upload the picture in the Yearbook Club office and paste myself into it. That's not lying. We really were here together. There are creative solutions to every problem. You just have to think outside the box. That's what makes me a good yearbook photographer: creativity and determination. Take that, Mariah Rourke.

They're finishing up here. Nico's taking one last shot of MacGraw head-on, and Laney is walking back to the Jeep. I wish I could ask them to come inside. *Stay, please come inside. Spend time with me. Don't go.* If only I had the kind of house with nobody home, snacks in the fridge that are not coffee cake, and all the right songs by rappers with capital-letter names playing from hidden speakers in the ceiling. *We can order a pizza. Do you like garlic knots?* I want to say. But that's not my life. I will die before I let Laney Villanueva and Nico Fiore see *SVU* and Gran in her no-slip socks and her nasty

Metamucil fiber drink on the folding TV table.

"Thank you for the ride," I say. "It was really nice of you guys."

"It was the least we could do," Nico says. "You're sure you're okay?"

I hold my elbow, which is ballooning as we speak. "Yeah. I'll put ice on it. I'm all right."

"Good." Nico pats my other arm. Our second touch and counting! I feel my cheeks redden. "I'm so sorry again."

"Not your fault," I say. "I'm a walking disaster."

Nico laughs. I memorize the sound. "Thanks for the photos. Love the car."

"Take care of yourself, Rafi. Maybe take some Motrin," Laney says, and she means it. She wants me to feel better.

They're driving away. Goodbye pleather, goodbye St. Christopher medal that hangs from Nico's rearview mirror. It's okay, though, nothing is lost. I shouldn't be sad this time, because look at everything I've gained. The proof is right here on my phone. It's a bounty: a picture of Laney and Nico standing in my driveway. You don't drive someone home or step onto their driveway, you don't care about a person's elbow unless you're friends. We have more quality time in our future because we're friends now, and friends come back. My life is plush. *Behold St. Christopher and go your way in safety.*

Inside, I grab an ice pack and hurry to my bedroom. I can't open my laptop fast enough. There are so many things I need to learn, and I want to learn them tonight.

EXO is pronounced as the individual letters, E-X-O. He says so himself in this online interview. *People want to know me.*

They hear the music, and they wonder. Who is he? What's this man all about? I tell 'em, I'm E-X-O.

This music video has the lyrics scrolling across the screen, so here I go. I hold the ice pack against my elbow, ready to play "Crash! Damn! Boom!" (featuring Matt King Kole) on replay for the rest of the evening, because I have some muthafuckin' words to learn, ya dirtyass bitches.

10

Rifling through Mom's old high school notebooks is an act of desperation, but I'm too lazy to read *Of Mice and Men*. The title alone bores me. Who cares about mice or men? I know, I know, it would probably take me less time to read the thing than it would to find it in Mom's notes. I don't even know if she studied it in the first place. It's the shortest book I've been assigned since *The Outsiders* in eighth grade. But, what can I say? Sometimes I just like to make life harder for myself. What makes this extra sad is the fact that Mom was maybe a C-student, so not only am I spending my time looking for someone else's work, I'm spending my time looking for someone else's bad work.

I was sure this blue notebook would be English, but it's Algebra II. I always use a red notebook for math and a blue notebook for English. This is another example of why Mom and I will probably never get along. Clearly, numbers go with red, words go with blue, social studies goes with yellow. Her notebooks are all wrong. Lavender for American History? What's so American about lavender?

Here it is—English. Green? Huh.

This notebook is from her senior year. There won't be anything about *Of Mice and Men* in here. It has Shakespeare and *The Things They Carried* and—

—notes between Mom and a friend, their slanted handwriting squeezed into the left margin:

Are you going to Missy's party tonight?

In theory.

Huh?

I'm saying I'm going to Missy's but really going to Carlo's.

That's hot.

His parents are away.

Code for boww-chicka-woww-wowww?

A lady never tells.

So, sex, right?

Obviously.

Get yours, girl!

You're such a loser. Are you going to Missy's?

Yes—in actuality.

Ha!

Mr. U. is wearing these pants again.

Maybe he has ten of the same.

Unlikely.

Unlikely as me passing this final. I'm lost.

Me too. I can't remember any of this.

Me either. I give up. Shoot me.

I don't know who Mom was writing to here. There are other notes between them, but no name. It doesn't matter. What *does* matter is that she was talking about Dad, and the date on the Shakespeare review notes says June fourteenth. My birthday is nine months after that.

I read the notes again and again. Now I'm convinced of it: that night, the night of Missy's party, changed my parents' lives. June fourteenth was the night I was conceived.

I don't know what to do with this information. What is there to do? I comb through the rest of the notebook, but nothing else seems important.

Did you watch the show last night?

So dumb! Season 1 was way better.

Yeah, right? I don't care about the new people.

But hello Billy Newman with that haircut holy shit.

I know. Stupid hot.

I flip back and reread June fourteenth. I think about Mom lying to Poppy and Gran about the party. I picture Poppy dropping her off at Missy's house, seeing her girlfriends there hanging out, and then Dad picking Mom up and the two of them going back to his place.

It's what I do. I drop you off, I pick you up. Poor Poppy had no idea.

Would Mom make the same choice if she could go back in time? I can't stop staring at this dumb green notebook filled with half-assed notes about half-read assignments. These are Mom's final moments of youth. Her final moments of freedom.

Ding! My email sounds. I look up.

You're invited!

My mouth falls open. It's from Laney Villanueva. I touch the screen. This is real. This is 100 percent not a joke. It's an actual invitation.

It was well worth risking broken bones for this. I would do it all again. I'd throw myself at that Jeep again—headfirst. And then I would show up to this party in a full-body cast if I had to. I take a screenshot of the email and stare at the invitation some more. There is no taking this away from me. It's mine, with my name on it: *Hi Rafi!* Exclamation point! She's excited to invite me.

> *Thank you for your donation to Leadership Club!*
> *PARTY TIME: Saturday 8pm*
> *WHERE: 717 Dunbar Street*
> *HOSTED BY: Fernando Villanueva*

This is the best thing that's happened to me since . . . this is the best thing that's ever happened to me.

xo Laney Villanueva

XO. Pronounced *ex oh,* meaning kiss and hug, which is exactly what I'm going to do when I see her and Nico at the party (our third touch and counting). I can see it now, a crowded house with the music loud, my classmates in street clothes, their exposed skin in tank tops and short skirts, sneakers with loose laces tucked into the tongues. I can practically taste salt and vinegar chips. I can smell beer in the air.

I imagine them—Laney and Nico—being their jeans-and-T-shirt selves, welcoming me in. *You came! We're so glad you're here!* They'll let me into their lives. Life. Their one singular life together.

This is even better than I could have dreamed—it's at Fernando Villanueva's house. Fernando, Laney's cousin and Nico's best friend on the planet. I'll be in a Villanueva house, a house where Laney's family members blow out birthday candles and open Christmas presents, where Fernando and his brothers breakdance in the basement under strobe lights.

Don't tell me his house isn't like that because it is. Everybody knows about the strobe lights and the disco ball in the basement hung by Fernando's father, and old DJ equipment that splices the V-Boys' competition mixes: *Rage, rage, rage! Freeze! And pop pop pop to the top! Let's ride it! Let's ride it!*

Just search for "V-Boys" on YouTube. This is how they live, with barbecues in the backyard with roasted pig, noodles served out of a huge pot, crispy egg rolls, and cardboard boxes splayed flat on the deck so that they can spin on their knees and backs and heads. It's not a grainy, muffled music video. It's the Villanuevas on a Saturday afternoon.

I look again at the notebook in my lap.

Are you going to Missy's party tonight?

In theory.

Missy was Melissa "Missy" Knoll: gymnastics team, SADD, orchestra. Dark, curly hair, big smile, bright pink lip gloss, as seen in Mom's yearbook pages 16, 30, 42, and 99. Melissa Knoll had invited Mom to a party. Melissa Knoll had made a playlist and had bought sodas and chips and beer. Melissa Knoll had hidden her family's breakables and had dimmed the lights and had opened her door. But Mom and Dad never walked through that door. They had said they were going, but it had been a lie. Instead, *boww-chicka-woww-wowww*.

And so, here I am.

I'm going to Fernando's party. If you want to break a cycle from one generation to the next, this is what has to be done: make different choices. Put English in a blue notebook instead of green. Accept an invitation. Show up where you're expected, and take hold of what the universe has to offer.

RSVP: Yes, thank you for inviting me, Laney. I will see you there! Exclamation point!

11

"It looks like this is where the action is," Poppy says. He slows the car on Dunbar Street. Seniors are parked on either side. There's no black Jeep, but Laney and Nico might have gotten a ride with someone else. If they're planning on drinking, it's the smart thing to do. They're very responsible.

"That's it ahead," I say. The lights are on at Fernando's house. A group of juniors walk up the driveway.

"You're meeting some friends inside, you said?" he asks.

"Laney, the girl who invited me." I wrap my hand around the door latch. "She's a senior."

"A senior, huh?" Poppy inches the car forward. "That's something."

"You can drop me off here."

"No, no." He pats my leg. "Nothing but five-star door-to-door service for you."

I unbuckle my seatbelt. "I can walk three houses."

"Hold on, now."

I release my belt and sigh.

"When your mom went to parties, I worried that she'd have too good a time." Poppy rolls slowly, very slowly, toward the house. "With you, I worry that you won't."

"I *will.*"

"That's the kind of talk that concerns me. Don't put so much pressure on yourself. Sometimes we build these things up in our heads and they don't live up to the hype, as they say."

"I haven't built it up, Poppy."

"The thing about parties is that they're hit or miss, you see. Sometimes we have fun. Sometimes we don't. No big deal." He stops in front of Fernando's driveway. Finally!

"Thanks for the ride, Poppy." I fling the door open and slam it behind me.

It's a warm night, but I wanted to wear my jean jacket, so I unbutton the cuffs and roll the sleeves up, which is how the other girls have been styling theirs anyway.

This jacket is perfect because of all the pockets: pockets on the hips, small, buttoned pockets on the chest, and deep pockets on the inside. I don't need a purse because of the inside pockets. They're also useful in case I want to take a souvenir (nothing valuable, nothing anyone will miss), just a little something from Fernando Villanueva's house that I can keep.

I recognize the song that's playing inside the house, I even know the words: *Crashin' toward you like a meteor, ain't no stoppin' gravity, we're collidin' like a tragedy.* Here I come, Rafi Wickham, stepping into this party as I mouth the lyrics like *a really cool girl.*

Laney and Nico aren't here yet, but that's okay. I can look around and get used to everything so that I feel more at ease when they get here.

"Hi! I'm Fernando. What's your name?" Fernando touches the back of my arm, which is almost like being touched by Laney since they're related, or Nico since they're best friends.

His touch counts. Fernando is wearing a silver-and-black track-suit and bright white sneakers. His hair is freshly buzzed on the sides and sculpted in the center to form a wave. He looks like someone famous. Father Philip will have a word with him about his haircut, but Fernando is well liked, so he won't get any demerits or detention. Father Philip will secretly like this haircut. He'll probably tell me as much.

"I'm Rafi," I say. I also tell Fernando that Laney invited me, because I want him to know that I belong here.

"Yeah, sure," Fernando says. His black eyes will lead me into a world of backyard barbecues and pyramid backflips. I'm ready for all of the Villanueva family things. "Welcome!" he says. "There's drinks in the kitchen and snacks in the dining room. Help yourself to whatever." He's sincere. I could fix my-self a bowl of cereal, and he'd be fine with it. "And if you want to sing something, you put your name and your song title in the hat."

His brother, Archie Villanueva, the biggest, strongest V-Boy who is always the one to toss Fernando in the air, taps the mi-crophone as Celine Dion lyrics begin to crawl across the screen.

"Heeey!" Fernando calls. "Here's my boy!" I follow his gaze. They're here. Nico is carrying a heavy bag of ice. He's wear-ing a new Adidas jacket. It's navy with white—

My jaw drops. A dozen other girls turn and notice at the same time—Laney got highlights! Wow, she looks so different—good different! The streaks range from her natural dark to caramel to brassy blond. I would've cried had I known she was going to color her hair. I wouldn't have wanted her to do it. Her hair had been perfect as it was; why would she want to change it?

But now that it's already been colored, it's beautiful. She looks so . . . glamorous.

Her friends gather around her. They squeal and touch her. They're nuts over her new look. Laney makes her way into the living room, thanking everyone for the compliments. In her yearbook pictures, Laney will have two looks: without highlights and with highlights. This party will mark the night of her makeover.

On the side table, there's a photograph of all the cousins at the beach together. Laney's hair is jet black, even under the sun. I glance from Laney to the photo and back again. Before the party: dark. After the party: highlights. This must be how Mom feels about the night she skipped Missy's party to see Carlo Tedoro. Before Missy's party: no baby. After Missy's party: baby.

As Nico rushes to the kitchen with the ice, Archie points at him and sings, "'Cause I'm your laaady! And you are my maaan, Nico Fiore!"

Nico is loved in this house. He's so obviously a friend to Laney's entire family. If I had to name a quality that is completely unnecessary but extremely sweet in a boyfriend, that would be it.

He's in the dining room now, saying his hellos and high-fiving, but he keeps sneaking proud glances over at Laney. He's not only happy with her hair color, he's happy that she's happy. If I had to pinpoint one thing that's absolutely necessary to make the perfect boyfriend, that would be it.

Even when they're on opposite sides of the room, you can tell that they're together. If it were a game, you'd be able to guess that they were a couple out of everyone at the party. It would be easy, even for lazy people who don't notice much.

But if you're like me, someone who notices, you'd also see Tomás Diaz in the far corner. Tomás Diaz, the boy Laney had been *this close* to going out with last year, right before she ended up with Nico, has been staring at Laney since she walked through the door. Tomás Diaz is not over it.

Laney is talking about Carson, her hairstylist. She had shown him a picture of the color she'd wanted, and he was able to copy it exactly. She tells her friends that Carson is at the Spiral Haircase in Oyster Bay. His appointments are backed up for weeks, but it's worth waiting for him if you want the job done right. Laney's friends agree. He's worth the wait and the price. Your hair is one thing you shouldn't be cheap about.

On the Spiral Haircase's social media there are pictures of the back of Laney's head: before and after. 289 likes. I screen-shot both photos and file them away.

"Oh, Nico loves it." Laney gathers her hair in both hands and smooths it over her chest. "I think he was a little afraid when I told him I was going to do it, but he really likes it now." She glances at her boyfriend, who has migrated to the pool table. He catches her eye and winks. How does he do that? How does he know when she's looking at him? It's as if they have radar for one another.

To my left, Jenna and Sydney Bergen exit from the kitchen with beers in hand.

"I didn't know you were here," I say, surprised. I wonder who they know. I'm sure it isn't Laney. Maybe they know one of the younger V-Boys, either Fidel or JoJo.

"We were in the kitchen," Jenna says.

"You're drinking?" I laugh at her beer can. "Be careful, Goody Two-Shoes. You don't want to get wasted. Someone might tell a teacher. You could get a three-day suspension."

"Excuse me," she says, inching by.

"Let's go find a place to sit." Sydney Bergen leads Jenna by the arm the way she leads her pink unicorn back to the barn.

I want to go outside, but it's starting to rain. People are coming in from the deck. I head to the kitchen. There are finger paintings on the fridge and an abandoned house of cards on the table. On the corner chair, I spot Laney's puffy tote bag. I can find a memento. Just a tiny party favor. I should take something quickly before anyone walks in. A lipstick or a mirror or maybe a—

"So, you're still talking to him?" A senior, Kevon Knight, storms in with his girlfriend, Sasha Grady. "Tell me you're still talking to him so I know where I stand."

I spin around and stand stupidly in front of them.

"I'm not *still* talking to him. I have spoken *to* him. There's a difference," Sasha argues. I see her point. There is a difference.

"Oh, and I'm supposed to let you off on a difference? On semantics?" He puffs his chest like a tough guy. Then he turns to me. "What are you staring at?"

"Don't yell at her." Sasha points at him. "You see? That's your problem. You have no respect for women. You're so damn rude."

"Tell me what my problems are again, and I'll give you a problem."

"You mean besides annoy me to death?" she says. "Excuse

my boyfriend." She faces me. "He's an asshole. Do you need something?"

"A soda?" I say.

"See that?" Sasha says to Kevon. "She wasn't staring at your ass. Why do you think everything's about you?" She turns back to me. "Coke or Sprite?"

"Ginger ale?"

She reaches for a Seagram's and hands me the cold, wet can. "Here you go."

"Thank you." I turn to leave them alone with their drama.

"No problem." Sasha leans back against the fridge, arms crossed. The two of them stand silently.

I want to say hello to Laney and Nico now. Their other friends have had enough time to greet them.

Sasha and Kevon hold the school record for longest-dating couple. They've been together since freshman year, believe it or not. But they're not in love. They're addicted to the roller coaster. Here's how they operate: they'll fight in front of the beverages for a few more minutes. Then they'll each find their friends so that they can complain about each other. Their friends will spout their opinions: *He's a dick. She's a bitch. Break up already!* Sasha Grady and Kevon Knight don't want to be content. They want to be the talk of the party.

"So, are you still talking to him or what?" Kevon says behind me.

They'd better not win the Cutest Couple superlative for the yearbook. It's not about longevity. It's about "cutest." There's nothing cute about their public displays of dysfunction.

"Ni-co! Ni-co! Ni-co!" I hear the crowd chanting in the living room.

I rush back, pushing past two guys who are tossing M&M's into the fish tank.

"Nooo!" Fernando yells at them, dashing toward the tank. "They're saltwater fish! My mother loves them more than she loves me. She'll have a freakin' heart attack!"

Nico's friends pass a microphone toward him. On the television is a video of Elvis Presley in a white jumpsuit. Nico's shaking his head no but making his way to the front of the room. He accepts the mic and takes a stance—legs apart, one knee jiggling. Everyone's clapping and cheering at the intro to "Suspicious Minds."

What! Nico Fiore does Elvis? I peer at the girls at the front. Laney is sitting on the carpet, covering her face.

"I'm not responsible!" Laney says, laughing.

The vocals kick in, and Nico begins, singing that he's "caught in a trap" and "can't look back."

On the screen, the women in Elvis's audience squeeze their fists and reach out to the King while they lose their minds. I understand how they feel. Nico's voice . . . is *good*. It's smooth and deep. It reverberates. Nico Fiore can sing.

I know that he means this act to be funny, but it's not funny to me. His friends are hooting, and he's circling his hips, but his actual voice isn't a joke.

All of a sudden, it's obvious; I know how and why Laney and Nico got together last year. Tomás had been buzzing around Laney for two months. I had seen him hanging around her locker, catching up to her in the hallways, stopping by her lunch table to talk. She'd been attracted to him, I could tell. Who wouldn't be? Look at him. He's Tomás Diaz.

I've seen Tomás's parents. His mom is Black with dark skin.

She's tall and has model cheekbones. His dad is Latino with an intense face and broad shoulders. Tomás got the best of both of them, curls and black eyes and that smirk. At school, he's forever wearing giant headphones around his neck. Whenever I see Tomás Diaz, he's either silent, retreated within himself, or sweaty and riled up with his circle of friends.

For two months, Laney leaned forward when Tomás spoke to her. She crossed her legs in his direction and touched her collarbone or the ends of her hair as she listened. I saw Laney straighten his tie as she laughed at a joke. I thought they were about to become a couple. It seemed inevitable.

On a Friday I walked past them outside the choir room. He asked her if she was going to Gabby Hollis's party. Laney said yes, and he was happy to hear it. "I'll see you there, then," he said. "Don't change your mind." His voice was gravelly and sexy, which was a tone I'm sure no one else had ever heard from Tomás. She said that she wouldn't change her mind. She would be there, definitely. When Tomás turned the corner, Laney squealed with her friends. Laney Villanueva and Tomás Diaz were on the verge.

But on Monday morning, Laney Villanueva wasn't coupled up with Tomás Diaz. She was holding hands in the junior hallway with the dirty-blond, clean-cut Nico Fiore. How had that happened? What had Nico Fiore done to stop that train from rolling full speed ahead?

I've been wondering about this ever since. But it's clear now; there had been karaoke at Gabby Hollis's house. And Nico Fiore had sung Elvis.

Tonight, Nico is here, curling his lip, eyes closed. Even as a few boys heckle "Elvis suuucks!" and "Elvis is a thief!" Nico is feeling it. He's reaching a hand toward his girlfriend, singing that he loves her *too much, baby.*

Tomás, who's over in the corner with his friends and a plain girl in tight French braids, shakes his head at the performance. It's been almost a year, but he still can't believe he lost his chance with his dream girl over karaoke. He can't take Nico's charisma and Laney's highlights any longer. He and his buddies are headed for the door. It's useless to compete with Elvis and too painful to stand by and watch.

Tomás will never be able to listen to this song again, or any Elvis song, without feeling a pang in his chest. When he's middle-aged, his company will send him to a conference in Memphis. He'll feel unsettled without knowing why. He'll check into his hotel while this song plays in the lobby, and then he'll remember: Laney Villanueva and Nico Fiore. Damn.

"Wow," says Greta Novak, suddenly standing next to me. How is Greta constantly popping up beside me like a Muppet from behind the furniture? "He's really good."

I clutch my phone inside my pocket. I want to take a video so bad, as Nico stretches his right leg to the side and bends deeply at the knee. I could record him easily; I have a clear view between Noel Dillard and Franny Lutz. But Mr. Bryant's voice is in my head: *Delete it. Delete it right now. Let me see you delete it.*

"Lunge, Elvis, lunge!" someone yells. "Wooo!"

Other kids are taking videos: Jacqueline Chen and Eva Tyson, Jamel Drinkwater. They'll post their videos, and then I'll be able to watch those.

Nico holds a pose and adds a karate chop. Rising, he sings louder as he shakes his hips. Someone throws a dish towel at his chest. He wipes his face with it and then drapes it around his neck. He raises a hand and squints away from an imaginary spotlight.

How many times has Nico done this act? A dozen? More? Does he rehearse in his bedroom with a hairbrush? I laugh to myself, imagining that.

I make a mental note of everyone who's recording so that I can look them up later and watch their clips from every angle. I can combine them, edit them together, and make one full video. My secret file is getting better and better.

Nico tosses the dish towel into the cheering crowd.

"That's *your* boyfriend!" Laney's friends holler and point.

Nico takes a bow.

Laney is laughing-crying. "I've never seen him before in my life!"

"I'm done, man. Elvis has left the building!" Nico catches his breath, hands on his knees. He reaches into an upturned catcher's helmet. "Who's next?" He swishes his hand around before pulling out a piece of paper. "Angela! And she will be singing"—he squints at the paper—"'A Whole New World'!"

Nico passes the microphone to a squealing Angela Fortunato. Angela jumps into place. She may be the lead of all our school musicals, but she's not the star here. No one can follow Nico Fiore.

"God, he's so cute," Greta squeaks dreamily—to me or to herself, I can't tell. What's the difference? The truth is the truth, no matter how you say it. Now I'm starting to feel bad for

Greta. The way her googly eyes follow him into the kitchen makes me sad for her and her future boyfriends who will never be as cute as Nico Fiore.

"He's nice, too," I say, reaching for my phone. "We hang out sometimes." I show her the doctored picture of me with him and Laney. I did as I'd planned—I pieced it together the next day in the yearbook office. The Piktura software is amazing.

Greta stares, impressed.

"This was at my house. They drive me home sometimes. He has that black Jeep in the senior lot. You know the one?"

"Uh-huh." Greta nods.

"Nico is obsessed with my grandfather's car. He's been begging me to drive it, but I don't know." I shrug. "That Road Runner is my grandpa's baby."

Greta looks up at me with her chapped lips slightly parted. Has she never heard of Vaseline?

"Nico took a bunch of pictures with it." I swipe through the other photos. "Laney, too."

Greta leans over my camera. Her hair is greasy at the crown. I slide my phone back into my pocket. "Maybe I'll let him drive it around the block. On a special occasion—maaaybe," I say.

Greta purses her mouth. Her envy fuels me. I can't get enough. I'm unbeatable tonight at Fernando's house party. I'm a girl with a movie-star car, a girl who's friends with the most beautiful couple at Holy Family High School.

"You know who else used to love my grandfather's car?" I say.

"Who?" Greta asks.

"Jenna," I say. It's true. Jenna has always thought MacGraw

was so classic. She used to call the car Ali, as if the two of them were on a first-name basis.

Greta and I look over at Jenna and Sydney, who are talking by the French doors. Their foreheads are nearly touching. What could they possibly be laughing about? Horse-Camp-Sydney is as dull as a tongue depressor.

"It's too bad we're not friends anymore." I rub it in like sandpaper against a sunburn. "She could have hung out with us—me and Laney and Nico." Someday we're going to pile into the Road Runner and go cruising, like in a scene from a teen movie. Regrets—that's all Jenna will have left of me.

"Oh," Greta says.

She'll go and tell Jenna everything. Jenna will hate that I have a better, more exciting group of friends. She'll resent that I'm healthy now and doing well without her. *So well.*

"But Sydney Bergen seems like a barrel of fun, too," I say flatly. I realize I've been holding the cold ginger ale against my left elbow. I guess it still hurts a little. I'm still black and blue here and there, but I've been trying not to think so much about the pain. I like to remember that afternoon as the time Nico and Laney gave me a ride home just because they wanted to. The reality of that day is fading along with my bruises.

Nico and Laney and the V-Boys are dancing near the china cabinet. Fernando is trying to teach Nico a crisscrossing move with his feet that ends with a turn and a half split. Nico is trying, failing, and laughing.

"You almost got it! Just put your toe on the floor to turn your body around. Go again! Go again!" Laney cheers Nico on. I can't get over her hair color, all those cascading highlights.

Greta's eyes travel from Nico and Laney to Jenna and Sydney. "Yeah. They're tons of fun." She lowers her gaze.

I still haven't spoken to Laney or even thanked her for inviting me. But I don't need to. Being in this house with her, with them, is enough. On the microphone, Angela Fortunato's "A Whole New World" begins to build. I swipe a tiny slip of paper off the coffee table: *Nico: Suspicious Minds*. A gem of a find! I slide it into my breast pocket, against my heart. This is the happiest I've ever been. In the Villanueva house, filled with cousins and corny ballads, life is shining and shimmering. It's splendid.

12

The glass doors rattle. I snap to attention. Tomás Diaz bursts in like he's about to set the office on fire. He hooks past me, straight toward the principal's office. Father Philip is in there, talking to Omar Douglas and Vinny Unger.

"Uh . . ." I say.

Father Philip sees Tomás through the glass. He holds up his hand. "One moment," he mouths. Tomás grumbles and spins around. I'm stuck out here with him as he paces and slaps notices off the bulletin board.

"It might be a while," I say. "You can sit on the bench . . . if you want."

"Fucking bullshit!" Tomás says, smacking a penholder off the table.

I sink onto my stool. "Or not."

Tomás backtracks toward the office again.

"I wouldn't go back if I were—" I say.

Father Philip is patient as far as principals go. He takes the time to chat with me, not just about what I'm doing. He likes to know how I'm feeling, which is a really nice thing to be asked. I wouldn't recommend busting into his office uninvited, though.

Tomás pushes Father Philip's door open. Trying to control his anger, he asks, "Why do they get to talk to you first?"

"Mr. Diaz," Father Philip says, "I will invite you in when I'm ready for you. Close the door, please."

"But why them first?" Tomás insists. "Why can't I talk to you first?"

"I can assure you, Tomás, it will have no bearing on how I assess the situation."

Tomás lets the door go. He paces again, from the front door to my counter. Finally, after his fifth time back and forth, he plants himself onto the bench. He leans back, bouncing his right knee up and down.

I know how he feels. You wouldn't know it to look at us, but Tomás Diaz and I have something in common. I've been summoned to the office, too. I've smelled Father Philip's cinnamon Tic Tacs and calculated the number of tiles under his desk. I've read the diplomas and certifications on his wall. Father Philip is actually a certified child and adolescent therapist. He is also scuba certified. He frames everything.

The front door swings open again, gently this time. It's Laney, carrying a big cardboard box. Seeing Laney and her pretty new highlights, Tomás groans, dropping his head into his hands.

Laney glances at Tomás and then balances her box against the counter. "Hey," she says to me softly. "Uh, these are string lights for the Safe Halloween maze. Mrs. Bardot needs them a week early so the custodians can set them up."

"Okay," I say.

"Are you volunteering for Safe Halloween?" she asks. "It's a cute event. Younger siblings come, and the kids from the elementary schools. It should be fun."

"Yes," I say, deciding only now. "I mean, I've been meaning to sign up."

"Oh, I can put you on the list if you want," Laney says.

I want anything you want, Laney Villanueva. "Yes! Thanks."

"Thank you for your time," Laney says.

"Of course," I say. "You can put the box on Mrs. Bardot's desk."

Tomás watches Laney walk around the counter and set the box down.

"Tomás?" she says, on her way back around. "Are you okay?"

He catches Laney's eye for only a split second. He's embarrassed to be here. More than that, it hurts him to look at her. "Just stupid shit going on."

I open my Spanish textbook and hide my face at an angle. *Yo estudio, tú estudias, él estudia, nosotros estudiamos.* She's inching toward him, closing in on a boy who's not her boy, but who wants to be.

"I'm sorry," she says. "Is it bad?"

"It's Omar and Vinny, man." He gestures to the office with both hands. "It's not me. I don't do drugs. You know I don't do drugs."

Drugs? This is bad. No wonder he's freaking out. He could get expelled. He lives in West Ingram. That's a terrible school district. I hope it doesn't come to that.

Laney sits on the bench beside him. He moves his leg away slightly. It's overwhelming to be near her.

"I know you don't do drugs. You don't have to convince me," Laney says. "I believe you."

What else does she know about him? How close had they been before she got together with Nico?

"They're in there talkin' shit about me first. Now whatever I say's gonna sound like bull." He stares at the floor because Laney Villanueva doesn't belong to him. He's already said more than he should have; the top two buttons of her shirt are undone, and he shouldn't look there. Even in this time of distress, he's forcing himself not to stare at her there. "I'm fucked," he says.

"Not necessarily. Is there a third party?" she asks. "Someone else Father Philip can talk to who'll back you up about what happened?"

"I don't know, I don't know," he says, dismissing her. He won't turn his head, won't look to her for support; she isn't his girl.

Laney puts her hand on his. She's touching him, this other boy who isn't her boy. But she doesn't want him, doesn't crave Tomás the way she craves Nico, deep in her core. If she did, she wouldn't touch Tomás at all, wouldn't even sit this close to him. Why play with fire? It would be too dangerous. That's how I know she isn't tempted. She's only imagining what it would have been like to be with him, which is perfectly innocent. She's thinking that if she were with Tomás Diaz, this would have been her problem, too. Their problem. She would find that third party and fight for him. And Tomás would fight for her if he ever needed to. It wouldn't have been a bad life with Tomás, just different. But it wouldn't have been Nico.

Tomás stares at Laney's hand. It's obvious he wants her hand on his, but he also doesn't want it—this is what he's been missing—Laney Villanueva's touch.

Yo toco, tú tocas, él toca, nosotros tocamos, I read in my textbook.

If Tomás were a threat to Nico, I'd take care of it. I'd switch him out of seventh-period European History so that he wouldn't pass Laney anymore when she came out of Mrs. Ribero's class. I'd move his locker to the south end so they'd have to enter through different doors in the morning.

"Father Philip's fair, though. He'll listen to you. He will." Laney checks the clock. "I can miss the rest of homeroom. Do you want me to stay and wait with you? It sounds like this might take time to—"

"No." Tomás pulls his hand away. She's not his girlfriend. He doesn't want to rely on her kindness. He's thinking that Laney should comfort her own man about his second-place soccer team or his grueling ab routine. "Nah, I'm good."

"Oh. Okay . . ." Disappointed, Laney stands slowly. "I hope everything turns out all right."

"Yeah." He shifts and peers back at the office. Of all the things he would miss if he had to leave Holy Family, he would miss Laney the most.

She pauses to look at Tomás's profile, sharp and dark and pained. He's the reverse image of Nico, her Nico. She leaves. Her loafers clip-clop across the floor.

Tomás collapses forward when the door closes behind her.

BE THE LIGHT.

He exhales into his forearms, as if the conversation caused him physical pain.

Yo lastimo, tú lastimas, él lastima, nosotros lastimamos.

"*Good morning, Holy Family. Let us pray.*" The morning announcements begin on the Holy Family TV station. The monitor on the wall blinks. A single black line travels slowly from the bottom of the screen to the top. I make the sign of the cross and fold my hands as Mackenzie Hagar leads us in praying the Memorare.

Mrs. Bardot and her steaming coffee mug are back. WORLD'S OKAYEST SECRETARY is the most accurate coffee mug there is. She's a nag who constantly looks over her shoulder at me. She checks and rechecks my work and asks me personal questions about other students. *Why is Alexandra Floyd living with Tara Wolenski's family? Is it true that the Solernas are downsizing as an experiment? Is Patrick Britton really related to that actress with that reddish-blondish hair on that drama?* As if I would tell Mrs. Bardot anything I know about anyone (Alexandra's parents are fighting, Mr. Solerna lost his job but is telling everyone that downsizing is an experiment, and no relation).

Mrs. Bardot notices Tomás on the bench and the boys with Father Philip. She lifts her brow at me. She usually asks if she's missed anything, but obviously it's been a dramatic morning. Mrs. Bardot and I both know Father's regular schedule: Monica Reilly has counseling appointments with him on Mondays, Aaron Paige sees him on Tuesdays. This is Tomás Diaz's first appearance.

Mrs. Bardot bows her head and waits for the end of the prayer. When the song begins— *"We sing our praise to the Lord most high"*—she sets OKAYEST on the table and picks up the memos that Tomás tore down. She misses the penholder that Tomás smacked under the chair, but I don't say so. Who knows where the pens landed?

"Let us stand for the Pledge of Allegiance."

Mrs. Bardot and I stand with our hands over our hearts. Inside his office, Father Philip stands, too, and Omar and Vinny do the same. Tomás slides off the bench and rests one knee on the floor.

"... *with liberty and justice for all.*"

The screen changes from the flag to Mackenzie Hagar in the media center newsroom. Tomás pushes himself back onto the bench and crosses his arms. His leg has stopped bouncing.

"Laney Villanueva dropped the string lights off for Safe Halloween," I tell Mrs. Bardot. "I'm volunteering for it."

"How nice, dear. Helping others is food for the soul," she says, setting the box on the radiator. "I don't see any Halloween decorations at the Leeland house this year. Do you think their parents are out of town again?"

"I don't know, Mrs. Bardot." (They're vacationing in Miami. The five Leeland kids have been running amok for a week. Perry Leeland's throwing a party on Friday. I wouldn't go to that one even if I were invited. Stoners.)

Safe Halloween will earn me six more volunteer points. Just a few more events and I can be an official Leadership member.

"*The nominations for yearbook superlatives are now in,*" Mackenzie says.

They're in! Yearbook Club nominated students yesterday. I wanted to nominate, but only seniors were allowed.

"*Ballots will be distributed in senior homerooms now. Be sure to submit your votes in the lobby by the end of the day.*"

Laney and Nico have to be on the ballot, they just have to.

Father Philip's door opens behind me. He steps out of his office and sets Omar and Vinny free. They blow silently past Tomás, out the doors, and then split off down separate hallways.

"Mr. Diaz," Father Philip says, poker-faced, "you may come in now."

Seventy-eight tiles: that's how many are under Father Philip's desk. Tomás is about to find out. I wish him good luck in my head. If Laney believes him, I believe him. He isn't a threat to Nico. Tomás envies him. I'm sad for anyone who pines over Laney Villanueva. It's a no-win situation.

"So, please, seniors. Vote for your top choices in all categories, including Most Likely to Succeed, Most Likely to Have a Reality Show, and Cutest Couple!"

Tomás rises. He steps forward, holding his chin high. It takes courage to face the music and the girl he can never have in the same morning.

13

I think I'll wait here at the top of the front steps. This way I can see everyone as they come off the buses. If enough sophomores are wearing costumes, I'll put on my Devil horns and tail. If not, I won't.

I'm standing in the very spot where Lisette Moss stands on page 80 of the 2008 yearbook. It's the photo of the year, in my opinion. Every yearbook has one—a standout that defines the class. The 2008 photo shows students pouring out of these eight doors, lugging backpacks and instruments down the stairs. In the midst of the chaos is senior Lisette Moss on this exact step, watching someone or something in the parking lot. She's the only figure in sharp focus, while the world whizzes around her. She's perfectly still, with the most heart-wrenching look on her face. I could stare at her for hours. Who is she looking at? What does she see? I get restless wondering about her sometimes.

Bus J is pulling in now. It screeches to a stop, engine running. The door opens, and students step down. Okay, here come some costumes. A ninja, Cruella, and dalmatians. I'll put my horns and tail on. I have a real costume for Safe Halloween later. Laney added me on the list to work with the little kids.

My horns and tail are fine for class, but I have something special planned for tonight.

I'm ready. I think I got my tail straight. I'm going in. I'm not nuts about Halloween anymore like some people, but the seniors are making it fun this year. It's really sweet how they decided ahead of time to do a pajama theme. That alone, deciding to do a theme, is so spirited.

The energy in the lobby gives me goose bumps. Something important is happening, I can feel it. Seniors stream in, checking out one another's costumes, squealing, "Look at how cute you are!" "You're adorable!" It's so wholesome, like third grade again. Some even brought jack-o'-lantern buckets for candy. Last year Mr. Bryant gave full-size chocolate bars, not the dinky fun-size ones the other teachers hand out. He was popular for the right reasons. I miss him. No, I don't. I'm fine.

There's Jenna, near the cafeteria doors, wearing bumblebee antennae and a yellow-and-black striped sweatshirt. Sydney Bergen is dressed as a nerd (not much of a departure for her, if you ask me), with taped eyeglasses and pigtails and a pocket protector.

Jenna and I dressed as Shaggy and Scooby in third grade, Minions in fourth grade, and cookies and milk in fifth. Notice how she and Sydney aren't coordinating today. Just saying. They probably won't go back to Jenna's house to watch horror movies and throw water balloons at trick-or-treaters, either. Sydney isn't the horror-movie-watching, water-balloon-dropping type. Literally. I heard she has a latex allergy.

The V-Boys have entered the building! This is not a drill! I'm literally laughing out loud. They're wearing plaid onesies in red, blue, green, and gray, as if they've just rolled in from a lumberjack sleepover. Fernando is in a hunting cap with earflaps and is carrying a bundle of logs.

"I brought my morning wood!" Fernando announces, and then the V-Boys break into dance steps. Their costumes are killing me. How funny are they, spinning on their plaid backs with their white footies in the air?

Nico! Here he is, sauntering in dressed as Hugh Hefner, with his hair sprayed white, a burgundy smoking jacket, black silk pajamas, and leather slippers.

"Hef!" Fernando and his cousins swoop toward him. Nico holds a pipe to his mouth as the guys give him hugs and high fives.

Laney looks so cute, too, in Playboy bunny ears and flannel pajamas with rubber duckies on them. She's carrying a fluffy stuffed animal that looks just like her dog Panda. Nico takes the pipe out of his mouth and hugs her. He dips her so far back that her bunny ears touch the boy behind her. She laughs and apologizes. The boy smiles. He liked her bunny ears against his back. But Laney is out of his league. He knows this, even with a Superman "S" bursting through his suit jacket.

Laney pets Nico's robe, saying, "Silky!" Everyone is trying to snap as many pictures as they can before we have to leave our phones in our lockers at the first bell.

"Over here!" I say, holding a hand up. From the corner of my eye, I can see Jenna's bumblebee stripes facing me.

Everyone pivots in my direction — they trust me, they know me, we're like that. I have the Nikon around my neck, very profesh. Everybody wants to be in the yearbook, especially twelfth graders. Laney and Nico pose front and center. Their friends fan out behind and around them. This reminds me of the 2019 photo of the year, which was snapped at a basketball game at the exact second the ball swooshed through the basket. You can practically hear the final buzzer and the student body roaring as they jump up and down. That photograph is alive.

Focusing my camera now at all the smiles and the costumes, I know . . .

"Say trick or treat!" I call, because you can't say the word "treat" without smiling.

"Trick or treat!" the seniors cheer.

The V-Boys say, "Smell my feet!" like elementary school kids.

A few girls chant back, "Give me something good to eat!"

. . . I know, when I click the shutter, as light filters through the stained glass window: *this is the photo of the year.*

"Jenna!" I run to her, my camera outstretched. "Look at the picture I just took!"

She leans back, surprised. I feel foolish standing here. Why am I showing her?

She looks at the photo. "Wow. That's good. It's really vibrant." Her compliment stings me and flatters me, equally.

"Is it for the yearbook?" she asks.

I pull my camera away. What a stupid question! It's something a complete stranger would ask. "I'm the yearbook photographer!" I yell.

"How am I supposed to know that?" she asks, antennae shaking. "You haven't spoken to me in six months, unless you count telling me off at a party. I thought you were passing me a note in Mass, but then you didn't. Now this? Do you want to talk to me or not?"

"Not," I say. Turning to her was just a bad habit. "Thank you for reminding me." I step away and disappear into a jangle of court jesters.

"Come on, Rafi," she says behind me.

It's been too long. Jenna doesn't know me anymore. She's out of my life. But I have other things now. Don't I? Better things? I lift the camera again. I have this—this one glorious picture. I have ghosts in Emily Dickinson nightgowns carrying lanterns. I have babies in onesies and bonnets, big-headed aliens, the walking dead, prom Carrie, the T-Birds and Pink Ladies. I have the lumberjacks and Fernando stroking his wood. I have Nico with his white hair and Laney in her bunny ears. I have them. I do. I will always have them.

14

I've only ever seen Nico Fiore's little sister from afar. Millie
Fiore must be seven, maybe eight. A couple of times last year,
she was in Mrs. Fiore's car when they came to pick Nico up
from school. It's safe to say it was Millie that second time, even
though I couldn't see her face. She was wearing what I think
was an astronaut helmet.

Here are three things I want to know about Millie Fiore:

1. Is Millie a nickname? If so, what is her real name?
2. Does Millie Fiore spend a lot of time with Laney
and Nico?
3. There's something else I want to know, but I'm
not going to admit it yet because I don't want to
jinx it.

I recognize Mrs. Fiore right away in her nurse's scrubs and
white sneakers. She's so impressive. She even has ID tags still
clipped to her top. Imagine having a mom who's essential per-
sonnel, a mom who's needed by greater society. It's no wonder
Mrs. Fiore has raised such a good son.

That's Millie beside her. She's unmistakable this time in a

furry, head-to-toe kangaroo costume. Too adorable. But Millie looks like she's about to cry, poor kid. She's telling her mom that her friend Alexa isn't here, even though she promised she was going to come. I get it. I feel like crying, too, just hearing about it. Alexa's parents must have gotten too busy to bring her. Alexa is probably just as upset. It's the worst—to tell a kid you're going to do something and then disappoint her. I think of Alexa dressed in her costume, all ready to go. What is wrong with some adults? Mrs. Fiore came straight from the hospital and made it here on time. If something is important enough to you, you make it happen; it's not complicated.

Safe Halloween plus clothing donations plus serving food at Senior Banquet gives me fifteen Holy Family volunteer points. Twenty more points and I'll be a full-fledged Leadership Club member. Then I can attend meetings with Laney and her friends. Sometimes Leeyah Shepherd holds meetings at her house in Garden City. I've always wanted to see inside those houses off Stewart Avenue. Twenty more points and I'm in.

Millie Fiore is the cutest trick-or-treater at Safe Halloween. I'm supposed to guide the kids through the cafeteria, which the Art Club has transformed into a Halloween maze. I introduce myself and welcome Millie to Safe Halloween Night. Mrs. Fiore is downright tickled, because isn't it such a coincidence that Millie is a kangaroo with a pouch and Rafi is a koala bear with a pouch?

"Look at that, Millie!" Mrs. Fiore says. "Isn't that sweet? Aren't you two a match made in marsupial heaven?"

We are. It's not important that I overheard Laney ask Nico what Millie was going to be for Halloween, that our costumes aren't a coincidence at all, and that the second I pulled my phone out of my locker that afternoon, I clicked on two-day delivery for a koala costume and a stuffed animal koala (the description of the costume said *stuffed koala bear not included*).

I stick out my belly to show off the baby koala in my pouch. Millie, the cutie-pie, smiles and pushes her belly out to show the joey that's sticking out of her pouch. Mrs. Fiore can't help but clap, we are so dang cute. Millie Fiore and I are a sight! She was near tears a few minutes ago, but now she's giggling. I am Mrs. Fiore's new favorite person.

Mrs. Fiore is taking our picture. Her phone case has a picture of Nico and Millie in a hammock. I ask if I can take a photo on my phone, too. I know this isn't pushy, because how many chances does a person get to take a photo with a fellow marsupial? Only one. This is the chance.

We pose, featuring our pouch babies. Do you see how we are instant pals? Rafi and Millie. We're like a kids' television show that has action figures and an opening song.

Some people think that if you look into the lens, the camera takes part of your soul. If this is true, I possess a piece of this child now, a fraction of her seven-year-old soul, and since I also have photos of her brother, I own a fraction of Nico Fiore's soul, too.

I offer to take Millie through the Halloween maze. She's so happy she's literally hopping in bursts of three. *Hop, hop, hop.* Pause. *Hop, hop, hop.* Pause. Mrs. Fiore is pleased to wait for us at the exit. She's a hardworking nurse. She deserves a break, no matter how cute her daughter is.

I extend my arm, and now Millie Fiore is holding my koala

paw with her kangaroo-costumed fingers. Everything I know of Nico expands to include this little girl who is collecting candies from the other volunteers and stashing them inside her velvety pouch. When she gets home, her chocolates will be soft and warm from body heat.

We start the trick-or-treat maze, which isn't really a challenge since there are glow-in-the-dark arrows on the floor. Up ahead are a T. rex, Batman, and a stormtrooper.

Millie stops. Her hand grips mine.

"What's wrong?" I ask.

"I don't like him," she says, leaning back.

"Who?"

"Ethan Jackson," she says. The T. rex falls behind his friends as he picks out candy from a cauldron.

"The T. rex?" I ask.

Millie nods. "He called me a dog A-S-S."

I side-eye the T. rex. "Don't worry about him. I'm here." I coax her forward. "Come on. We'll have fun, okay?"

The arrows lead us to an Under the Sea display that's bright and fun, not spooky, which is good, since Millie is in need of something lighthearted.

"Let's pretend we're underwater!" I say.

We hold our noses and swim through the seaweed paper streamers and balloon "bubbles" hanging from the ceiling. Making fish faces at the camera, we take selfies in a clamshell. Our pictures make Millie laugh. I tell her I'll send them to her mom. Mrs. Fiore will have to give me her phone number. I'll have a direct connection to Nico Fiore's family.

I want Millie's memories of tonight to be as happy and as

perfect as possible. I click Edit on my phone and crop out the background and sharpen the image 4 percent. It looks a lot better.

"Heeey!" Millie yells. "That's mine!"

I look up and see her at the end of the sea display, with a volunteer dressed as Ariel the mermaid. The T. rex is laughing, holding a Pez dispenser.

"That was for her!" Ariel says.

I race past Ariel and chase the dinosaur around the corner, nearly tripping over my koala feet. Someone needs to teach this mini asshole a lesson before he grows to be a big asshole. Behind a life-size cardboard cutout of Spider-Man, I grab Ethan Jackson by the tail. I twist the green felt and shove him against the wall.

"Oww!" he yells. "Hey!"

"Listen to me, T. rex," I hiss, trapping the sides of his costume in my fists. "If you ever bully Millie Fiore again, I will knock you so hard you'll wake up in the Jurassic period running from meat-eaters. Do you understand?" I rip the Pez from his stumpy hand.

He bucks in my grasp and tries to kick me beneath his fat dinosaur belly. I am doing Millie Fiore and every little girl in this kid's future a favor.

"I said, 'Do you understand,' *Dog Ass*?"

"Yes! Yes!" he blurts, spittle snapping between his lips. "Jeez, get off me!"

I shove him toward the exit. He hurries away as quickly as a kid in a *Tyrannosaurus rex* costume can hurry, with the weight of his head and tail forcing him to lean to the left.

I turn, and there's Millie staring at me, eyes wide. I show her the Pez, and then I toss it to her. She catches it.

"Shhh," I tell her, holding my paw up to my mouth. "Our secret." I pretend to lock my mouth and stuff a secret into my pouch.

Millie cracks a smile. Her eyes shine beneath a string of Laney's twinkle lights. "Shhh," she says. She giggles, lifting the candy to her lips and then pushing it into her pouch.

Look out, everyone! We are Rafi and Millie, watch us roar! Our TV theme song crescendos in the background. We fight for the innocent! We rid the world of candy-stealing punks like Ethan T. Rex Jackson!

Free from bullies, Millie and I take our time through the final exhibit. It's the spooky portion, where someone wearing a pumpkin head and a black leotard gives us a map and flashlights. He tells us to wait for two minutes before going in to avoid a traffic jam.

We weave through hay bales and corn stalks and scarecrows. We're bonding, strengthening our friendship with every twist and turn. It's symbolic, really, this journey we're taking. At Point A we were strangers, but by Point Z, we're a dynamic duo.

Here it is, number three out of the three things I want to know about Millie Fiore: "Millie, do you have a regular babysitter?" I ask.

I wait for her answer as we duck under an archway of polyester spider webs. This is a fire hazard, this whole exhibit, but I will risk my life for the idea that's been brewing in my head.

"I have Diana, my neighbor. She has ladybugs in her garden. She buys them at the flower nursery and adds them on her leaves on purpose. Or sometimes her son Aaron comes when he's home from college," she says, pulling one of her kangaroo ears from the web.

We check the map for the next turn, a right at the glow-in-the-dark skull. "No one regular, though, like who comes all the time?" I ask.

"Nuh-uh. My nonna and nonno moved to Florida."

"Oh, that's too bad. But I'm sure they're much happier there without snow and everything," I say.

"Yes." Millie points her flashlight left and right and then chooses the path to the right. "Nonno likes his toes in sand."

"I don't blame him," I say, getting ready to reel her in. "Well, just so you know, I'm a babysitter." It's a lie. I've never babysat before. Little kids are sticky and germy, and they tell maddening stories that go on and on without a plot. But for Millie Fiore, I'll be a babysitter. I'll be a babysitter for any kid who lives in Nico Fiore's house. "But the little girl I usually take care of just moved, so I'm looking for someone new," I lie again.

"You can babysit us!" Millie says, waving her baby kanga-roo at me.

"Really? I can? That is such a good idea!" I crouch down and hug the stuffed joey. "Would you like that?"

"Uh-huh!" Millie's ears bob up and down as she nods. I want her to wear this costume forever. I'm sad already, thinking of her wearing anything else.

"Tell your mom, then, okay?" I hold her kangaroo palms in my koala bear hands. We are best animal friends. Between fighting crimes, we sing songs in the Australian Outback and teach biology by narrating footage of wombats giving birth.

Millie's eyes are the same hazel as her brother's, the very same. Those eyes make me want to go home with her. "Ask your mom if I can babysit as soon as we get out. Ask her right away."

Millie Fiore's eyes, Nico's eyes, tell me that she will.

15

Allegro Dance School is smaller than I remember, and dustier, too. I haven't been here since my last year of jazz class. I was so sick of that "Puttin' on the Ritz" routine. I did love those little white gloves, though, from the recital costume. It's funny how I wore them around the house with my nightgowns, pretending I was dressed Victorian.

Those gloves and Laney Villanueva were my silver linings at Allegro. I was ten and in elementary school when Laney was twelve and in middle school. I remember her stirrup tights that showed her calloused dancer's feet. She also had purple stretch bands that helped her to press her chest all the way down to the floor when she pulled on them. And she had her own cell phone; she listened to her own music while she warmed up at the barre. Middle school—so mature.

I'd thought that once I got to middle school, I might magically become poised and elegant. Maybe I'd become someone to look at. It still hasn't happened. It's not the end of the world. I'm not waiting for a transformation anymore. If we all grew up to be Laney Villanueva, who would there be to envy?

Millie Fiore is a riot. Look at her through the one-way glass. She's a beat behind her class dancing the Charleston because she keeps pulling at a wedgie. Millie will never be elegant either. She couldn't care less. All she wants is for her underwear to stay out of her crack. Priorities.

After Gran's car accident, she didn't want to drive anymore, so Poppy drove me the rest of the year to finish "Puttin' on the Ritz." When he dropped me off today, he said, "Well, this brings back some memories, doesn't it?" It does—memories of moms watching the other girls through the window. Memories of me asking Poppy to wait for me in the car because I didn't want people to know I lived with my grandparents. Memories of Gran deciding that there weren't many things worth leaving the house for anymore.

I find brochures at the reception desk. The photo on the front is of Laney doing a stag leap in midair, her hair whipping wildly. Photography credit: Philippe Turpin. I google him immediately. Philippe Turpin: 28, *Dance Magazine, New York Times* magazine, *Climbing.*

"Rafi?" It's Laney, coming out of the office. She wrinkles her forehead at me.

Startled, I slip the brochure into my back pocket. "Laney! Hi. I didn't know you were here."

She has a hickey on her neck, very low, close to her collarbone, a faint, freckly circle of blood cells underneath a faded layer of makeup. I'm staring. I'm thinking about Nico's mouth attached to her flesh and her hands up the back of his shirt.

"I work here on Wednesdays," she says, adjusting her sweatshirt to cover the hickey. It's Nico's purple sweatshirt, the one he wears on cool mornings. They're together even when they're apart! "What are you doing here?"

"I, uh . . ." I have temporarily lost my memory.

I'm here for you. I'm here to make my way into the Fiores' home and slip quickly and seamlessly into your life. But I can't say that. *Back off, back off.* The music from the studio, the Charleston, turns louder, reminding me.

"I'm here to pick up Millie," I say. "I met Mrs. Fiore at Safe Halloween. She asked me to babysit."

Laney glances into the studio. Millie is dancing with a partner. "Ohhh." She exhales. Her shoulders relax the way a good dancer's shoulders should.

"Chin up, shoulders down!" Millie's instructor yells.

"Well, her class should be out in a minute. Thanks for doing that, by the way, Safe Halloween."

"Of course!" I say. "It was fun, just like you said."

"Good." She smiles quickly before turning back into the office.

I'm soaring! I can feel my heartbeat in my brain. I hadn't planned on seeing Laney, but here she is. So much good is sprouting from this plan. This encounter adds another dimension to our friendship. She now knows I'm trusted in the Fiore household, and I know her schedule. Next time I babysit on a Wednesday, I can say, "I'll see you later at the studio, Laney," and she'll say, "See you then!"

What a joy to be back here at Allegro. The studio is full of surprises. Who would have thought it? I can almost taste red Gatorade on my tongue. I'm back at Allegro dancing again— on the inside.

16

I'm here, in his space. This is Nico Fiore's house. It's toasty warm from the sunlight shining through the bay window. I'm breathing his air—fruit punch, Elmer's glue, garlic, wood shavings. I'm standing inside Nico Fiore's life.

His backpack is right here in the front hallway. I dig my hand inside it, like it's a grab bag at a Christmas party. Tangled earbuds, pens, coins, index cards. I pull out crinkled dollar bills, Tylenol, strawberry ChapStick. I uncap the ChapStick and swipe it over my lips. It's as if we're kissing. I pretend that we are—I close my eyes and kiss the back of my hand. This is Nico, his strawberry-flavored lips, we are kissing goodnight in his front hallway. This is his mouth that sucked blood to the surface near Laney's collarbone.

Millie is rattling around in the mudroom off the kitchen, where a radio is playing for her rabbit. The rabbit listens to "today's top hits" while the family is at school and work. Millie rinses and refills his water bottle and sings along to a mattress jingle: *"Trust Sleepy's, for the rest of your life!"*

I watch her move comfortably through her routine and imagine her brother here, too. Nico Fiore, kidding around with his little sister, pouring himself an iced tea. Nico Fiore, wearing an old comfy T-shirt and Pringle-stained sweatpants and thick tube socks.

Throughout the Fiore house are happy messes: soft sweaters tossed over the banister, catalogs stacked into piles, a paint project of greens, blues, and yellows on an easel to be continued, baking ingredients waiting on the counter, and a Lego village on the carpet in mid-construction.

On the fridge, beneath a Busch Gardens magnet, is last year's report card for Camille Fiore. First grade with Mrs. Houser. My first question has been answered. Millie's real name is Camille. She has an old lady's name. Millie is a seven-year-old Golden Girl who is "inquisitive and enjoys a challenge" in class.

Camille Fiore has turned the rabbit's radio off. She's snacking now, reaching her skinny arm into a box of Lucky Charms and watching a Kidz Bop music video on her tablet. The Kidz change the word *liquor* to *water,* which is good, I guess. Seven-year-olds shouldn't bop to a song about drinking liquor, not that I would've stopped Millie from watching the original video. It's not like I'm a real babysitter; I don't know what I'm doing. For example, I should have told her to wash her hands before eating that cereal, but here we are.

Above the rabbit hutch, the hand-painted sign says *Buster Brown's Home Sweet Home.* I bend down to say hello to Buster. He's hiding. He's just a puff of breathing fur sticking out of a little wooden shelter. In the photo that's taped above his hutch, I can see that he's brown with white feet and brown eyes. Thank goodness. I don't think I could handle red, beady eyes. Those are just evil. I shiver just thinking about red eyes.

On the stone floor are Nico's cleats, his running sneakers,

and shin guards. Real-boy necessities. I slip my right shoe off and slide into his Nike and wiggle my toes. I feel small as my foot disappears inside it.

The doorbell rings.

"The pizza's here!" Millie yells.

That was fast. We ordered early before the dinner rush. Millie thunders through the family room. She has heavy footsteps for such a small, fragile-looking person. She's going to be very entertaining at her dance recital.

I slide out of Nico's sneaker and balance my foot above the cold floor. I don't know why, but I feel a sudden sadness that I can't explain.

"Money, please!" Millie calls. *"Dollas, dollas, holla, holla,"* she says, imitating a rap song.

I can smell marinara sauce and mozzarella from here.

Every two minutes I have a mini revelation: I'm washing my hands in Nico Fiore's sink. I'm pulling plates from Nico Fiore's cabinet. I'm opening a pizza box on Nico Fiore's counter.

I'm eating pizza at Nico Fiore's kitchen table, and this must be the best pizza I've ever tasted in my life. The delivery was so fast that the cheese is still gooey and the crust is still crunchy. The driver must've really gunned that gas pedal. I hope the rest of the family isn't expecting leftovers. The Fiores must order from Gino's Pizzeria often, because Mrs. Fiore knew exactly how much money to leave for a large cheese pie, including a generous delivery tip.

Millie Fiore eats with her napkin tucked into her collar and does a happy pizza dance by shimmying her shoulders as she chews. What if I need to do the Heimlich maneuver? That's something real babysitters know how to do. When Jenna took a babysitting certification course at the library, she had to learn CPR and basic life-saving skills. I'll look that stuff up tonight so that I know for next time. In the meantime, if Millie chokes on this pizza, I'll grab her tablet and watch the Heimlich online.

Everything ok? Mrs. Fiore texts, as if she could sense trouble from afar. Not to point fingers here, but she's the one who's a nurse, she should have asked me if I knew first aid.

Yes. Pizza is here. It's really good!

Great. Enjoy! Nico Fiori's mom is texting me while I'm sitting in her kitchen: another realization.

It's important for me to answer her texts right away. I want to make it clear that I'm responsible and reliable, and that Millie adores me, so that she'll ask me back for every possible occasion.

Here's how it will be: I'll be the Fiores' regular babysitter. Some nights Nico and Laney will come home before Nico's parents. Nico won't know where the money is to pay me, so I'll have to stick around and wait for his mom. Nico and Laney and I will sit at the counter and chat about Millie and school and Holy Family in general. It'll get late. We'll move over to the sofa and watch television (you really get to know people through the shows they watch and the comments they make). He'll put his feet up on the coffee table, and she'll rest her head on his shoulder, and I'll sit cross-legged on the other end—we'll be very casual by then. His parents will walk in together carrying Chinese takeout, and they'll say, "Hey, since it's dinnertime, why don't you stay and eat? We ordered enough to feed an army!" because that's something happy families are always saying, that they have enough "to feed an army."

That will become our regular evening routine. These are

the moments that make a person a part of the family. What I'll do is make extra dinner for Poppy and Gran the night before I babysit. It won't be a problem.

I lift a sweatshirt off the back of my chair so I can lean back. It's white with a red Adidas logo across the front. I recognize its coconut-and-almond scent right away as I hold it up to my face.

"That's Laney's," Millie says.

"Oh, I'm sorry." I drape it over the chair to my right. "It's really soft," I say. Laney sits here, in my exact chair! I picture her name carved into the wooden table.

Millie juts her chin forward. "Do *you* know Laney?"

"I do."

Millie nods. "Laney is afraid to wear white when we eat spaghetti."

This dinner table has five chairs: one for Nico, his dad, his mom, Millie, and one for Laney. She has a chair here. She dines with the Fiores and takes her sweatshirt off before eating red sauce. They're used to her, she's not "company" anymore. It would be no big deal to welcome one more person. It'll be easy to pull a sixth chair in from the dining room. There's plenty of space for me. Enough space for an army.

I see and feel Laney's presence everywhere in this house. I picture her flicking her shoes off in the mudroom, grabbing an apple from the fruit bowl, cutting it up for Buster Brown, and eating half of it herself.

I look up the stairs. Laney has been up there, too, and she's taken off more than a sweatshirt. I want to be up in Nico's room. I want to see where they go to be alone, to be together, to be a *we*. I'm going up there tonight. Goal setting is the key.

Know what you want ahead of time. That way, as soon as an opportunity opens up, you can seize it.

"Do you know what?" Millie says, covering her mouth as she chews.

I lean forward. "What?" *Tell me more, anything, I need to know all about them.*

"My teacher, Ms. Ryder?" Millie begins. "She's doing *Tidying Up with Marie Kondo* to her house, so she brought her junk drawer to school and gave away her junk for prizes."

"Her junk?" I slump in my (in Laney's) seat. Here we go, a maddening story without a plot.

"Uh-huh," Millie says, scarfing down a hunk of crust.

Don't talk with your mouth full until I know the Heimlich. "Who would want a teacher's junk?" I ask.

"*Everybody!*" Millie spreads her arms wide. "It was so cool! She brought in the whole drawer. Her cabinets are white with gold handles."

All right. Ms. Ryder is sort of hilarious, dumping her old crap off on her students.

"So, what was in it?" I'm genuinely interested now.

"Lots of stuff. Um . . ." Millie swallows and takes a sip of water. "First, Alex Poole won a dice key chain from Las Vegas."

Ms. Ryder is promoting gambling among her students. A very funny woman indeed.

"And then Mackenzie won a ticket stub from *Ant Man.* And then Rosie got a busted TV clicker, but she traded it with Mikey Cho for a watch with the band broken. And then Mikey Cho pretended to freeze everybody with the clicker, so then Rosie got mad because she wanted the clicker back." Millie presses an imaginary clicker and then freezes. She clicks it again and freezes in a different position.

"That's junk, all right," I say. Ms. Ryder is a comedian. She should have a show called *Welcome to My Junk Drawer.* "What did those kids do to win prizes?"

"Uh, being quiet, sharing a snack without being asked, working very nicely." Millie counts each good deed on her fingers. "And I can't remember what Mikey Cho did. A clean desk, I think."

"What about you?" I ask. "You didn't win anything?"

"No, because I'm always good," Millie says, matter-of-fact.

I pause. "That doesn't seem fair."

"You have to be bad and then be good to win something," she explains.

"But you should get a prize for being consistently good," I say. "That's an injustice."

"Don't tell me. Tell Ms. Ryder." She shrugs and bites the tip of a second slice.

Ms. Ryder is a bitch.

●　●　●

Millie is coloring her poster for the National Fire Safety Month contest. She has drawn herself throwing Buster Brown out a second-story window. The rabbit is smiling in midair as flames blaze from every part of the house.

"Come on baby, light my fiiire," Millie sings as she colors.

It's peaceful to do homework with a seven-year-old. It's also motivating, because I have to be a good role model and stick to my work. I don't check anyone's social media, not even once.

> *Dear. Ms. Ryder,*
>
> *It has come to my attention that you have been reward-
> ing students for good behavior, but only the children who
> usually misbehave. For example, your junk drawer prizes
> are rewarded to students who show improvement.*
>
> *It is my belief that students who consistently "work very
> nicely" should be rewarded as well. Please do not take
> well-behaved students for granted.*
>
> *Thank you.*
>
> *Sincerely,*
>
> *Dr. Kristina Churchill, Principal*
>
> *Great Harbor Elementary School*

Okay, this is not exactly homework, but it is school-related. It practices persuasive writing and formal letter format, which are required skills according to the New York State Regents scope and sequence (posted on the wall in Holy Family's main office). I'll utilize graphic skills, too, because Great Harbor Elementary has a really nice website with a principal's letter under "Administration." I can copy the letterhead using Piktura and then paste my letter onto it.

"Done!" Millie raises shaky fists over her head. *"Light! My! Fiiire!"*

The poster is nightmarish—she's added black smoke and tears. "Looks good," I say.

"I have to do my timed reading." Millie sits on the carpet

with a big Ziploc bag. Inside are a paperback, a purple pencil, and what looks like log sheets. "I need to read for twenty minutes. You have to time me."

I look up the stairs again, wondering which door is Nico's bedroom. It's getting late, and by late, I mean, it's about time I get up the damn stairs. "Do you want to go upstairs and read in your room?" I ask.

She pulls the bag open. "Nuh-uh."

"You might be cozier reading in bed," I say. I could at least see his room if we're up there. Maybe I can step inside if she uses the bathroom.

"Nah." She pulls out her book.

I could scream.

"I like reading in *my* bedroom," I try again. "It's much comfier."

"That's okay." She takes her log and pencil out.

I want to smack that book out of her sticky little hands. *Breathe, breathe, breathe* . . . I'm sure she'll want to play upstairs once her homework is done. I'll just flat-out ask to see her bedroom. Kids love showing people their rooms, don't they?

"Time me . . . starting . . . *now!*" Millie says, opening to her bookmarked page.

I set the timer on my phone for the longest twenty minutes of my life. Millie's version of twenty minutes of required reading is skimming the book for specific answers she needs to record in her daily reading log.

While I wait, I make a mental list of my priorities in Nico's room, things that I can achieve in mere minutes. I want to look inside his dresser, peek inside his bedside table, find something of Laney's, touch his pillow, and take a souvenir. I also plan several topics to chat about when Nico and Laney get home.

Beep! Beep! Beep!

"Time's up!" I say.

Millie looks at her page number, slams her book shut, and starts filling in her log. Ah, the joy of reading!

"Millie, show me your bedroom!" I say, acting all excited so that she gets excited.

"Okay!" She pops off the floor and puts her things back into the Ziploc.

Now we're in business. I'm off the sofa, ready to go. I'm only seconds away from—

"Hello? Mills?" The back door slams. Mr. Fiore.

"Daddyyy! You're early!" Millie barrels toward him and jumps into his arms. He's patting her back. She's hanging from his neck. They're unreal, disconnected from my life. It's like watching a commercial.

"Get your coat," he tells Millie. "Let's get some frozen yogurt."

Millie runs for her coat.

Invite me. Invite me. Invite me. I'll get cookies 'n cream on a cone. Nico and Laney will be home when we get back. I'll be prepared. Discussion topics: Superlatives layout, Millie's fire poster, Millie's bitchy teacher, Gino's pizza, karaoke, the Halloween photo.

Mr. Fiore turns and smiles. He's handsome, an older version of Nico.

Invite me, older version of Nico!

He pulls out his wallet to pay me.

I'm not invited. Millie's rabbit is scratching and rattling his hutch—scratching and rattling inside my brain. No frozen yogurt. No bedroom. No Nico and Laney. Not tonight. Only scratching and rattling, scratching and rattling.

Ask me back. Ask me back. Please, ask me back.

17

Best Eyes. Best Body. Best Dressed. These are the dumbest superlatives, the ones that are based on looks. I mean, Best Dressed? We wear uniforms. I did the best I could with it, anyway. This picture turned out not so bad. Tia Lang and Logan McHugh are standing in front of open lockers that we stuffed with their fanciest street clothes. Tia is in her faux leopard coat, and Logan is wearing his Gucci jumpsuit, A.K.A. the tackiest getup I've ever seen. Logan has a friendly smile, and Tia's haircut is so sleek. I had to ask her how she gets it so shiny. "I'm Asian," she said, deadpan. Fair enough.

I don't know what to do about Tomás Diaz. I said, "Tomás? Hi, I'm Rafi. Remember? From the main office? I'm the yearbook photographer. Can you come by the yearbook office after school? I need to take your picture for Best Hair," and he said, "Yeah, I'm not doing that." My role as yearbook photographer has brought me closer to everyone but Tomás.

Matt Dorian and Ulla Posey came to me the very day the winners had been announced. They asked if I could style their photo to look like a seventies album cover, "something between a James Taylor and a Doors vibe," Dorian said. So, the next day, after I had looked up what those albums looked like, that's what we did. Why can't Tomás Diaz play along, too?

Dorian's streak of skunk white in his black hair photographed so sharply. Ulla Posey looks like a girl out of a Woodstock documentary, long braids and no makeup. I can't believe they climbed onto the dumpster with their guitars. It stank like warmed puke behind the cafeteria.

"Anything for art," Dorian said. He'll be famous one day. A lot of people from this area have become huge celebrities, like Jerry Seinfeld, and Eddie Murphy, and Natalie Portman, and okay, okay, Mariah Carey.

The photo is dreamy, isn't it? Dorian is strumming his guitar, sitting with his legs hanging off, and Ulla is gazing straight into the camera. I'll size it into a square now, to make it look like an album cover. I'll add their names and MOST MUSICAL in the same yellow font as the James Taylor cover from 1968. I'll make it sepia-tone, more yellowish than brownish, so it will look more seventies than forties.

I should show Poppy. I learned a lot from his album covers, especially his favorites displayed on our mantel, the ones with cars on them. The best one is THE WHO ON TOUR: MAGIC BUS with a photo of a big flower-power hippie bus. It's so funny that he displays the Cars album, which says THE CARS but doesn't actually have a car on the cover. Poppy has a subtle sense of humor.

I've photographed Helene Zuniga for Best Hair, so that's done. We'd gotten tired of waiting for Tomás. Helene and I carried a ladder out to the football field. She lay in the grass in her yellow dress with the Peter Pan collar. I brushed her long blond hair all around her like a sunburst and then took her picture from up high. The photo looks like summer. She asked for a copy to frame at home. I should tell Father Philip about that.

Tomás Diaz, on the other hand? Nope. Every time he sees me, he ducks in the opposite direction. I hate it. He associates me with this idiotic thing, and I don't know how to change his mind. With Tomás, it's about more than the yearbook. I want to spend time with him the way Laney did. Close proximity to Tomás Diaz—how does that feel? I just want to know. Is that so wrong? Would Jenna consider this un-profesh? Should I be stripped of my Nikon once again? Jesus, just let a girl live!

There's a knock at the doorway.

"We're here to take our superlative photo," Laney says. "Is this a good time?"

They're here. Her delicate neck. His strawberry-flavored lips.

"Yeah, perfect! Super."

"Great," Laney says. "Because I got up early to do my hair, and I never want to do that again." Her hair is bouncy and curled at the ends.

"It looks pretty," I say. All those highlights. "Can I show you guys something first?" I lead them to the round table, where there's a stack of old yearbooks for reference.

Nico pulls Laney's chair out. He's a gentleman, a dying breed. I lay an old yearbook on the table, turn it for them, and open to page 113. I don't need to look at the page to know what they see. Every detail is seared into my memory.

"Senior Superlatives," Laney says.

Most Likely To Succeed: Meredith Voight and Trayvon Reeves, wearing suit jackets and power ties. Most Dramatic:

Kate Hoppy and Owen Young, posing on the *Romeo and Juliet* balcony, and Cutest Couple on the dance floor.

"Aw, look, Nico. Cutest Couple." Laney touches Nico's arm and pulls him toward her.

Nico takes a look. "This kid had great hair."

I stare at the kid's hair. It's moussed up high, and naturally wavy. It was great. It still is, just not as high.

"I love her dress," Laney says, admiring the deep purple satin. "I'm all for short dresses for formals. This must've been the homecoming dance."

"It was," I say. "These are my parents."

"No way! Really?" Laney grasps my forearm. "They went here?"

"Seriously?" Nico asks.

"That's them." I nod. "They loved it here."

Every day I imagine Mom and Dad in this building—young and laughing, his arm around her shoulders. Her uniform skirt is hand-stitched, tight against her thighs. Sometimes I think I see them from the corner of my eye, but they're always turning around the bend. I call to them in my mind—*Wait! Please! Stop!*—but they never slow down, and I can never catch up.

Laney lifts her hand. Heat from her touch lingers and then evaporates. "That's amazing that they went here."

"Yeah. They were really popular—like you guys."

Laney smiles a little. It was an awkward compliment. *Stay cool*, I tell myself, *back off.*

"Carlo Tedoro and Bianca Wickham," Laney reads softly.

She's looking at my father in his rented tux, at my mom, who's clutching her satin pumps in her hands and laughing into the camera. Dad is hugging Mom from behind. I realize that I've seen that exact pose before, in a photo of Laney and Nico on social media. I stare at her and at him. Do they see what I see?

"They were so cute," Laney says, without a hint of recognition.

"Thanks," I say. "They were."

It's hitting me—here we are—me and Laney and Nico and Mom and Dad and Dad's high hair, hanging out together after school. This is why I fixed the Superlatives. I could not let Kevon Knight and Sasha Grady steal this from us. I'm glad I took a ballot from the yearbook office and made copies. I'm glad I hid in the bathroom and checked the boxes using a dozen different pens. I'm glad I stuffed the ballot box. Laney and Nico deserve Cutest Couple more than anyone. I'd had a vision of us ending up this way, and it's come true.

"You look like them," Laney says.

"I don't," I answer. She's only being kind.

Plum—that's what my mom called the color of her homecoming dress. Her lipstick, also plum, matched perfectly.

"Yes, you do," Laney says. "You have the same eyes. And you have your dad's cheekbones."

I don't see it. Mom and Dad were magnetic.

Laney checks the front cover to read the year. "So, your parents are really young, aren't they?"

"They were eighteen when they had me." Nine months after Missy's party.

"Wow," Nico says. "Are they still together?"

"Nico." Laney pushes him lightly. "Don't pry."

"It's okay," I say. We've reached this level. Friends are supposed to get personal. "But no, they're not." Mom and Dad don't speak. Mom's voice tightens whenever she mentions him.

"Sorry," Nico says.

"That's all right." My parents have only been in the same room together a couple of times that I can remember—my First Communion and middle school graduation—but they stayed on opposite sides of the room, and those were big rooms. "They were never married. My dad travels. He's a roadie."

Nico leans forward. "Like, with a rock band?"

"Yeah." I say. "Sons of Orwell."

"No way, really? They're great," he says. "I have them on my rotation." He starts scrolling through his phone. "I love Jay Monroe's voice. He's so soulful. They have this one song that I listen to ten times a day, uh . . ." He swipes through his playlist. "'Song to Myself.' It's so mellow."

"My dad's in that video," I say. I'm proud of Dad all of a sudden. I want to thank him for giving me this—a real connection with Nico Fiore.

Nico's eyes widen. "He is?"

"He didn't act in it or anything," I say. "He's in the background pushing a dolly. Sons of Orwell doesn't 'make' videos. They use live footage."

"Ah! That's so cool." He looks to Laney.

"We'll have to watch it!" she says. I imagine them watching it and pointing out my dad. We are friends, aren't we? They wouldn't watch a video of just anybody's father.

"They're touring this year," I say.

Tonight they're in Portland. Thursday night, Seattle. Next

week, Tucson. I keep his tour dates on my lock screen. Soon he'll be back on the East Coast. What I don't tell Nico and Laney is that the "Song to Myself" video is the only way I see my dad these days. The last time I saw him was sixteen months and five days ago. That's a long time. His job is overnight hours, long, hard shifts, lifting and hauling. He works so hard. Somebody has to. He sends checks for my tuition.

"Does he send you stuff from tour? Concert merch?" Nico asks.

"T-shirts and tour posters, yeah."

"Niiice."

I sleep in the oldest concert T-shirt, and the current tour poster is on my bedroom wall. Whenever I look at it, I feel sad and guilty. Sad because I miss him, and guilty because he could've gone to college, could've had a suit-and-tie job right here on Long Island or Manhattan, if only . . . I'd rather not think about it.

I've searched all the videos for Dad. Some I've watched a dozen times, slowing them at certain points to see the faces, but Dad's only in "Song to Myself." He shows up after the second verse: *"Singin' alone but never lonely, me, myself, and I, I, I—I don't mind, I don't mind, I don't mind, whatever it is I find."* He comes out right then from behind the truck and walks across the lot with the dolly. Dad, in his jeans and black tee.

"What about your mom?" Laney asks, looking again at the yearbook. "Did she keep the dress?" Her eyes are hopeful. "You should wear it."

"I'm not sure—" It dawns on me. I remember slinging an armful of dresses from the back of my closet into a Hefty bag.

"I think . . ." I feel my throat closing. "I . . . I think I might have donated it."

Laney's mouth turns down. "Oh, no . . ."

My parents are slipping further away from me every day. I want to cry, and Laney and Nico know it.

"I'm so sorry." Laney bites her lip. Nico places his hand on her back. "Well, you have this." Laney smooths her hand over the yearbook. "And it's such a special thing to have this picture of them in here."

Laney is so sweet and so thoughtful, looking at me with pity. It makes me want to cry even more. But she's right. I do have the yearbook and the photo. That's why all of this is important—we have to stop time.

"Thanks for showing it to us," Nico says.

I nod slowly, still thinking about the dress. "I thought you might like it."

"We do," Nico says, trying to be cheerful.

"It's amazing." Laney closes the book carefully. She slides it over as if to push my parents closer to me. "Thank you, Rafi."

"You're welcome." I swallow my emotions. "But your picture's going to be even better."

What's done is done. No point in wallowing. This is Laney and Nico's year, it's their time, and I'm going to immortalize them. It's what friends do; we make each other's lives better.

"We can take the picture however you want and wherever you like," I say. "We can go out to the soccer field or in the dance studio or the stage. Or Nico's car?"

"Maybe we can take it on the roof?" Nico whispers to Laney.

"We could," she whispers back. "But then everyone will know that we go up there."

"By the time the yearbook is printed it won't matter anymore," Nico says.

He's right that they won't get in trouble for it anymore, but he's wrong about it not mattering. The photo will matter forever. And it will exist because of me.

Laney laughs. "True. Okay, then." She turns to me. "Can we take it on the roof? Above the north wing?" She adjusts the gold chain around her neck. I see Nico's class ring dangling at the end. They're an old-fashioned couple, "going steady."

L.V. & N.F.

"Wherever you want," I say. She has no idea that I've worn that ring and have touched the initials. My thumbprint is probably still there. I'd forgotten to wipe the inside. On *SVU,* detectives would interrogate me in the room with the metal table and the harsh lighting. Gran would shake her banana at the TV. *Let her go! She's just a little girl! She wouldn't hurt a fly!*

"We go up there sometimes to be alone—ninth period, actually." Laney gestures to me, acknowledging that ninth period was my gift to them. "Thank you for that, by the way."

There it is. Better late than never. I knew she appreciated me.

"You're welcome. It was nothing." We've shared so much now, the three of us.

"It's quiet up there, and it's right above the dance studio, which is really convenient," Laney says as Nico rubs the back of her neck. "The door's open. But it locks from the inside. There's a dumbbell against the wall, you need to use it to prop the door open."

"We learned that the hard way," Nico laughs.

"We got locked out once. Luckily for us there's a gutter

down the side of the building, so we were able to climb down."
She nudges him playfully. They tell the story as if they've rehearsed it. "Someone was a scaredy-cat, though."

"It was rickety!" he says. "It's not bolted securely to the
brick!"

"Ohhh, so scary! One flight up, save me!" Laney teases him,
and then she turns to me. "You won't tell anyone that we go
up there, right? It's, like, the one place nobody knows about."

"No. Never." I cross my heart. I'm collecting their secrets
like souvenirs.

"Of course she won't," Nico says. He trusts me. We are
friends, friends, friends.

The George Orwell quote on the Sons of Orwell "Present
and Past Tour" poster says, WHO CONTROLS THE PRESENT CON-
TROLS THE PAST. As Laney and Nico lead me up to their secret
meeting place, I think about the extra ballots I fixed for them
and the photo I'm about to take. I think about how I'm con-
trolling the present so that someday I will have controlled the
past, and I think I understand.

I follow Laney Villanueva and Nico Fiore—them, and then
me. *We.* They show me the tricks on the way to the roof. The
doorway marked STAIRS feels like it's locked but it isn't.

"See?" Nico explains. "The knob spins so you can't get a
grip on it, but you don't have to. You just have to pull it with
your weight and it'll open." He pulls, and we're in.

"The stairwell smells like bologna, sorry," Laney says, as if
she should've cleaned up before having a guest. It does smell
like bologna, but who cares? I've been invited.

"Whoa . . ." I stop. There are hundreds of names scrawled

on the cinder blocks. They're the names of couples in hearts pierced with arrows, couples with initials, couples with first names, nicknames, first and last names, couples with dates and quotes and phone numbers going back over thirty years, back to when the school opened. I run my index finger along the bumpy surface. *Brent luvs Heather '99*. I trace the heart around *Jenny + Max 2004*. My eyes land on *Tina Shepherd + Ryan Vermeer 1992*. These are real people who are grown now, living their lives somewhere in the world.

"You coming?" Nico calls from the top of the stairs.

"Yes, I"—I step back to take in as much of the wall as I can—"I just want to see something." I scan the letters in bold black marker, others in weak pencil strokes that have somehow survived for this long: *Jon and Bonita, Call Suzy Q for a good time, Rolling Stones, JJ luvs Anika*.

"Oh my god, that's right," Laney says, stepping down a few steps. "Do you think your parents are here?"

"I don't know." I crane my neck to read the words at the top. *Don't let the bastards get you down, Abby and Brian 4ever, The Aboff twins suck dick*. I sigh. "It would take forever to read them all."

"How cool would it be to find them, though?" Laney's big eyes scan the wall.

"So cool," I say. "Are you guys on here?"

"No," Laney says. "I've always thought of it as something from the old days. But maybe I'll add us. I don't know. Maybe at the end of the year."

"Nah, I don't think I want us on here," Nico says.

"Why not?" Laney asks.

"You don't think this is kind of dingy?" he asks.

"No, it's not dingy," she says. "It's . . . historical."

"Phone numbers," I whisper. There are so many. Why would couples leave their phone numbers? The older numbers must have been landlines, those old-fashioned telephones with the curly cord. In classic movies, girls were always getting called for dates and twirling the phone cord around their fingers.

Who were these people? What do they remember of Holy Family? Of this staircase? Would anyone answer these numbers if I were to dial them?

"You can always come back to search for them," Laney says. "Read them a little bit at a time."

"I will." I'm going to do exactly that. I start up the stairs, reading the cinder blocks as I go. I'll take a picture of the wall on my way back out.

Nico pushes his body against the heavy steel door. It's so sunny. We cover our eyes and stumble like survivors of an apocalypse, emerging from our bunker. I grab the doorknob as I step up. It leaves my hand smelling of rust. Nico wedges the dumbbell in the doorjamb.

I look around. It's disappointing. The roof isn't the most picturesque place for a photo shoot. It's only a brick perimeter, a bubbled skylight at our feet, huge air ducts, and heating and air-conditioning machines that are bigger than washer/dryers.

There's nothing special about the roof. But Laney and Nico are magical enough to make this work. I want to know what happens here. What do they talk about? What do they do here when they're alone?

Laney's phone buzzes in her jacket pocket. Her phone case has a picture of her dog on it. "Hello?" she answers. "No, I haven't checked. You did? When is it? Wow, that's soon."

Nico eyes her. "What?" he mouths.

"I'll check right now. Okay." She hangs up and scrolls through her phone.

"What?" Nico says aloud.

"Wait. One second . . . ugh, the signal up here sucks," she says, running to the corner that faces the soccer field.

She scrolls some more and then shrieks, "I got the audition!" She runs back to Nico and squeezes him. "NYU."

"Ahh, that's so amazing!" Nico squeezes her back.

Laney Villanueva and Nico Fiore have forgotten about me. See how comfortable they are in my company? I'm honored to disappear into their background.

I lift the Nikon camera to my eye and watch quietly as Nico kisses her. His fingers slide lightly down her neck as he pulls away. They smile at each other, at their fortune, and their future.

I hold my breath. I capture the Cutest Couple through my lens and press the button.

Look at this photograph.

Just look at how beautiful.

18

Millie doesn't want to order pizza this time. She says there are "good leftovers," so I open the fridge. I'm raiding Nico Fiore's fridge.

She was right. There's eggplant parmesan! Laney wasn't at Allegro when I picked Millie up today. I was so disappointed. But my luck is turning. There's nearly half a tray of parm left.

"Mmm . . ." Millie stares as I take the lid off. "We can finish it. Whoever's first gets it, that's the rule. Losers weepers."

My stomach growls. A home-cooked dinner made by someone who isn't me! "No weeping for us," I say.

"We just have to make more angel-hair pasta." Millie pulls a pot from the bottom drawer. "We finished that part last night."

I'm boiling water on Nico Fiore's stove. I'm clearing Nico Fiore's dinner table. No big deal, just being a good babysitter. Under Millie's notebooks and folders are financial info packets: Hunter College and Baruch. New York City schools. I'm squealing inside!

We set the table for two while the pasta boils. Millie says angel-hair is her favorite pasta because it's the fastest. I have to agree. You can't beat the flavor of a four-minute cooking time.

Millie digs the colander out of the cabinet, but I don't let her drain the water. I make sure to do it myself. I'm getting so good at this job.

This is the same meal Nico and Laney ate last night. Her sweatshirt is still hanging over the chair. I eat slowly, savoring each bite. I'm ready with topics if they come home first tonight. *Please, please, please come home first.*

How's it going over there? Mrs. Fiore texts.

I reply ASAP, *Delicious eggplant parm!*

I'm so glad you like it. Don't worry about the dishes.

After dinner, Millie "reads." I rinse the dishes and put them in the dishwasher, clean the kitchen table and the countertop, fill the parm tray with soapy water, and leave it to soak. This is how to get invited back.

The twenty-minute timer on my phone rings. "Time!" I say.

Millie slams her book shut. Then she speeds through her reading log questions. It's her only homework tonight, so she says. I should check her memo pad to make sure, but whatever. I still have my own English and Religion homework. I can't concentrate, though. I have an agenda.

"I didn't get to see your room last time," I say. Tonight is the night. I *will* see Nico's bedroom.

Millie rushes to the Legos on the carpet.

"Do you want to play upstairs?" I ask. I need to feel closer to them—I've been staring at their Superlatives photo all week.

"Nah," Millie says. "I'm making a swimming pool and a pool house and a horse ranch and an ice cream shop and a theater—a drama one, not a movie one—because that's a waste of village money. Anyone can watch movies at home, it's modern times." She rolls her eyes. "And a ski slope, and a tunnel."

"But aren't you tired?" I ask.

"No."

She must be joking. I did everything I could to exhaust her this time, no exaggeration. I took her to the park after dance class, I showed her the squat thrusts we did in PE and challenged her to do more than me, which she did, twenty-two to my eighteen. I raced her across the monkey bars, we did an army crawl under the rope net, and we practiced cartwheels on the white lines on the baseball diamond. My shoulders are sore, and I might have done something weird to my ankle—it's a little sensitive when I turn it to the right. Millie should be passed out, not building a metropolis in the middle of her family room.

I sigh and plop down to join her. "How are you going to make a tunnel?" My wrists hurt, too, and my right elbow. I hadn't cartwheeled since sixth grade. And, yes, it hasn't been long since Millie's brother hit me with his Jeep, but that's in the past, so why dwell?

"I'm making an entrance to the tunnel that I pretend goes under the carpet. And I'm making an exit to the tunnel that I pretend comes up out of the carpet." She digs lines into the tan fibers with her fingers. "You can travel underneath with a car or you can walk on the sides because there's guardrails and lights. It's a shortcut because if you travel on top of the land you have to go all the way around the stores and everything. So it's better to go underground unless you want to be slow, like maybe you want to stroll out in the sun on a date."

A date. She's definitely Nico Fiore's little sister. "What do you know about dates?"

"I know stuff. I'm seven." Millie gestures to the television. "I have TV."

I laugh.

"And I have an older brother."

Now she's getting somewhere.

"Does your brother go on a lot of dates?" I ask, trying to sound casual.

She groans, red-faced, trying to pull two Lego pieces apart. "Ugh. Stuck."

"Let me try." I hold out my hand.

She passes me the Legos. "They won't go," she says. "There's dried Play-Doh inside them."

"So, your brother goes on dates?" I ask again. She needs to learn to focus. That's the problem with kids today. Too much screen time causes a short attention span.

Millie sighs. "He has a *girlfriend*."

"I know. Laney. Does that bother you or something?" It seems like it does. I thought that she would idolize Laney and that she'd talk on and on about her. I don't know where her negative attitude is coming from. Maybe she's walked in on them when they didn't expect it and they yelled at her to get out, or maybe she's jealous of the time her brother spends with her.

"See, this is the entrance to the tunnel." She shows me a red arched piece. "And this one is the exit." A yellow arched piece.

"Clever." I give up on separating the Legos. She was right, the pieces won't budge. I'm not about to rip my nails trying. "Sorry. I can't do it." I pass the pieces back.

"See?" She shakes her head. "Play-Doh."

Millie doesn't want to talk about Nico and Laney or their dates—it's driving me crazy. *Give me something, Millie Fiore, come on. Do they sit together on this sofa? Do they watch movies and snuggle up with popcorn? Have you seen them make out? Tell me, Millie. Tell me!*

"This town needs a moat," Millie says.

Gaahh!

I turn the TV on and click to the news because I need her to get tired and fall asleep, and the news used to make me sleepy when I was her age.

On tonight's *NBC Nightly News,* fires in the California canyons have spread; twelve-year-old Kaitlyn Bellows, who had gone missing sixteen weeks ago, has been found alive; the dirty secret behind what really happens to our recyclables is revealed; concert ticket scalpers are facing harsh penalties. Totally boring grown-up stuff. Perfect.

In the bathroom, there are three gummy bears underwater in the sink. Red. Orange. Yellow. They've expanded to about three times their size. I remember soaking gummy bears when I was a kid. It's funny because everyone's soaking them again in high school, except in vodka. I guess it's true that "everything I need to know I learned in kindergarten." I'm not sure how long these gummy bears have been in here, but they look close to disintegrating. I should remind Millie about them. She'll want to see them before they turn into juice.

The Fiores' medicine cabinet is shocking. Parents should really lock up their medications when they have small children in the house. This is a tragedy waiting to happen. Cough medicine and ibuprofen can be dangerous for little kids. Mrs. Fiore should know better. Parents need to take full responsibility for whatever happens.

They have Benadryl. The other morning, people called the radio station, complaining about how airline travel has become unbearable, with its shrinking seats and rude passengers. A caller said that he and his wife give their kids Benadryl to make them sleep on the flight. The DJ said that's probably a terrible thing to do. I had to take Benadryl for a bee sting when I was nine. It knocked me out in two seconds flat.

I could crush one. I could mash the Benadryl powder into some ice cream. I'm sure the Fiores have ice cream in the fridge. Every happy family has ice cream, even those that go out for frozen yogurt. Especially those. Then Millie will fall asleep, I can go upstairs, and no one will know a thing.

I put one pill on the counter and crush it little by little with the bottom of a cough syrup bottle. All I need is something to put the powder in. These drawers are a mess. Millie should bring this junk to school and give it away as prizes.

A contact lens case! It's empty. Exactly what I need. I brush the Benadryl into it, careful not to leave residue behind.

"Millie?" I call, stepping back into the family room. "Did you forget that you have gummy bears in the sink? They're about to—" I stop to look at a photo on the wall of grade-school Nico on his bicycle. Too adorable. His wavy hair was lighter then, almost pure blond and out of control, sticking out every which way. "Hey, Millie? Should we have some ice cream?" I hope they have chocolate. I suddenly have a craving. I'm sure the white powder will just mix right in.

Millie isn't constructing her moat anymore. She's curled up on the sofa under a Sponge Bob blanket, sound asleep. Asleep! Her head is pressed into a stuffed hippo.

I hover over her for a moment and watch her take long, steady breaths. The *Nightly News* is describing the miraculous rescue of Kaitlyn Bellows from a cabin in rural Vermont. Cops should automatically search cabins in rural Vermont as soon as someone goes missing. That's where kids always end up in the movies. I pick up a handful of Lincoln logs and drop them into the Lego pile to make noise, but Millie doesn't stir.

"I don't think the tunnel should go here. I'm gonna put it *here*," I say, pointing to the other side of the Lego town. No response. She's thoroughly zonked out in the heavy-headed way only little kids can be thoroughly zonked out.

She won't know, then, if I lift Laney's sweatshirt off the chair and hug it, will she? She won't know, either, if I put it on, or if I take a selfie wearing it.

And what will it even matter that I'm walking up the stairs? That I'm on the second floor, opening every door? Or that I'm standing in her brother's bedroom? Good night, Millie Fiore.

This is where Nico and Laney do it. Laney's parents are home in the mornings since Allegro opens in the afternoon. But the Fiores work early—a nurse and social worker. They save lives. No time is too early to counsel distressed patients or to defibrillate.

I fondle Nico Fiore's real-boy clothes: the uniform shirts and slacks that hang in the closet, his jeans and sweats on the shelves, his soccer jersey and his T-shirts. I'm giddy, I'm lightheaded, I'm even happier and luckier than Kaitlyn Bellows who has been found alive in a cabin in rural Vermont. I love everything in Nico Fiore's bedroom, from the PowerBars in a shoebox to his college prep books; from his Darth Vader mug filled with coins, to his hamper with a towel, underwear, and a flannel shirt in it. I notice a fat yellow hair tie on his nightstand. I pick it up and put it around my wrist.

I love this frame on his wall—a collage of him and Laney and their friends. Who even prints pictures anymore? Laney Villanueva, apparently. Here's the photo I saw online—they're on the beach at sunset, he's hugging her from behind. I remember this one, too, of Nico kissing Laney's dog. And I love this shot of Laney in a full split-jump over a heart that had been drawn in the sand. It is just . . . wow.

I'm taking pictures of the pictures, storing their memories away for myself. It isn't stealing if they aren't losing. They won't feel a thing. I'm taking this one: a picture of them at a water park. There's a tall slide behind them with people zooming down in yellow inner tubes. And this one: Laney and Nico in red theater seats holding Playbills up to their faces. *Hamilton.* Damn it, I still haven't listened to *Hamilton.*

Written in the corner of the sunset photo: *Happy 17th Birthday, Nico! I love you, Laney.*

And I love them for not using cutesy nicknames. If they were Honey Buns or Lovey Doveys, I couldn't bear it, I swear, I'd turn and run, watch my dust. But no, they are Laney and Nico, plain and true—take me as I am! I spin in the middle of Nico's room, imagining a heart carved in the carpet at my feet.

Their energy is here. I picture them doing homework in this room, reading, listening to music, watching Dad's Sons of Orwell video on Nico's laptop . . . which is . . . on his desk . . .

I open Nico Fiore's computer and touch the keys that hold a million of his fingerprints. It feels like . . . like I'm crawling into his mind. It's exactly where I want to be. On his desktop screen: Holy Family High School Varsity Soccer Schedule.

There's a home game next Tuesday and an away game at Naza-reth High School on Friday.

He's made folders for each class? He is such a good student. His notes are organized by date, and there are spreadsheets for his grades. He has a 96 average in physics? I knew he did well, but I didn't know he was a brain. Is he thinking about med school? I think that's eight years and then longer for residency. It would be tough on him and Laney. But they can manage. She has her own goals, too.

There must be more on his computer than schoolwork. Every-one has a secret file; I should know. There's got to be something personal, something juicy, something morsel-y—"morsel-y" as in delicious, a tasty morsel.

Maybe in this untitled folder? Let me check. I've seen these pictures before. A video from a soccer game. A video of Laney's dance practice. Laney's dance showcase. His dad's surprise birth-day party at Marone's Restaurant. A video of . . . what is this?

Play.

It's them. Laney and Nico are on the screen. I lean close. They're lying on their backs in his bed, *this* bed. It's the same sheets, light blue on the inside, dark blue comforter, white pil-lows. Laney Villanueva and Nico Fiore are warm and bed-headed and bright-eyed, right in front of me.

Nico steadies the camera. He centers their images from the shoulders up. Laney hides against his neck. He slips his arm be-neath her head and kisses her forehead.

I slide the volume up as Nico whispers into her ear, "Do something."

Laney laughs.

"Please," he says. "For me."

My breath catches. This is Nico, his truest self—Nico Fiore behind closed doors—his needs and his real-boy fantasies.

"Do something," he whispers again. "I'll watch it every night."

Laney nuzzles into his gray T-shirt, covering her eyes. She's reveling in his request, loving it. She takes her time, thinking. He gives her that, but he's anxious, excited, breathing more quickly now. She's going to do something. For him. For me. He twirls a strand of her hair, watching the side of her face in the camera. How does it feel to drive Nico Giovanni Fiore wild?

I wait and I wait, and Nico waits and he waits, and I cannot believe what we're seeing and have no idea what's coming—something so morsel-y—he's nearly drooling.

And then, a smile in the corner of her mouth. She turns to look into the lens. It's as if she's looking up at me, into me, her eyes soft and deep. Nico strokes the top of her head. He can't stand this, the torture. How do you do it, Laney? *Teach me.* He watches as she lifts a hand to her left shoulder and pushes the strap down so, so slowly. He kisses her on the temple. The camera shakes.

Nico whispers to her again, something I can't hear. What do you need, Nico? What do you want? God, I wish I could hear. Laney shifts, turning over onto her belly. The camera jostles. Pillow. Headboard. The back of her head. He is above, looking down over her. He sweeps her silky hair off her back like a curtain. She wriggles under him.

Very lightly, barely skimming her shoulder, he slips her other strap down.

He pauses.

With his index finger, he traces a short line on her smooth

skin and then a longer line: *Y.* Then a circle: *O.* He dips his finger down and then up again: *U.* Another line, a curve, a slant: *R.* He bends forward, kissing her behind the ear, punctuating the word. Nico continues, snaking his finger lower: *S.* Another line, diagonals, straight, up-down-up: . . . *K* . . . *I* . . . *N.* Another kiss, ending the second word. He touches her again, drawing lines, slants, curves: *M* . . . *A* . . . *K* . . . *E* . . . *S.* Nico kisses her a third time, moaning softly. I know what's coming. I recognize the lyrics. I can hear the tune in my head. *M* . . . *E.* A longer kiss this time. He rises. His finger completes the sentence: *C* . . . *R* . . . *Y.*

She turns to kiss him. The camera rattles. Blue sheets. Ceiling. Lamp.

Realizations flood over me: I'm crawling under Nico Fiore's covers. I'm in Nico Fiore's bed. I'm tasting Nico Fiore's strawberry ChapStick. I'm pressing my head against Nico Fiore's pillows. What else can I do? I have no other choice but to watch it again.

19

I smell roses. I look up to see a full bouquet of perfect pink buds approaching my counter. I'd like to cradle the bouquet in the crook of my arm and wave from a pageant float.

"Delivery for a . . ." The delivery guy reads from his clipboard. ". . . Laney Villanueva."

Ohhh! I reach for them. They're heavy in my arms, with thick stems and thorns curved like cat nails. I inhale them.

"Sign here, please."

My hand shakes as I sign.

"Have a great day, miss."

An envelope stapled to the plastic wrapping has a gold sticker from Blue Grove Florists. It's easy to unbend the staple with my thumbnail. I pull out the card, which is white with red hearts in the corner.

> For my beautiful Laney,
> Your favorites — pink like your ballet slippers.
> Thank you for the best year of my life. Happy 1st
> Anniversary! I love you so much and forever.
> Your Nico

It's Nico's handwriting, slanting to the right, trying hard, extra effort on the neat punctuation. After he cleaned his locker out the other day, I took some of his papers from the trash: AP Euro practice test questions, *Othello* list of characters, facts on the Globe Theatre. He likes bullet points, uses them in all his class notes. He draws the tiny circles with the tip of a very sharp pencil and then fills them in.

• *The Globe was built in 1599 by the Lord Chamberlain's Men, Shakespeare's playing company.*

Nico must've gone to the florist to order these flowers in person. Imagine Nico Fiore walking into Blue Grove Florist, asking for a dozen pink roses the color of ballet slippers, and then choosing the perfect card off the spinning rack. Buying these roses was at least a ten-step process. Very good work for a real boy.

The Xerox machine is already warmed up and humming. I copy the note on a color setting so that I can capture the red hearts and the exact color of his ink. I cut the paper down to size, rounding the corners exactly like the real card. It fits in my wallet behind my library card. I slide Nico's card back into the envelope. The office stapler is the same size as the one at the florist. I'm able to staple through the same holes.

Laney will fall asleep with these in a vase on her nightstand. Her dreams will be filled with the scent of roses. I swirl my fingers around each bud: one, two, three, four, five, six, seven, eight, nine, ten, eleven, twelve, thirteen. Thirteen? Is this a mistake? Shouldn't there be twelve? There's an extra.

The bouquet is full enough. It'll be fine if I take one. Laney will be so happy; she won't miss it. This one. It's the smallest, hiding beneath the larger ones anyway. That's probably how it got here. It's so small that it went unnoticed. If I take it, it'll get the attention it deserves. And I'll have my own little piece of Laney and Nico. "You smell so sweet, you cute little rose. Happy Anniversary," I say. "Your Rafi."

I fold my sweater over it, hiding it carefully. I'll bring it to my locker and stand it in my water bottle.

The bell rings as I gather my things.

"Ah! They're here!" Nico is in the doorway, beaming.

I can barely look at him. If I do, he'll see right through me and know . . . we've been intimate. I've been under his bed-sheets, have seen him slide her strap down, have watched him trace an *S* between her shoulder blades. He'll know that I took a video of that video, stored it in my secret file, and that I watched it at home again and again.

"Are they yours?" I ask. "I've been wondering who they were for."

"Yeah." He picks the bouquet up. "Well, they're Laney's. It's our one-year anniversary."

Do something. I'll watch it every night.

He closes his eyes and inhales them. The plastic wrapper crackles in his arms.

What if he ordered thirteen roses? What if he counts them? It'd be just like Nico to order one more for good luck. One more to prove how much I love you. One more that means you're my one and only. One more to represent one life to-gether.

"She'll love them, won't she?" Nico grins. He's not going to count them. He's pleased with the roses as they are.

"Yes. They're beautiful," I say.

He rubs his thumb against an unopened bud. "Hey, Rafi." Nico lowers his voice. "Laney and I might come in a little late tomorrow morning . . ."

My face must be bright red. I glance at Father Philip's office. He's out. "I'll take care of it."

"Yeah?" Nico's warm eyes are ever so grateful.

Pillow. Headboard. The back of her head. I can't stop remembering.

"Happy anniversary," I say.

"Thanks." He smiles. My brain short-circuits. "Gotta run!"

Nico Fiore bursts out of the main office. He rushes into the chaotic hallway. His shirttail pulls out of his slacks as he lifts the roses over the crowd. I memorize this image of him—I fold it carefully in half, in half again, and then once more—and I store it deep inside my heart. When I'm an old lady, I will unfold it petal by petal, and it will make me feel young to remember Nico Fiore this way.

20

There's a systematic way to search an expansive space like this cinder block wall. When search parties look for a body, volunteer groups walk in a grid pattern, with each group assigned to a coordinate, so that no piece of land goes uncombed. I'm trying that here in the stairwell, reading one cinder block at a time, starting from the bottom left corner.

Cinder blocks A3 through A6 are mostly couples from Holy Family, the early years: *Michelle and Greg always and forever, Vi + Mike '88, Paul loves Bobbi '86, Holy Family Sux Ass.* Mostly. My newest hobby is jotting down the names and then seeing if I can find them in the old yearbooks. Yesterday was a huge success! I found *Cherie and Kevin '89.* They were seniors that year. There's a picture of them with classmates in a toboggan at the Frost Valley Winter Retreat, page 44: STUDENTS ENJOY A SNOWY RIDE DOWN RABBIT RUN. Big smiles, green froggy mittens, Jets scarf, permed hair, earmuffs. Seeing their faces fed my soul. But I'm hollowing out again, wondering. Where are they today? Who are they? Do they still know each other? Do they even care?

Laney and Nico will meet on the roof today, I'm sure of it. It is their first anniversary. They need time to be alone. And I need to be there. We're celebrating. I push against the heavy steel door and step up and out, allowing the lock to catch behind me. I'm not afraid of climbing down. Anything they've done, I'll do. My lungs fill with fresh air. I'm proud of the roof. There wouldn't be *ninth period on the roof* if it weren't for me.

I hear the doorknob turn. They're early. The hinges are squeaking. I scrunch behind two of the heating/cooling machines and push all the way back until my back presses against the brick wall. I created their time here. I'm allowed to share in it, even just a little. The door opens and then closes slowly. This is it. His eyes. Her dimple. His fingertips. Her *S . . . K . . . I . . . N.*

"Dude, you here?" someone calls. It's not Nico. Heavy boots cross to the far corner.

"Dorian?" He's calling for Matt Dorian, Most Musical.

The door opens again and then falls back into place. Sneakers come to a stop less than two feet away from me. "Metal?"

It's Matt Dorian now. The first boy is Joey Metalia, his friend who does stand-up comedy. These guys are going to ruin everything.

"Hey. I haven't seen you all day," Metal says. "How's your dad?"

A lighter strikes. I smell a flame.

"Not good, man, not good. Broken collarbone, three bruised ribs."

"Oh, damn. Sorry."

Pot smoke wafts over my head. I nestle my face into my forearms and breathe into my blazer. Get lost, potheads. If Laney and Nico see you, they might not stay.

I wiggle my toes to keep my circulation moving and

alternate tensing my muscles and then relaxing them. The last time I hid was in Mr. Bryant's Volvo. He never locked his car doors—his one bad habit. It was comforting in there, like a cocoon. There was reading material: *Goosebumps, Caps for Sale,* dinosaur books, *Sharks,* Bed Bath & Beyond catalogs. I took some of those for Gran—the coupons never expire, they're her favorite currency.

"How's your dad's bike?" Metal asks.

"Totaled."

"Shit."

There was an open box of Lorna Doone shortbread cookies in Mr. Bryant's car, too, with an entire sleeve left. I hadn't eaten those since Gran got old and traded shortbread cookies for her coffee cake. Mr. Bryant's shortbreads were delicious.

"Damn, time's up," Dorian asks. "Ms. Fleiss is gonna kill me."

I hope she does. Then he won't come to the roof anymore.

"You didn't do that thing?" Metal asks.

"No. Why, did you?"

"Handed it in yesterday."

"You did not."

"I had to. If I fail I can't do my club gigs, and I'm screwed."

"Oh man, I'm dead."

The bell rings inside the building. I feel the vibration beneath me. If they don't leave now, I'll shove them off the roof myself.

They each inhale. Metal smashes out the joint with his boot.

"Clean it up."

"I got it."

"Get the whole thing."

"I'm gettin' it."

Metal and Dorian shuffle away. The door yawns wide and closes heavily. *Click.* Thank you, God! I stretch as the air begins to clear.

My knees are stiff and "creaky," as Gran puts it. Me, Gran, and Camille Fiore: the new Golden Girls. I place my hand on the corner of the big whirring machine and do a set of pliés in first position. Then grand pliés. Second-position grand pliés on my toes. I'm Laney Villanueva. Watch me relevé, balancé, piqué turn. My theme song is playing. I'm doing it, leaping across the floor. The little kids are watching me with their noses pressed against the window. They admire me, they want to be me as I flow into one last arabesque —

The doorknob jiggles behind me. It's them — for real this time. I crouch again, watching the door crack open. I'm panting as I duck behind the machinery and tuck my legs in.

"It looks amazing, really. It's so professional. The choreography is unique, it's entertaining, and it's beautifully executed, of course."

Nico.

"But the lighting, do you think I should —"

Laney.

They're here. The Cutest Couple and the scent of a dozen pink roses cut through Dorian and Metal's smog. The sun has lowered. I can see their shadows on the concrete. I feel cocooned again, but thrilled, too. We're finally alone.

"No, no, no. Don't change a thing," Nico says. "It's great how it's darker when you start in your opening position and then it's brighter where you end up by the window. That's perfect."

"But it could be distracting."

"Didn't you do that on purpose?"

"No. It's just the lighting that time of day."

"I thought it was on purpose because it works with the whole composition, the silent film theme, and the progression of the piece."

"Really?" Laney asks.

"Yes. That's the one. That's it. No more messing around with it, all right?" Nico says. "It's the winning take."

"Okay."

"You're all set, then? It's final?" Nico asks. "We're sending it in?"

"Yes. We're sending it in!"

We. Their shadows move closer together, only a sliver of light between them.

"Congratulations," Nico says.

"Don't say that! You'll jinx it."

"Impossible. They're going to love you."

"I hope so."

They're quiet now. I wait. He waits. *Do something. Please. For me.*

"Remember when I said it didn't matter, that I could go to any choreography program and be happy?" Laney asks.

"Yeah."

"I lied."

"I know."

"I mean, of course I want San Francisco and Boston to like

my video—I want to have options. But I really want my live audition to go well. I want to go to NYU."

I used to watch Laney study herself in the mirror at Allegro. I couldn't imagine what it felt like to see that reflection. Soon she'll walk into a dance studio at NYU and see herself in a new mirror. Nico will choose a school in the city. It will be autumn in Manhattan, a new beginning. She'll wear tall brown boots and carry her pointe shoes in her floppy tote. He'll meet her on the corner wearing a chunky sweater and peacoat. They'll have a usual restaurant, which they'll walk to without having to discuss it first.

"Then that's what we'll pray for," Nico says. Their shadows meld into one. I'm all warm in the middle.

Laney laughs.

"What?" Nico says.

"The 'composition and the progression of the piece'?"

"Why is that funny?" Nico asks.

"You're very choreographic."

"Dance has a vocabulary," he teases. "I learned that from someone. She was pretty hot, too."

"Oh, was she?"

"From what I remember."

They kiss. Their mouths, their souls, join. I touch my lips.

"Sorry, ugh, I smell pot," Laney says.

"Metal and Dorian," they say simultaneously.

I officially hate those guys.

Laney sighs. "Should we get going?"

"In a minute. Let's watch your video one more time."

"Okay. One more time."

I hear Laney's music, something jazzy, or is it bluesy? I think it's Etta James because it sounds like something Poppy would play. I didn't know his music was cool.

Laney's song spills over my head—a soulful rhythm that sways back and forth.

"Ah, that's so nice," Nico says. "I love that opening."

"Thank you," Laney says. "I changed it eight or nine times, but it's finally right."

Etta's passionate voice fills the air. "This is my favorite phrasing."

"Ah, I knew it. And I love this spin with one hand up and the other at your heart, that's beautiful, Laney," Nico says.

"Thanks. That part, I never changed."

In my mind, I see her turning beneath the spotlight and then stopping on a dime. She opens her expressive arms and then wraps them around herself. Suddenly I miss being eight and nine and ten, though I don't know why. I was already incomplete back then, watching Laney's eight-counts melt into motion, and longing for her beauty to seep into my pores.

In the fall, Laney Villanueva and Nico Fiore will sit inside a Greenwich Village coffee shop on Saturday afternoons, sometimes with their new college friends, sometimes without. Either way, you can find them there.

Etta James sings that she'd rather go blind than lose her lover. The bass *thump-thump*s above me . . . Listen to my heartbeat fall in time with Laney's song.

"This part right here is so intense. See the line from your hand down through your leg?" Nico says. "I would love a picture of that position right there."

I could photograph her. I would love to do it. I have to. I will, just like Philippe Turpin. I keep the Allegro Dance School brochure on my mirror at home. Some nights I stare at Laney suspended in midair until the photo turns into pixels. I fall asleep that way, with her image dissipating into gray dots. It's so strange how it gets harder and harder to see her the closer I look.

21

Mandy & Ryan 2009, Lina luvs Michael, R.U. + J.L. forever. There seem to be more and more names every day. It's a scab that I never should have started to pick, because now I can't quit. I have to find Mom and Dad. Or I have to know for certain that they aren't here. Either way, I want to know. Do I have to have a reason?

Anita & Tom were here at the same time as my parents. I'm trying to think if I've heard their names before, if Mom has ever mentioned them. I don't think so. I can't be sure. But they must've known my mother. Everybody loved Bianca. She was in their senior yearbook seventeen times. *Seventeen.* Smiling every time.

There's a phone number beneath Anita on cinder block E4. I still don't know why these people wanted their phone numbers here. I can't understand it, but I'm dialing. It's ringing. I walk up the stairs to get a stronger signal.

"Hellooo!" a cheerful man answers.

". . . Hi." I don't recognize my own voice. "I'm looking for Anita?"

"Anita has flown the coop. This is Anita's dad," he says, proud to be Anita's dad. "Who's this?"

"Bianca," I say. Mom's name feels foreign in my mouth. "This is Bianca Wickham. I went to Holy Family with Anita."

"Oh, one of her old high school friends?"

I don't know. Am I? "Yes."

"Super! Swimmer or partier?" he asks.

"Oh, uh, swimmer."

"That's too bad. You should've lived it up while you had time!" Anita's dad laughs. He is the best type of dad, the type that laughs at his own jokes. "This adulthood stuff is a real crap-fest, isn't it?"

Mom would wholeheartedly agree. "Yeah, it is."

"Don't say we didn't warn you. Well, Anita moved down to Virginia, going on four years now. Long Island is a tough place for young families. Are you still around here?"

"Yes, I am. Still in the area."

"Well, good for you, if you can manage it. It's getting pricier by the minute. Whoop, there! It just went up another two percent!" He chuckles. "Anyway, Anita's in Norfolk, but she did leave behind this slobbering, wrinkled hound of a dog, if you're interested. Adopt, don't shop, as they say." He sighs. "I'm just kidding. He's grown on me, the sloppy bastard." The dog howls in the background. "What can I help you with, Anita's old friend from swimming?"

Is Tom with Anita? Does she still know Tom? Whatever happened to Tom?

"Oh, it's nothing, really," I say.

"Any message for her? Backstroke tips? Butterfly advice? She still swims. The weather's better down there. Lots of pools and sunny days."

Did you know my mom and dad? What were they like? Did every-body envy them?

"No . . . no message, thank you, Mr. . . . uh, Anita's dad."

"Would you like me to pass her your number so that she can call you back? Or maybe she can find you on the Facebook. Let me get a pen so I can write down your info. You'd think I'd learn to keep a pen by the phone, but I'm a numbskull. Hang on."

I sink onto the top step and picture Anita's dad at the diner after a swim meet with Anita's teammates and their parents, because of course that's who he was, a Community Parent.

"Alrighty. Go ahead," he says. "Bianca? Still there?"

I hang up. Immediately, I regret it. I should have asked him. He would have been glad to answer. He's so happy, Anita's dad who's home at 2:51 in the afternoon. Anita can go back to him whenever she wants. Her dad and her dog and her old bedroom with her high school swim medals on the wall will still be there. I should have asked Anita's dad so many things.

22

I got a new envelope from Mom in our mailbox. It's a card with a bulldog wearing a pink bow.

> Hi Rafi,
> Let's go to dinner for my birthday. Can I pick you up from school? Hope you're having a good week. Here's some spending cash. Selfie, please!
> Love,
> Mom

Only five dollars. But she's coming soon, so that's okay. I text her not to pick me up at school because the parking lot is congested, and I want her to meet me at the diner.

When Mom and Dad went to Holy Family, Astro Diner was called Apollo Diner. It had brick on the outside and a sticky floor and greasy tables inside. Mom told me she used to order grilled cheese with tomato, and Dad would order the bacon cheeseburger. When the new owners turned Apollo into Astro Diner, the sign got a rocket ship logo and the interior got murals that show the view of Earth and other planets from space. Mom hasn't seen it redone. She'll like it.

"Hi, Gran." I flick my shoes off and hang my jacket. I forgot to research penny loafers again. I'm such a slacker. "How was your day?"

"There's a favorite-guest-star marathon today," Gran says. "Come sit. It's Brooke Shields."

"That's good, Gran. You like her. I have homework, but I'll sit with you when I'm done." I check the fridge. We have frozen chicken meatballs. I can boil pasta, quick and easy, which will give me some time to relax. "You know the Cutest Couple I photographed for the yearbook?" I say over my shoulder.

"Brooke Shields!" Gran says.

"It's their anniversary today. They've been together for exactly one year," I say, bringing her a banana. "Here's your potassium."

She reaches for it, eyes glued to the TV. "Thank you, Bianca."

"I'm Rafi, Gran," I say. "Remember, I took their photograph on the roof? Do you know if Mom and Dad ever hung out on the roof? Or the stairwell?"

"She starred in _The Blue Lagoon_ in 1980 with that Christopher Atkins. He wore nothing but that piece of cloth over his privates," Gran says, transfixed on the screen. "That poor little girl with that awful stage mother."

"The school roof, Gran, or the stairwell," I repeat. "Did Mom and Dad hang out there?"

"They hung out all over the place. That was their problem. Everywhere! Behind our backs, mostly." Gran unpeels her banana. "We should've sent her to that girls' school, What's-It-Called."

"Our Lady of Grace," I say.

"That's the one!"

Our Lady of Grace: the road not taken. "What could have been" still looms over Poppy and Gran, and maybe Mom, too. Imagine Bianca in an all-girls school? I can't. They used to argue about it right here in this living room. They'd threaten to transfer her whenever she got out of hand. Mom would have a fit and promise to be better. They'd cave. She would behave for a few weeks and then act up again . . . repeat drama until graduation. Poor Poppy and Gran.

"Where's Poppy?" I ask.

"You know, tinkering with the thingamajigs," she says. "*The Blue Lagoon* . . . what were they thinking? She was naked in that movie!"

I open the garage door. "Hi, Poppy."

He's on his stool reading *Local Boat and Auto*. "Rafi, my girl! Come over here and read this number for me, will you?" He points to the page. "I need to put a brighter bulb in here. The sun's on the wrong side of the house in the afternoon."

"Every day," I agree.

"Indeed."

I take the magazine and read the ad. "Reese Motors?"

"That's it. Gary Reese and sons. Too bad his sons never learned a lick about cars. All they ever wanted to do was throw a ball around and join fraternities."

I read the number. Poppy writes it down.

"And what are their hours? What's it say in the corner?" he asks, adjusting his lamp.

"It says eight to four."

"Eight to four, huh?" He scratches his ear. "Well, of course."
The clock reads 4:09.

"Sorry, Poppy," I say. "You can try them in the morning."

"Eight a.m. sharp," he says. "Every unanswered phone call is
a missed sale. Remember that."

"Mom's celebrating with me for her birthday. She's meeting
me at Astro Diner after school," I say, as Poppy returns loose
tools onto the pegboard.

"Uh-huh." He nods. "It's that time of year again, is it?" He
holds up a bolt with a metal ring attached. "Do you see another
one of these anywhere?"

I look around a little. "No."

He doesn't want to get into it about Bianca. He hates when
I get my hopes up about her. But it's different this year with her
at that office job. It's what she needed to feel good about herself. She just needed that little boost so that things could fall
into place. And she invited me this time. I didn't ask her to dinner. That's progress.

"We'd better watch where we step till we find it. It'll cramp
your style if you step on that sucker." He puts the single bolt in
a clear drawer.

"Okay, Poppy."

"And stay away from those fraternity boys and their lambda-
beta-theta-hoopla parties, you hear me?"

I turn to go inside. "Thanks, Poppy. I'll be careful."

23

Laney Villanueva and Nico Fiore are here late, as promised. They're walking toward me. She's holding sneakers. Gym clothes. Water bottle. He's carrying his black Jansport and wearing his purple sweatshirt that's ratty at the cuffs, the one he wears on cool mornings and carries home on warm afternoons. Their wet hair, and their hands, tightly clasped, say, *We had sex!*

Behind them, the decals on the window say, HOLY FAMILY HIGH SCHOOL: BE THE LIGHT! Laney Villanueva and Nico Fiore are on fire. I'm melting.

"Good morning!" Laney says, bounding toward my counter.

"Hey." Nico grins from ear to ear. I guess they've gotten better at "parallel parking." "We're just getting in. We were . . . uh . . ."

"At the DMV?" I smile.

"Yeah," Nico says. "Something like that." An inside joke! Just look at us.

"Nico said you would sign us in?" Laney says, peeking at Father Philip's empty office. This is it—we're a team now. "Just this last time, we promise. We don't want to get you in trouble."

"Don't worry about that." I shrug. No biggie. "I got this."

"Thank you, Rafi," she says. The sound of my name falls

so naturally from Laney's mouth now. This is our routine; it's who we are.

Nico whispers to her. He says they should do something special together after the craziness of rehearsals and exams die down. They'll think of a plan for just the two of them. He's touching her cheek, and she's nodding without breaking his gaze. How could anyone look away from Nico Fiore, whose skin is clear this time, and whose voice is saying so sweetly, *Just you and me, just you and me?*

I'm drinking them in, watching how happy I've made them. It's my pleasure to do it—whatever they want. Remembering their late passes, I reach for the pad. I write them up and mash the stamp in the ink.

Father Philip has gone to visit the cafeteria, and Mrs. Bardot is a caffeine addict, so I stamp freely, feeling the satisfying *thump* of rubber hitting paper. It's only the three of us here, free and clear. What a day to be alive!

EXCUSED

EXCUSED

Laney hugs her gym sweats. Nico tosses his Jansport over his shoulder. They're ready to go. I splay the passes in my hands like winning lottery tickets. This time, I feel drunk from belonging.

"For you." I hand a pass to Nico.

"Thanks," he says.

"And for you." I hand the other to Laney.

In three . . . two . . . one . . .

Laney leans forward. "You're the best, Rafi."

Bam.

I am! I am! I am!

They exit through the glass doors: BE THE LIGHT!

Holy Family's Cutest Couple, my friends, burn my retinas.

Just you and me.

And me.

"Did I miss anything?" Mrs. Bardot lumbers in. She turns her little radio on to *Your favorites from yesterday and today!* which is a pretty wide time span, and since yesterday outspans today, I hardly get to hear anything new. I need to catch up at home on the new songs, the ones that Nico and Laney sing in his car.

"Nope," I lie. "Not a thing." I add a yawn for effect and return to stuffing invitations.

"Well, this is how we like to start the day, isn't it? Nice and quiet," Mrs. Bardot says, referring to the Tomás Diaz incident with his ex-friends, Omar and Vinny, who have since been expelled. Laney had been right; Father Philip is fair, and he is a good listener. Tomás is still a member of our Holy Family.

"You wouldn't happen to know why the Cavino kids have been out this long, would you?" Mrs. Bardot asks, checking the attendance sheet.

"No idea," I answer (Caribbean vacation for their grandparents' fiftieth anniversary).

I notice my fingers: they're bright, inky red. There's red everywhere—red smudges on the counter, red on my cuffs, red on the edge of my palms, red fingerprints on the envelopes I've been stuffing for Season of Giving donations.

We don't want to get you in trouble. I hear Laney in my head. *Trouble.* It would be a disaster.

Keeping my back turned to Mrs. Bardot, I grab a wad of tissues from my backpack and wet it with my tongue. Then I rub and rub and rub. It won't come off. It's been on for too long.

"Are you all right, Rafi?" Mrs. Bardot asks.

"Yes, I—" I squeeze antibacterial gel onto my skin and rub harder. If Mrs. Bardot finds out about the late passes, she'll tell Father Philip. He'll think I haven't changed at all. He'll think I'm back to my old habits. But I'm not, I swear, I've changed. I volunteer for things. I'm a babysitter. But the gel isn't removing the ink. It's smearing it and turning my hands pink.

"Did you use the stamp pad, Rafi? For who? Did you collect their doctor's notes?" she asks sharply over her oldies station playing the Lovin' Spoonful.

"No. No, I didn't use it," I say.

My hands are turning raw. I know that I hated working here at first. I hated that Father Philip put me here as a punishment. I hated being under his watch every morning. And I hated cleaning dirty birdcages every Wednesday while he pestered me with questions. But I don't hate it anymore. Look at everything this job has brought me. I need this. I can't let Father Philip take it away from me now that Nico and Laney and I are a *we*. "I was just . . . I was only . . ."

"You shouldn't play with that stamp pad, dear. These things are messy and costly."

"I know, Mrs. Bardot. I wasn't," I say, rubbing the counter hot pink.

Father Philip will strip me of my Leadership Club points. He'll ban me from yearbook again. I won't be able to photograph the Senior Awards Brunch. The radio is getting louder and louder, singing "Summer in the City" . . .

It's mocking me with one of yesterday's favorites. And Cat Lorrey's grass-stained cleats are still in the lost and found, taunting me, threatening me. Any day now, Cat will figure out that I stole her shoes, that I was the reason she missed practice, I was the reason she couldn't flirt with Nico, and I was the reason she had to buy new cleats. I googled them—they cost two hundred dollars! She'll come after me. Then Father Philip will know, and then Poppy and Gran, Mariah Rourke, Jenna, and then . . . Nico and Laney. If I lose them I might die. I'm already on my second and final chance. I won't just lose my job here. I won't just get kicked off of yearbook. I'll be expelled. I can't let that happen. I love Holy Family. My parents are here somewhere. As soon as I can, I'm throwing those cleats into the dumpster.

"We'll have to ask the custodian for the proper kind of spray to clean that." Mrs. Bardot won't stop nagging, and now she's involving other people in my business.

Why does everyone care so much about what I do? She's treating me like a delinquent. This red ink is a lie. It's too severe. I haven't hurt anybody. I've been helping. I had promised Nico and needed to show them that my word is good, so they'll need me in their life as badly as I need them. I wasn't playing. This isn't a game at all.

24

The train is slowing down. We're almost there. Penn Station. There's nothing wrong with what I'm doing. It's much safer, actually, to follow them around Manhattan rather than in school. It was scary the other day, almost getting caught, but it was a good reminder that I need to be more careful. Mrs. Bardot has zero power over me in the outside world, and Father Philip can't ever find out. This isn't strange. This is smarter.

We're stopping at the platform. Passengers are gathering their bags, winding their scarves around their necks, and stepping into the aisles. It was a close call, catching the same 10:22 train. I should've been on the 9:37. Gran's laundry took forever. I hadn't planned on washing her bedding, too. Thank god I saw Laney and Nico before they saw me and was able to sneak on to the train after them. I'll keep them in my sight and lie low.

The doors are opening. They're exiting the train car ahead of mine. Lucky for me, her teal hat is easy to spot as I follow them out and up the staircase. Penn Station is packed during the holiday season, which works well for me. I'm nothing but a tiny speck in this sea of humans. Getting lost in a crowd is my talent.

We move toward the downtown subway. I drop all the coins from my coat pocket into a Salvation Army bucket. I don't need anything weighing me down. The Salvation Army Santa rings his bell. "Ho-ho-ho!"

Laney holds Nico's arm as the subway pulls in. A mom beside them tussles with her little kid, trying to wrangle an iPad away. An old guy is pushing trash over the platform with his cane. A college girl is trying not to drop her fat bag of laundry. City people seem to live for the past or some better future. Laney and Nico are living for the present and the future simultaneously. Comparing them to everyone here, it's obvious how different they are. See how he's swinging her arm as they wait? They're so excited. So am I. Why wouldn't I be? Today is morsel-y. A morsel of promise. Today will change the course of everything that follows.

We're boarding. I let them step into their car, and then I enter the one behind them, along with the old man with the cane. It smells like apple juice in here. I see a wet spot that's spreading and running underneath the seats.

I know just what Laney and Nico are talking about. Her hands are probably sweaty from being nervous, so she's probably taking her gloves off. Nico's telling her that she's going to be a superstar, that she's more than prepared, and that she's a natural. He's reminding her that what they're looking for is "raw talent" (from the website), and the admissions committee would have to be blind not to see that in her. Then they're chuckling because that's the title of her audition song, "I'd Rather Go Blind" by Etta James. (It *is* one of Poppy's songs!) "Ha! So funny." They're laughing, and that's breaking up their nervousness.

There's no need to be nervous, Laney. I'm right here. I'm here to cheer you on. I'm here for moral support and positive vibes.

She's trained her whole life for this. I know she'll do well.

But true friends show up. They support each other to reach their goals. They don't bail during challenging times.

We get off at Astor Place. I follow them up the staircase to the city above, and behold! This is the Cutest Couple in Greenwich Village among makeup artists carrying clear cases filled with brushes and compacts and round cotton pads, and blue-haired musicians in combat boots, and married people walking their sweater-wearing rescue dogs. This is Laney Villanueva and Nico Fiore walking past the park, on the very street where they'll be next year, "strolling like on a date or something," as Millie would say. Next fall, it won't just be a date, it will be their life.

I had to come. I want to be the first to know how the audition goes. Once we find out that she'll be here at NYU and he'll be at Baruch or Hunter, the pressure will be off, and I can put my worries aside. Think of all the worry-free partying at Fernando's and hanging out at the Fiore house and going for fro-yo we can enjoy together. The three of us can coast easy till June. They can have senioritis like Cat Lorrey. They can come in *late*.

We made it to a brick building with skinny trees in front. He's holding her arms, wishing her good luck. Laney takes her hat off and shakes her hair. She wants it flowy, in all its glory. She steps back, no final hug, because she's so ready for this audition and for everything else to begin.

"Go!" Nico laughs, loud and clear.

Laney nods. She runs inside, grasping her dance bag. Nico stands for a moment, staring through the vestibule. Then he checks his phone and seems to follow its directions up the street.

The audition could take a while. There's no telling if they're on time or if they've fallen behind schedule, and if so, how many dancers have to audition before her.

I left home in a hurry without having eaten; I'm so hungry now. I slip into the bagel shop across the street. Inside, the heat is on full blast. My cheeks feel like they're burning. I order an everything bagel with tuna salad. After the first bite, I can't eat fast enough. I scarf down the rest, leaving nothing but poppy seeds on the wax paper. I definitely can't let Laney and Nico see me now, because that bagel was potent. I stink of garlic and tuna.

I don't usually drink iced tea because the caffeine makes me jittery, but I'm treating myself today. It's a special occasion. I put my earbuds in and play the Etta James song, which I added to my playlist after Elvis and EXO featuring Matt King Kole and Radiohead. Damn, I need to add Broadway songs but keep forgetting. Laney must be auditioning by now. I pray for her while repeating her song. *Feel my strength, Laney. I'm here. You got this.* Besides Nico, I'm her only other friend who came. Doesn't this make me her *best* friend?

I duck into a boutique that has embroidered pillows in the window because it doesn't look like a place Nico would go. I can watch for him from here. Gran would like some of this oddball stuff they sell. This pillow says, HOME: WHERE I CAN LOOK UGLY AND NOT CARE. It might make her laugh. Or it might offend her. It would make me laugh to find out. These little pillboxes are cute, too. I actually like them for myself. I like hiding places. I think I'll buy the silver one with pressed flowers on its glass cover.

He's back. Nico is walking up the street, carrying a white

shopping bag. I can't read where it's from. I have to take a picture of him and then zoom in. Magnolia Bakery! Yum. They have the most amazing banana pudding. There's a Magnolia back at Penn Station. I saw it when we came in. I'll treat myself to one of those, too, on my way back.

Here comes Laney, bursting out the door, clutching her teal hat. She's rosy-cheeked and grinning madly. Nico opens his arms. He lifts her up and sways her back and forth. Now I know for certain—the rest of our year will be golden. We are going to live it up.

On the show *So You Think You Can Dance,* when a dancer is in danger of being voted off, the judges make them "dance for their lives." Gran and Poppy love a heated dance-off. That's what Laney has done. She gave it her all. It's good that I came. She felt my energy holding her up; I know she did.

Nico lets out a "Woo!" Laney laughs over his shoulder.

Several girls exit the building. They notice Laney and Nico in their embrace. Two of them smile as they pass by. The others roll their eyes, revealing their inner demons. Isn't it funny how cynical some people, even dancers, can be? If they could only see Laney and Nico the way I see them, they'd know that it's possible. There's real happiness to be had, ours for the taking.

I watch as Nico gives Laney the Magnolia bag. "You did not!" she says. She looks inside it and squeals. My cheeks hurt from smiling. Laney opens her pudding right there on the sidewalk. Nico hands her a spoon and some napkins, and she digs in. It's the sweetest thing.

Their future is unrolling like a red carpet. I can't wait to talk about it when we're back at school, or back at Nico's house.

(Even better!) I'll ask all the right questions; our shared memories are so intertwined now. *Did you take the train to the city? Did you wear the wine-colored leotard? I hope you celebrated afterward with a treat!* They'll be thrilled to tell the story. I'll think, *Yes, I know. I carried you every step of the way.*

25

Watch me hustle. I've just photographed the Senior Awards ceremony and am currently earning six volunteer points by setting up refreshments in the lobby. Leadership Club status, here I come! I'm on a winning streak today.

This morning, my yearbook layouts were Mariah Rourke approved. "These pages look fine, I guess," she said, which really means that the pages (football highlights, Halloween, grades 9–10 homeroom classes) kick ass and she's fully impressed, but it's killing her because she doesn't want to give me the satisfaction by saying so. I, however, am dripping with satisfaction, it's oozing from my pores. You cannot live without me, Mariah Rourke.

I designed a border around the homeroom photos with the teacher's name and homeroom number inset within the border. They look much more anchored and defined within the space. And the football highlights have wide-angle photos as well as close-ups. The mixture of the two adds depth and interest. Even if you don't know what a fumble is, which I don't, you can still appreciate an image of floodlights filtering through the fog, and the sharp profile of James Forsythe, number 10, praying on the bench.

Mr. Tosh, who is old but new to Holy Family, doesn't know my past and believes that I'm indispensable to Yearbook Club. "You've got a knack for this, Ms. Wickham," he said. Mr. Tosh is no Mr. Bryant, but that old-fashioned word has been bouncing inside my brain like a pinball: *knack, knack, knack, knack.* He'll like my photos from tonight, I'm sure. We have soft lighting in the auditorium. The photos have a sort of a golden tone.

My stellar day continues — these lemon cookies from Golden Edges Bakery are sensational. They're gooey and not too sweet. I've never called a cookie sensational before. I don't think I've ever called anything sensational. They truly, truly are. See how I've arranged them in overlapping circles on the table? This is the kind of attention to detail I can contribute to Leadership Club. Parents and students who've discovered these cookies keep coming back for more. I should stash a few in my blazer.

"Rafi!" Millie Fiore comes running toward me. "I got a junk drawer prize!"

"You did?" I say. I spot Jenna against the windows, pretending not to watch as Nico Fiore's sister hugs me. Do you see how close I am with this family, Jenna?

"We were supposed to pick up and throw away ten pieces of trash, but I picked up seventeen pieces, and then I helped Krista Berlin find enough for her ten, and then Ms. Ryder said that was very kind of me, and I won a junk prize!"

"That's amaaazing!"

"Wasn't it funny when the table fell off the stage?" Millie asks. "I snorted laughing."

"Hilarious!"

Mrs. Bardot had placed the award certificates on a small

table at the edge of the stage. When Father Philip pulled his microphone, the cord pulled the table leg, and down it went. Students picked up the certificates, but they got knocked out of order, so awardees received random certificates at the handoff. Father Philip announced that they'd sort it all out later.

"Whoosh!" Millie says, spreading her arms to demonstrate.

At graduation, grads get empty dummy tubes, purely for the photo opportunity. Real diplomas are sent through the mail.

Stop. Don't think about graduation. It's ages away.

I see Mrs. Fiore rushing over. She's angry. I watch her face and steel myself. What if they have a nanny cam? How had I not thought of this before? Maybe Mrs. Fiore keeps a hidden camera on the bookshelf. I'd been too excited to think straight. She must have seen me go up the stairs to Nico's room and not come back down for an hour. I've thrown Cat Lorrey's cleats into the dumpster, but I never considered a nanny cam. Please don't yell at me here, Mrs. Fiore. Please, not in front of everyone.

"Millie!" Mrs. Fiore says. "I told you to stick with your dad. I've been all over looking for you."

I exhale. It's fine. I'm fine. No nanny cam. *Breathe . . . breathe . . . breathe . . .*

"I'm with *Rafi!*" Millie says. Duh. Where else would she be?

"Hi, Rafi," Mrs. Fiore says, exasperated. "She needs to stop running off. We can't keep up with her."

"She has a lot of energy," I say. She's also comfortable with me here at Holy Family, her brother's school, my school, which will someday be her school, our home away from home.

"Too much," she sighs.

Can you hear how Nico's mom confides in me about the

challenges of motherhood and the Fiore family dynamics? We're tight this way.

I should ask Mrs. Fiore for a ride home. Maybe they're all going to the diner. They'll have to invite me. The Fiores, the Villanuevas, and me.

"And she's been talking about you nonstop," Mrs. Fiore adds. "It's been all 'Rafi this' and 'Rafi that' at our house lately."

Did you hear that, Jenna? Nonstop. Millie must've talked me up in front of Nico. He's heard about my sparkling qualities, like how I did cartwheels in the park and taught Millie to call "punch buggy red" when we spotted a Volkswagen Beetle in front of her school. She must've mentioned that I didn't force her to summarize the chapters she'd read, and that I built a Lego dining table for her rabbit. Nico probably heard that I'm so much fun, she couldn't help but fall asleep because of how fun I am. Of course he'll hang out with me now.

"I need to pee." Millie grabs her mom's arm and pulls her away.

"You'll have to sit for us again," Mrs. Fiore says.

"Tomorrow?" I didn't look through Nico's dresser drawers last time. "I can come tomorrow."

"Not tomorrow. Next week?" Mrs. Fiore calls over her shoulder. "Let me take her to the bathroom, and then we'll schedule."

"Okay. I'll wait right here."

This awards ceremony is for seniors, but I'm the real winner here. I'm going back to Nico's house, the Fiores do not have a nanny cam, and oh my god, these lemon cookies!

"You babysit for the Fiores?" Greta Novak has sidled up to

me again. Someone needs to put a bell around her neck. That someone should be me. I'll fasten it nice and tight, really tight.

"Like, you've been to their house?"

"Of course I've been to their house, Greta. Tons of times." I don't have to embellish. She's envious enough already, but I cannot be contained, this is my awards ceremony! Give me my trophy!

Greta stares at me with that Hansel-and-Gretel-lost-in-the-woods expression again. She wants details. Does Nico leave his sneakers in the hallway? (No, mudroom.) Are you there when he comes home? Do you talk to him? (No, and no. Not yet, but soon. But I would never tell Greta that.)

"Is there something you want?" I ask, as if my relationship with the Fiores is a casual, everyday matter.

"No, nothing," Greta says, because she is weak and doesn't know how to get what she needs. She probably wants to replace me. She wants to say that if there's ever a day I can't babysit, I should pass Mrs. Fiore her phone number. Well, that is never going to happen because 1) I will never be unavailable for the Fiores, and 2) Greta is never going to speak up for herself.

"Are you sure? You're standing here staring at me like you need something." I give her another chance. Come on, Greta. This is your moment. I'm leaving breadcrumbs all over the forest floor for you.

"No, I'm good," she answers, bending the stack of programs in her hands. She's not good at all. She's pathetic.

"You know what, Greta?" I feel sorry for her all of a sudden. "Don't be so shy. You'll never get what you want from being shy. I'm not saying this to be a bitch, it's just that I used to be the same way. I never said what I wanted, and it got me nowhere."

It's true. I wanted to be class treasurer in fourth grade. I was good at keeping records and checking boxes and keeping things safe in a tin box with a lock and key. But I didn't raise my hand during nominations because Derek Wise had raised his hand, and everybody liked Derek Wise, even though he wasn't good at any of those things. I should have raised my hand and listed my qualifications. I should have told my class that I absolutely lived for locks and keys, but I didn't.

I'd never been part of anything good until I decided to be, and look at me now. Who do you think tied the white ribbon around every single one of these Awards Ceremony programs? Who do you think photographed the programs on the table right before we opened the front doors? That's right: me. Because I'm not satisfied anymore with being "good." I want more.

Greta is staring sadly at her feet. She doesn't realize that this is kindest advice she's ever received.

"Here." I pull a cookie from my pocket and hand it to her. "Have one of these. They're sensational."

I need to get something to drink. It will also give me a reason to visit the beverage table where Laney is talking with her friends. Nico must be around here somewhere—

Why is Nico talking to Jenna? They have no reason to talk. She's never spoken to him before. I didn't even know Jenna was still here. She was supposed to help during the ceremony. She's not getting any more volunteer points for staying after. She must've been waiting for Nico, waiting to tell him something, waiting to humiliate me. It must've killed her to see me so close with the Fiores.

I push past dads in khakis and moms in cashmere scarves that smell of pressed face powder, past Leadership Club juniors carrying trays of punch made with grapefruit juice and ginger ale. I rush faster and closer to Jenna, who's about to hand Nico Fiore a cream-colored folder.

Are my photos in that envelope? Are those my mementoes? Nico's karaoke strip of paper from Fernando's party? Nico's anniversary note to Laney? Nico's class notes on the Globe Theatre? How did Jenna get them? It must have been Gran. She's been asking about Jenna for months. Gran must have let her into the house and allowed her into my bedroom. She must've gone through my middle school backpack. I have to stop her from—

"Jenna?" I step directly between her and Nico. "Jenna. Can I talk to you, please?"

"I'm busy, Rafi," she says, holding the folder.

"Now." I pull her aside.

"What is your problem?" she asks, trying to keep her voice down. "I thought you were done speaking to me."

"What are you and Nico Fiore talking about?" I ask.

She crosses her arms. "That's not your business."

"Oh, that's funny," I say. "Because you seem to think that everything I do is your business. You can't stand to see me happy without you, can you?"

"Rafi, get a grip. You're being loud," Jenna says.

"Are you talking to Nico about me?" I ask, gritting my teeth.

"Why the hell would we be talking about you?" she asks.

"That's what you do when you're jealous." Heat is rising in my chest. "You tell people about me, and you show them things so that they won't like me anymore."

Jenna whispers, "Don't do this, Rafi."

Last spring I was called into Father Philip's office. When I walked in, Mr. Bryant was there, and Poppy was there, and a Polly Pocket toy of a poodle with a green collar was sitting on Father Philip's desk.

There were always crumbs in the back seat of Mr. Bryant's car, but I would brush them off and settle in just fine. Sometimes I'd play with his daughter's Polly Pockets. I kept that one, the tiny poodle toy with a green collar. It didn't matter. She had so many: a kitten, a snowman, Polly Pockets in bathing suits and sunglasses, Pollys that lived eternal vacations. She wouldn't have missed just one.

It's come to my attention that you've been inside Mr. Bryant's car? And you've been to his house as well? Father Philip said the second I sat down. *This is highly disturbing behavior, Rafi, highly disturbing.* That was the end of Mr. Bryant and me.

"What's in the folder?" I ask Jenna.

She clutches it to her chest. "None of your concern!"

This is a gross violation of Mr. Bryant's privacy, Father Philip said. Poppy's eyes were watery; he grew older and more wrinkled as he listened. I was a disappointment to him, just like his daughter had been.

Mr. Bryant said nothing. He didn't even look at me, not even once, not a single glance, he couldn't stand to look at me. On the desk, the smiling Polly Pocket puppy taunted me.

"Give me that folder!"

"People are staring," Jenna says through clenched teeth. "Calm down."

"Calm down? Calm down?" I yell. "You called my *dad!*"
This was the worst of all Jenna's betrayals. It was bad enough
having to watch Poppy wither in front of my eyes. But to put
Dad through that, too? I will never forgive her. "You knew he
was working. He had to worry about me from across the country! What good did that do?"

"He needed to hear it," she says. "He needed to know that
you were—"

"What?" I lean forward. Dad called me from a motel in
Phoenix. He asked me what I'd done. Jenna had used that *word.*
He doubted me, I could feel it. "That I'm *what?* Go on. Say it."
Call me crazy again, Jenna, and I will destroy you.

She drops her head. "He just needed to know."

I settle back on my heels and smile. "Coward."

Jenna had been brushing her hair in front of my dresser
when I had left to go to the bathroom. When I came back, my
jewelry box was open. She was holding the toy between her
thumb and index finger. *Is this one of Bea Bryant's Polly Pockets?*
She glared at me in that maddening way. *No,* I said. *It's mine.*
It's my Polly Pocket. But she wouldn't let it go. *What are you*
doing, Rafi? Mr. Bryant is our teacher. You're obsessed. This isn't
normal. You're a stalker. You're crazy. That was the end of Jenna
and me.

I have no choice but to suspend you. During that time I will evalu-
ate the situation and determine if further disciplinary action, or possibly
even expulsion, is necessary, Father Philip said.

I can't let Jenna ruin me again. I grab the envelope from her
and rip the contents out: NATIONAL HONOR SOCIETY CERTIFI-
CATE: NICO FIORE.

"Father Philip asked me to redistribute the certificates to the correct students," Jenna says. "Are you satisfied?"

Nico steps toward us. His family and Laney and the Villanuevas are watching us from the exit doors. We were supposed to schedule babysitting. I was going to ask Mrs. Fiore for a ride home. I should be joining them for dinner. Instead, Mrs. Fiore is staring, pressing Millie hard against her side. "Uh, sorry to interrupt," Nico says, "but I have to get going."

I hand him the certificate; it's crumpled from my grip. He takes it and walks toward the double doors.

He overheard everything.

26

I've been here before, so this isn't weird. I'm not sneaking in.
I'm not prowling. They know me. I'm like a neighbor on a
Nickelodeon show who pops by casually to say hello. I'll ring
the doorbell like a normal person to remind them how regular
I am, how laid-back and fun, how I'm their favorite babysitter.
The argument between Jenna and me isn't who I am at all. That
was Jenna trying to make me look bad again. I have to rebound.

This isn't normal, she'd said. But who is Jenna to determine
what's normal and what's not? I'd done nothing wrong with
Mr. Bryant. Jenna is the one who made it into something sor-
did in her narrow little mind.

What did she mean by "normal" anyway? It's not normal to
look up to someone? It's not normal to want to be near them?
It's not normal to be passionate about something? We're teenage
girls! We're the same as the teenage girls who fainted at Beat-
les concerts and the teenage girls who marched for our lives in
Washington, D.C. To need and to crave and to want—this is
what teenage girls are supposed to do. Doesn't she know? Pas-
sion is our job.

I press the bell and hear it ring behind the shiny black door.
There's a holler inside the house and then footsteps. The door

opens. Nico Fiore. The sight of this real boy's body in low-slung sweatpants and a threadbare T-shirt ignites the teenage-girl instincts in me again — the need and the crave and the want.

"Rafi," he says. He is looking at me in that way — the same way Jenna looked at me — as though I should be dragged away in a straitjacket. *You're a stalker.*

I have to fix this.

I dangle my keys in front of him. "Ta-da!" I present Poppy's 1971 Plymouth Road Runner in Nico's driveway, sweeping my arms in its direction like I'm Vanna White on *Wheel of Fortune*. "Look what I stole for you!"

Nico's eyes grow wide, wide, wider.

"Who is it?" Laney emerges from the living room, hair mussed, eating from a package of Goldfish crackers. She's in yoga pants and a tank top, no white sweatshirt. It must be spaghetti night.

"Hi, Laney!" I say. My heart is thumping out of rhythm, in random thuds that feel out of whack. *Knack, knack, knack, knack . . .*

"She stole the Road Runner," Nico tells Laney.

Laney gapes at the car. "What have you done, Rafi?"

I'm being proactive, reclaiming control of a bad situation, taking the bull by the horns, as they say. Maybe Laney doesn't understand, maybe neither of them do, that me driving to them is symbolic of our first meeting. *Don't you remember? In the main office? Both of you lying about the driver's test? We were in on it together. And here we are again, me without a license, the three of us against the world.*

It doesn't matter. They'll think more clearly later when they reminisce. All the hidden messages will come together then. They'll appreciate it when it dawns on them.

"Are you surprised? Are you happy? Excited?" I ask. "She's ours for the night." I jingle-jangle the keys. It's a festive sound. I have come bearing good tidings. "We can go anywhere you want. Nico, you said you wanted to drive her. I heard you say it."

"Let me have those." Nico grabs the keys from my hand and heads straight to the driveway wearing his sweats. There's no time to change clothes, because he can't hold back his excitement. Even Laney is shoving her feet into her sneakers and pulling a random windbreaker from Nico's front closet. It's time to get up and go. Who can resist such an adventure?

In a movie, this scene would be about the hot car, the guzzling, growling beast let loose into the dark, dark night. The camera would hold on the front wheel picking up speed, and then it would pan over the letters, ROAD RUNNER, and then over the Petty blue shimmering under the moonlight.

In reality, this momentous night is about Nico wearing his at-home clothes, his strong hands on the steering wheel, and Laney still snacking on Goldfish in the passenger seat.

"Want some?" Laney turns and shakes the crackers. Somehow, in the dark, her eyes appear lighter than they do in daylight.

Yes, yes, yes! I want anything from you. Everything! "Sure."

She tips the package. The Goldfish come pouring out, too many at a time, like I've won a jackpot, and I have, I truly have. The slot machine keeps on giving. *Ding! Ding! Ding!* We laugh as I make a bowl with my two hands. I've struck it filthy rich in this car with Laney Villanueva and Nico Fiore.

As we speed across Long Island, I lift cheesy Goldfish crackers from my palms with my tongue. Nothing has ever tasted better. I feel as if I'm Laney and Nico's child, and they've whisked me out of bed for surprise late-night fun. I want to scream out the window, *Look at me now!* But no one would hear. So I say it to myself: *Look at me now! I am here with them.*

Nico turns the radio on. He finds *today's hits.* Take that, Mrs. Bardot! We're modern teens, breaking all the rules in yesterday's car. This is how memories are made. See us! Envy us! We're a spark of youth driving from the past into the present!

Laney and Nico sneak looks at each other. I see them, the lovebirds, out for a romantic night. Who would have predicted Nico and Laney and me and MacGraw, adding to Holy Family history?

We are only two songs into the evening, but it's happening, it's really happening, just as I planned. Playing now is "Crash! Damn! Boom!" by EXO featuring Matt King Kole. My every fantasy is coming true. I practiced. I trained hard. I am ready. I roll the windows down to prove it to Laney and Nico and everyone along Hempstead Turnpike. I rhyme and I rap, I'm exactly on beat and don't miss a single word. I make a megaphone with my hands, which smell of "flavor-blasted extra cheddar." I belt it loud and clear: *"Fuck this shit, the doom, the gloom. Here comes the sun, my son. Roll the stone from the tomb. We're back to the livin' now. Crash! Damn! Boom!"*

Laney and Nico are impressed. I can tell by the way they look back at me in awe. *Who is this gem of a friend we're lucky enough to have found?* they're thinking. *How blessed we are to have this daredevil, dear-hearted girl who took her granddad's most prized possession from the garage the second he fell asleep. She has risked it all for us!*

It's working. I'm erasing the Awards Ceremony from their minds. I'm fun. I'm light-spirited and spontaneous. *A really cool girl.*

So, this is what it feels like to be exhilarated! *"No way, not ever, not me, not you!"* Laney forgot to do the pointing. She wasn't ready because I've completely taken her by surprise. It's understandable. We'll do it next time — she'll point at me and I'll point to her — it's our thing.

There must be some sort of breathing method that performers use, a proper way to rap without getting winded. I'll learn it and use it next time. I'll apply it to singing, too, so that I can put my name and my song title in the karaoke hat at parties — what a hit I'll be! What is a duet with three people called?

Nico pulls into the Garden City Golf Club and parks. CLOSED, the sign says, but we are breaking rules together left and right. There are no barriers when it comes to this friendship.

"Why don't you two take a walk?" I tell them. "Have some time together."

Nico takes the keys with him, and they go. I climb on top of the hood and watch them walk to the edge of the golf course. They are "strolling."

Laney and Nico lean against the wooden fence. They whisper to one another what Poppy would call "sweet nothings." But they aren't nothings. When you love someone, their words are everything. I can't hear them, but I can imagine.

What a night!

Such a time!

What a life!

What's the one thing you can give to people who have everything? Time. They're walking along the grass now, his arm over her shoulders, her fingers laced into his. Talking softly and gazing at the stars, they're soaking up the night, not even taking selfies because they're appreciating life as we live it. *As we live it!* That's what Angela Fortunato told us to do when I photographed her in *Our Town*. Tonight, the three of us are Thornton Wilder's ideal youths.

I'm breaking through. I'm showing Nico and Laney that the drama with Jenna was nothing but a measly, insignificant blip. I have hit reset, and now I'm back.

I sway back and forth and start to sing Poppy's Billy Joel song about the king and queen of the prom because Nico and Laney are "Brenda and Eddie." I'm not talented like Nico at singing, but my notes are filled with emotion. I'm feeling it, creating a soundtrack to their evening. This song is coming from my heart.

They're walking toward the clubhouse. Their shadows move against the hill of the golf course as I end the song and begin another. Laney knows this one. It's her theme song, after all, the one that all of us girls from Allegro remember.

"It's the climb!" I toss my hand up and hit the high note. Laney glances back. I knew she'd recognize it. If she starts to dance I might faint from happiness.

I've never been to this golf course before, but maybe Nico and Laney have. Maybe this is where their parents play. I remember their dads comparing golf swings the night of the banquet. What is it like to have a father who plays golf on Sundays and comes home in time for dinner? My dad should have, could have been a golf dad, but he isn't because . . . because . . . never mind. Don't think about it tonight of all nights.

The Sons of Orwell are in Richmond. My phone says that's less than seven hours from here. I finish Laney's song and sing "Song to Myself" for Nico. He'll get it. He'll feel our connection. *"Singin' alone but never lonely, me, myself, and I, I, I—I don't mind, I don't mind, I don't mind, whatever it is I find . . ."* You'd never know from listening to me that I didn't like this song when I first heard it. I must've been too young for it then, but I love it now.

"Hey!" I jump to my feet. "You guys, the Sons of Orwell are in Virginia. We can leave now and catch the concert tomorrow."

Nico turns. "What?"

"The Sons of Orwell are in Richmond. Let's go!" I say. I took Jenna to a concert when they were here in New York. Dad brought us backstage to meet the band, which was fun, but she only knew a couple of their songs. Nico and Laney would enjoy it much more since they're fans.

I miss Dad's scrambled eggs. He made them for dinner once. If I could, I'd take Laney and Nico to his apartment and make them a plateful. That would be cool, to have a place for us to hang out, but strangers live there when Dad's away, which is all the time. It's as if he doesn't live anywhere. When I picture Dad at home, all I see are highways.

As I wave Laney and Nico back to the car, I envision the three of us road-tripping with bags of gas station junk food, and then applauding in the front row at the concert. After the show, they'll meet Dad, and he can introduce us to the band. There will be photos, so many photos, and Nico's smile will be courtesy of me, Rafi, *the best*.

Laney and Nico are walking back. She's wrapped in that big windbreaker that almost reaches her knees, and he's rubbing his arms.

"It's cold, Rafi. Let's get inside, and then we'll talk about it," Nico says.

I hop into the back seat and wait like their well-behaved daughter. It's funny how I'm not cold, not even a little. And I refuse to button my jacket. I want Nico to see my Sons of Orwell T-shirt. He'll want one. He can get one in Richmond.

"It's probably not a good idea to drive to Virginia in Mac-Graw," Nico says. "Our families will be looking for us. And I wouldn't want to hurt the car."

"Oh. Right, right," I say. He's so thoughtful, which is the perfect balance to my recklessness. We're such a good team.

"It was a great idea, though," Laney says. She would have gone if we'd planned it.

"We'll do it another time, right?" I say. "We'll plan it out. And we can take your Jeep." Nico's car could make it, and no one will be after us then. Virginia! We can go to Norfolk and visit Anita from the swim team and talk about Holy Family and the good old days.

Nico starts the engine. He's so excited to drive MacGraw again that he forgets to answer me.

"Did you have a nice walk?" I ask, watching Laney's eyes in the vanity mirror.

"We did," Laney says. "But we should really get MacGraw back to your house."

"No. It's all right, really." I pull myself forward. "My grand-father takes his hearing aids out before bed. We can drive around for longer." I don't mention that Gran wakes up a few times a night to pee. But I talked her out of her evening tea tonight.

"We don't want to get you in trouble," Laney says.

"You won't. Besides, this car will be mine someday, so what does it matter if I use it tonight?" I look from her to him. They're so serious, full of concern for me. I can see how much they care. But Father Philip isn't here. Why worry? "We're having fun, aren't we?" I ask.

"Sure we are," Nico says, eyeing me in the rearview mirror.

"Such fun, Rafi." Laney turns and gives me a tight smile.

I knew it. *What a night. Such a time. What a life.*

Her lip gloss has been kissed off. Time and kisses on the golf course under the stars—these are the gifts I've given them.

"So then let's not ruin it by getting caught, okay?" Laney says. "I don't want anything to spoil it."

She's right. Tonight is perfect as it is. Let's not be greedy. I settle back in my seat, feeling energy drain from my limbs until I'm fully relaxed. Among friends, you can sit quietly sometimes. You can close your eyes and be content. You can drift off. Let's have this one perfect memory together, the three of us . . .

We.

Deep down, if I really think about it, a part of me is afraid to catch up to Dad and the Sons of Orwell. I haven't seen him in so long. What if he doesn't know me anymore? What if all he can think about when he sees my face are the sick things that Jenna told him? He wouldn't come back to me even if he could. And I'd be sad to hear the band's music—their songs are all about real life—each one ends with goodbye.

We're back at Nico's house. A creamy warmth glows from the living room window. I still can't believe I've been inside this house and inside Nico and Laney's world. I've slid across his floor in my socks, stretched myself beneath his comforter. I've turned the volume on Kidz Bop up to ten.

When I step out of the back seat, Nico places his hands on my shoulders. Here it is, Nico Fiore's touch that makes my whole body tingle. Our third touch and counting. He peers deeply into my eyes. He's so close. His eyes—hazel and hazel—I'm diving into them.

"Are you okay now?" He snaps his fingers. "Look at me. Focus." He holds my eye contact. "Are you all right to drive yourself home?" He's emotional. It's been a lot, I know, this magical evening we've shared.

I feel it too, Nico. Hold me tighter, the way you hold her. "Yes."

"You're sure?" he asks again, keeping his strong grip on my shoulders.

"Yes. I'm fine," I say, although he is the one who is so fine.

"All right." He squeezes me before handing back the keys and sending me off. I shiver, remembering the way he touched Laney's back. *I'll watch it every night.*

Nico hurries up the steps to Laney, who's already waiting on the stoop. She lifts her hand at me, and then they disappear into the house. But it's okay—I'm fine letting them go this time because what we have shared, no one can take away.

"Rafi!" There's a voice from the second-story window. Millie is inside her dark bedroom, cupping her mouth against the screen.

I wave up to her.

"Look!" Millie loud-whispers. Her head disappears for a second before popping up again. "My junk prize! A melted spoon!" She holds the spoon up. It reflects light from the streetlamp. I can see that it's drooped like one of Dali's clocks.

I silent-clap. Yaaay! I'm still her favorite. I'm back in their good graces. I hold my index finger in front of my lips. "Shhh." I pretend to lock my lips and put the key inside my koala pouch.

"Shhh." Millie locks her mouth and slips her make-believe key into her imaginary kangaroo pouch.

There are secrets, and there are keepsakes. Millie has one, and I, the other.

27

Sneaking back in is harder than I thought it would be because I'm so hyped. I don't want to be quiet. I want to bang Poppy's metal car parts together, wake the neighborhood, and scream, "We are *friends!*"

Being super hyped has also given me super strength. I can lift the garage door by hand, no problem, no battery required. It feels light, even as I pull it up quietly, inch by inch. I'm small but mighty. Feel my muscle.

I also have X-ray vision. Here, in the semidarkness, I have spotted Poppy's missing screw with the bolt on it! No obstacle shall trip me. I am all-powerful!

I leave my sneakers and jacket in the garage and step into the kitchen. This is the squeaky door, but I squirted Poppy's WD-40 on it before I left, and it worked. I'm home.

"Bianca?" Gran calls.

I stop in my tracks. So much for skipping her evening tea. I could say I'm Bianca and let Mom take the fall, but I can't do that to Gran. She caught me. I surrender. "It's me, Gran. Rafi."

"Are you eating my coffee cake?" she asks.

I exhale.

"There are only two left," she says, shuffling closer. "I need one for my breakfast and one for my program."

"I'm not eating them, Gran." My heart is galloping—my body is one big pulse. I open the fridge. I grab the tuna casserole and turn around. Egg noodles, tuna, mushrooms, half an onion, celery, Campbell's mushroom soup, 375° for forty-five minutes.

Gran flicks the light on. "Tuna casserole? At this hour?"

"I'm hungry," I lie. I'm full on love and lust and the thrill of getting away with this.

Gran blinks at me. I'm wearing my Sons of Orwell T-shirt and sweats, same as always. There's no mistaking me for Bianca now. I'm not the kid in belly shirts who sneaks out.

"Well, you'd better warm me a plate, then," she says, pulling her chair out. "No one should have to eat alone."

28

I need to hurry up and finish copying these notes for Mrs. Dabrowski. I'm not writing them half as neatly as Mom did because I need to make it look like my own work. It's a blessing and a curse to work in the office first period. The blessing is that I can do my homework. The curse is that I can do my homework. Let's face it — if you go to bed thinking you'll finish something in the morning, you've already lost.

Father Philip is in his office reaming out Jason Traeger for an outburst he had during junior class assembly. His door is slightly open. I can hear every other sentence, including "complete and utter disrespect for authority," "last chance," and "look at me when I talk to you." Isn't that one the worst? I don't know Jason Traeger at all, but in last year's yearbook, he's wearing a smock and lab goggles and sticking his tongue out at the camera. He looks like a hot mad scientist.

Mom's tenth-grade biology notebook is pink. We had the same teacher, only now Ms. Rice is called Mrs. Dabrowski. Mom's notes are so weird. There are sporadic spurts of detailed, elaborate notes written in colorful gel pens, followed by days and weeks of chicken scratch and doodles of bubble-letter vowels and tornadoes.

It's sad to see that she had days when she tried really hard. She probably thought, *This is it! I'm going to buckle down and turn myself around.* Maybe those were the times she was trying not to get transferred to Our Lady of Grace. But then what would happen after that? I just don't know. Did she get distracted or bored or what? She always fell back into, *This sucks! Screw it!*

She reminds me of the quote posted in my English classroom: *The best-laid plans of mice and men often go awry.* It's too real.

Mom's pages on "How the heart pumps blood into the body" look like they were written by some type-A honor student cheerleader. If I didn't know her handwriting, I wouldn't believe it was hers. There's even a flowchart. She drew the arrows with a straightedge. The arteries, ventricles, and veins are color-coded: red, purple, turquoise. She even used a highlighter to emphasize "returning blood." Returning blood, apparently, has low O_2 and is carried by the right atrium.

I'm copying from her because I couldn't possibly do my homework after our Friday night drive in MacGraw. I spent the rest of the weekend thinking about the golf course. Mentally recapping a good time is as important as having the good time to begin with. It cements the memory in your head, not that I could possibly forget it. I added to my playlist, too, with songs we heard in the car and the ones I sang on the hood so that I can snap back into that night whenever I want, which will basically be all the time.

Mom's diagram of the heart has all its parts labeled. She drew the heart in pencil first and then traced over the pencil marks with a thin black marker. She wanted to succeed. I can tell. Not just to stay at Holy Family. She wanted to succeed in life. She might have, if only . . . stop it. What's the use in wondering what might have been?

The superior vena cava is the thick vein that carries the low-oxygen blood into the heart. Superior Vena Cava is the perfect nickname for Mariah Rourke, who still treats me like an inferior vena cava. She wants me to edit the pictures I took last week. "You'd better get the new batch edited," she said. She doesn't have to speak to me in such a bitchy tone. I'm happy to do it. I never said I didn't want to finish editing.

I took a fun picture of the science teachers trying to learn a dance step off the Internet. A bunch of freshmen are laughing while they're showing them the moves. I took a picture of the parrots, too. There hasn't been a photo of them in the yearbook for three years, which means they're due. I even went outside and snapped a few candids of classrooms through the windows. They're of Mr. Rossi and Ms. Suma in action with their students' hands up. These pictures belong on a Holy Family brochure—really, they're that good.

Wait till I get the new photos laid out. Mariah won't have a bad thing to say about them. The heart can't function without the inferior vena cava. The body would literally die.

"Can I get a late pass?" someone says.

I look up.

"Laney! Hi!" I pop off my stool. "I'm sorry. I didn't see you! Biology. Right ventricle, pulmonary veins," I babble, showing her my loose-leaf. "That was fun Friday night, huh? My grandparents didn't suspect a thing. I told you it would be fine. We should totally do it again. I can't stop thinking about you guys and MacGraw. It was such a pretty night, the air was so—"

"I just need my pass," she says.

"Yeah, sure." I tear a pass from the pad. "I mean, we lucked out with that weather. It was chilly, I guess, but invigorating. You were cold, weren't you? I'm sorry. But wasn't it the freshest air?"

Laney huffs. "Can you hurry up?"

She's pale. Her lips are nearly colorless, and her eyes are red. Has she been crying? I hope not. She hands me an actual excuse note. This is a first. The signature is Dr. Something Illegible, but it looks official to me. No wonder she's so pallid. She's legitimately sick. There's something going around. We're at our highest absentee rate of the year this week. There are so many people out that Mrs. Bardot doesn't know which of them to gossip about. Laney should have grabbed a warmer coat for the golf course. I wonder if Nico is sick, too.

"Ugh, I'm sorry you're sick. It must've hit hard. You were fine the other night." I say. "Do you think it's the flu? Or strep? When people are stuck indoors the germs just recirculate, it's like—"

"Will you just stamp the pass already?" Laney snaps. It's not like her to be rude, but true friends don't have to put on a polite act for one another. It sucks to come to school when you feel like garbage. She must have a test or a presentation today that she can't miss. We can recap when she's feeling better.

I fill out her pass and stamp it: *Laney Villanueva/doctor.*

EXCUSED

"I hope you feel better soon." I mean it, sincerely. She'll obviously need a few days off. What will Nico and I do without her? I'll miss her. If she needs me to, I can bring schoolwork home for her from each of her classes. I can email her later to ask her. I saved the invitation she sent me, not that I need it; I memorized her email address. I remember when I was at Allegro, whenever she was absent from dance class, the studio seemed lifeless. There was no one else worth watching. Following steps and mimicking the moves is one thing, but it seemed like no one else could really . . . *dance.*

Laney takes her late pass without a word. She leaves me and wipes her eyes as she goes. I bet Nico will duck out of class and meet her at her locker to see how she's feeling. I pick up Laney's note again to file it. The letterhead says, *Dr. Vivianne Cho, Obstetrics & Gynecology.* It screams at me like a neon sign:

Laney Villanueva is pregnant.

No, no, no, no. Noooo. This can't be happening. They're mature and dependable. They're on the honor roll. They pray. They're in the damn choir. They're *happy.*

I grab my books and bolt after her, cutting through the cafeteria and around the back way to the senior hallway. I'm so afraid of what's to come that my chest hurts. It feels like there's a fist inside me, trying to punch its way out.

In seconds, I'm in the north wing. From behind the trophy cabinet, I watch Laney walk slowly, very slowly toward Nico. He looks both terrified and courageous. I take a breath and hold still.

Laney's soundless footsteps press forward in slow motion. Three feet away from him, she stops. She waits. I wait. Nico gives her a defeated smile and shrugs with his palms up, like a kid who's just struck out in Little League. Laney goes to him. She falls into Nico's open arms, and collapses onto his chest. Her head lands perfectly beneath his chin as she starts to cry.

"Ohh, Laney . . . it's gonna be okay . . . we're gonna be okay," he says.

Laney covers her face and cries harder.

"Shit . . ." he says softly, "shit . . . shit . . ."

Suddenly, I'm crying, too. From relief. From hope.

Behind the classroom doors, school goes on. Mr. Tosh is droning on about the Hundred Years' War. Ms. Rowen is showing cartoons that illustrate supply and demand. The dorks in the library are reciting mnemonic devices for kingdom, phylum, class, order, family, genus, species. It seems wrong for Holy Family to continue while Nico and Laney's life has been turned upside down.

Nico wraps his arms tighter around her as her shoulders begin to shake. "I'm here, I'm right here," he says. "We'll figure it out, okay? You and me. We're still us."

We.

I can't tell if she's nodding or if she's only wiping her tears, but even if Laney doesn't believe him right now, I do.

He whispers to her, something I can't hear.

Do something. Please. For me.

"Nico . . ." Laney says. "My parents."

"Shh . . . I know."

"Please don't tell my cousins." Laney tightens her arms around herself. "Please don't tell Fernando."

"No, no." He holds her, swallowing her into his hug. "I won't."

Laney and Nico will keep this secret while their families and classmates continue breakdancing, collecting volunteer points, eating angel-hair pasta. Laney and Nico and *I* will keep this secret.

"What am I going to do?" Laney cries. "We're *Catholic*."

They stand welded together for a long while. I listen to them sniffle and inhale and exhale. My breathing and my heartbeat, I'm convinced, match theirs.

"I'm supposed to go to NYU," Laney says. "I'm seventeen . . ."

He rocks her slightly in his arms.

She pulls away and presses her palm against her chest to declare herself. "I'm a *dancer.*"

Nico cups her face in his hands. "You don't have to do anything you don't want to do."

"I don't want any of it." She shakes her head.

"I know . . . I know . . . I love you. You know that, don't you? God, Laney, I love you so much and forever." He pulls her close again. "I'm sorry. I'm so sorry. I'm so sorry." He repeats it over and over until, "Please don't hate me."

I settle against the wall and think about that first morning in the main office, the way he looked at her, the way he stroked her hair. *We're terrible drivers. It was the parallel parking.* How could Laney hate him? How could Nico even think that she would? I know they're going to make it. Deep in my heart, I know this because beneath all the fear, I see so much beauty.

Watching them in this pocket of time reminds me of the song they've been rehearsing in chorus—the lyrics rise from the open windows of the choir room up to my class on the second floor. When I listen very carefully, I can hear Laney's voice and Nico's, too, singing of the glory and the grace I've seen, and of how blessed I am to be a witness.

29

I don't know if I should put Mom's gift on the table or hide it under my jacket until dessert. It would be fun for her to walk in and see it right away. But it would also be fun to surprise her later.

I actually want to talk to Mom about real things tonight, not just BS about the weather or how Poppy and Gran are doing, or how time seems to fly faster every year. (Doesn't it, though?) I need to know how she felt when she found out she was pregnant, how Dad reacted, if he held her the way Nico held Laney. Were Gran and Poppy shocked? Did they scream and cry? Did she wish she'd gone to Our Lady of Grace? I wonder if they expected her to get married. If Laney and Nico want to talk to someone who's been through it, will she talk to them?

I hope Mom likes the gift I got her, a solid glass bar with her name etched into it, to put on her office desk: BIANCA WICKHAM. It'll add a professional touch. Poppy says he got her name from Bianca Jagger, the actress who married Mick Jagger from the Rolling Stones. It's weird that Mick Jagger is older than Poppy, because Mick is a rock star who plays stadiums, and Poppy alternates between two pairs of bifocals that hang from his neck.

Some of the engraving examples for Mom's gift included a title beneath the name. I don't know Mom's work title, so I only ordered her name. It's better this way because if she gets promoted or switches positions, her title will change.

I thought Bianca Jagger was only an actress, but it says here on Wiki that she's a human rights activist now. More so, she's a goodwill ambassador. People can change. They can live multiple lives. You don't have to fold sweaters forever or be an actress forever. A person can go from not needing a nameplate to needing a nameplate.

It's good that I had balloon-print wrapping paper left over from Gran's birthday and red ribbon from baked goods that a friend had sent to her. It was just the right length to tie around the middle of Mom's box and then into a bow.

Hopefully Mom's hungry since I ordered rings and fries already. I think I'll have the veggie burger because I've been thinking a lot about Allegro Dance. If I'd kept going with classes, I might have been decent at dancing (not talented, you can't become talented, you either are or you aren't), and I would have been in better shape. Since that didn't happen, I'm going to try to make small improvements in my lifestyle, like eating less meat and junk and eating more vegetables. Laney isn't the type to post pictures of her meals on her social media. If she were, I would just copy whatever she eats.

I don't know about Mom's diet these days. She's tried no carbs and then low carbs, no sugar, 75 percent fruits and vegetables, and other fads that didn't stick. She always looks great, but now that I've seen her old clothes, I can see why she doesn't feel like herself. But it is her birthday; she should eat anything she wants. She might get the grilled cheese she used to order. Or she might not want to be reminded of high school. This is something I'd like to know, too: does she like to think about when she was my age or not? I have so many questions.

The mini jukebox at the table is space themed. There's Elton John's "Rocket Man," "Fly Me to the Moon" by Frank Sinatra, John Mayer's "Gravity," "Space Oddity" by David Bowie, "Walking on the Moon" by the Police, and "Cover the Moon" by the Sons of Orwell. The band and Dad are in Atlanta tonight. The people in the booth behind me have just punched in a song. It sounds like robots and spaceships and boys rapping.

I like flipping through the titles. Turning the dial right and left is so satisfying. I can't stop. I keep turning and flipping and turning and flipping. Sure, you can play any song you want on your phone, but the jukebox is more fun. A touchscreen feels nothing like this. The robot song must be the Beastie Boys' "Intergalactic."

I fish a quarter out of my jacket, feed it into the slot, and select number 48. The opening guitar chords to "Cover the Moon" are loud and aggressive. But when the lyrics kick in, the song turns mellow.

I hear some kids horsing around in the back corner, so I turn to see. It's V-Boys in a booth, laughing over a video. I had no idea they were here. It's not like me not to notice. I've been a little scatterbrained lately. I can't imagine how Laney is doing.

The V-Boys are mid-meal, eating double cheeseburgers, baked potatoes, and Reubens. With the amount of calories they burn in one dance routine, these guys can afford to eat all of that and more.

Fernando is in the middle seat, holding up his phone, showing the cousin next to him a video. "Sick. That's sick!" the cousin keeps saying.

"I told you," Fernando says. "It's like he's flipping in zero gravity."

Nico has kept his promise to Laney. Fernando doesn't know about Laney. He wouldn't be here watching videos if he knew. All of the Villanueva cousins are blissfully clueless.

I wonder how Mom told her friends she was pregnant. And what did they say? She should be here any minute. I shouldn't have played Sons of Orwell. She might not want to hear it. There's no sign of her car in the parking lot yet. Hopefully the song will finish before she walks in.

I'm putting the gift on the table, I've decided. It will distract her from the song if it's still playing. Also, life is too short to save gifts for later. One of us could choke on a French fry, and what would happen to the gift then?

"Here you go. One order of fries and one order of onion rings," the waitress says, setting the food down. I thank her and take a fry. It's hot and crispy and not oily, which is good. Oily fries should be outlawed.

"Watch the next one!" Fernando says, getting loud at his table. "No, not them. Screw those guys. Skip their asses. Play the next group."

I remember seeing Laney and her cousins perform together once. I was nine. It was the end-of-the-year Allegro showcase. They did a traditional Filipino dance where two people kneel on the floor and tap long bamboo sticks on the ground while the dancers dance in between the sticks. What is that dance called? It was sort of like skipping double Dutch except with wood. The bamboo sticks hit the ground and smack together to clap the beat. From the loudness of the bamboo against the floor, you could tell it would hurt like hell if they stepped out of rhythm and got a foot caught. Jump ropes can sting if you mess up in double Dutch. But bamboo could break an ankle.

When I watched the Villanuevas' routine, I kept thinking about the number of hours it must've taken to rehearse it. They spend so much time together as a family and as performers. There's a plaque in the guidance office at Holy Family that says, "The family that prays together stays together." It must be the same for families that dance together, which is why it's a big deal for Laney to keep a secret from Fernando and the others. Nico is her chosen family.

I google "Filipino bamboo dance." It's called "tinikling." There are videos, too. The Villanuevas' tinikling performance might be online, but maybe not. It was a long time ago.

The bell over the door rings. It's Poppy walking in wearing his Sunoco cap. I didn't expect him to join us. It's nice of him; he didn't have to come. Once in a while, Poppy surprises me. I can still ask Mom some of my questions with Poppy here. I wasn't really going to ask her all of them anyway. It's hard to go from talking about nothing much to, "Did you consider having an abortion? What made you change your mind?"

Poppy sits in front of me and drinks from Mom's water glass. "Bianca isn't coming. That job of hers didn't work out," he says, matter-of-fact. "She's embarrassed. She didn't know how to tell you. I'm sorry, kid."

I stare at the red ribbon and balloon-print wrapping paper.

Why is this so hard to believe? Shouldn't I have known? There are too many fries on this table now and too many onion rings. No one is going to eat any of this. I sink into my seat, hearing the vinyl squeak against my back.

"Let's not be too mad at her," he says. "It is her birthday."

HEART → LUNG → HEART → BODY → LUNG

Bianca had used a ruler to draw the arrows, but in the end, her notes fell apart. I don't know why she doodled tornadoes. She must've liked how it felt to draw the spirals, wide at the top and then narrower and narrower until they came to a point at the bottom.

Poppy waves for the waitress. "Can we get a box for these? And the check, please. Thank you, dear."

We're not staying. The diner is where happy people come after winning baseball games or watching Pixar movies. Poppy and I belong at home, nursing our wounds.

The door opens, ringing the bell again. It's the track-team girls, the biggest badasses of Holy Family, dressed in matching black tracksuits. Other teams complained because the girls had matching practice outfits for every day of the week—black caps, black ASICS, black tanks, black crewneck tops with thumbholes. Why didn't volleyball get them? Why not boys' track? What about basketball? Favoritism! Well, these girls had bought the clothes themselves. That shut everyone up.

"Maybe it's for the best." Poppy points at the onion rings. "Anyway, these'll warm up just fine."

The track girls are taking the long table, sliding their chairs back and picking up menus. Tonia Lowe, the team leader, all legs, laughs and flips off the cross-country boys who are settling into booths. The Community Parents at the end of the table remind their daughters to ask for separate checks and to skip the sodas (too much sugar), all while Poppy is boxing up our food.

"Well, we'd better get back home to your gran before she starts to miss us." Poppy sighs, leaving cash sticking out from under the napkin dispenser.

In my parents' yearbook, the photo that defined the seniors was taken in this parking lot. I can practically see their class out there now—some sitting on top of a wide Buick, some waving out of its windows, some crouched in front of the hood ornament. Some were still in the school uniform. Others wore flared jeans and zip-up hoodies. A few had Holy Family varsity jackets. It's a wide shot with the Apollo Diner behind them, lights gleaming. Through the front window, you can see them—Bianca Wickham and Carlo Tedoro—at this exact table where Poppy and I are seated, where Mom should be right now.

In the picture, their hands are clasped across the table. Carlo watches the action outside as his classmates pose for the shot. My mother's face is in profile. Her ponytail is secured on the crown of her head. She looks like one of those silhouette cutouts framed in a nursery, a template of the perfect girl. She's smiling at Carlo, maybe even laughing. Bianca Wickham and Carlo Tedoro. *They.*

Why couldn't they stay as they were? How did the Cutest Couple end up not speaking, not caring, not striving, not loving anymore?

What's the point of even asking, when I already know? I know, I know, I know! They should have gone to Missy's party.

The bell above the door rings again. This time, it's me

running out of the restaurant. "Should have" is useless. Nothing could've stopped Mom from meeting Dad that night. Not Poppy, not Gran, not Our Lady of Grace. Not even the looming possibility, the threat of me, had stopped her.

"Rafi!" Poppy calls. The door slams on his voice.

My sneakers hit the asphalt. I imagine my parents' senior class here mugging for the camera. I speed through the parking lot and leave them all behind. I don't look back at the window. I'm afraid I'll see Bianca and Carlo still sitting there, hands joined. Or I'm afraid that I won't.

I race uphill. My calves burn from the hard concrete. Gran has been right for years—there's no reason to go out—it's comfortable at home. Nothing good happens out here. At home, it's warm, and Gran keeps twelve kinds of tea in the cupboard. We watch entertainment news starting at seven o'clock every night. We each have our own fleece blankets; mine is yellow, Gran's is blue, Poppy's is red. Out here, the temperature has dropped a good ten degrees. I'm only wearing my thin jacket, and I'm running against exhaust fumes from the traffic.

When Mom left me with Gran and Poppy, did she know she wasn't coming back? Is this how she'd planned it? Had it crossed her mind to tell me flat-out so that I wouldn't wait, so that I wouldn't hope for her to pull her act together and take me back?

I should have seen this coming. Once I turn eighteen, it will be over—the chance for her to be my mom will be done. Is that what she's been waiting for? I should have known.

I'm bolting down Sutter Boulevard past the gas station, the 7-Eleven, and the back end of Holy Family baseball field. Faster, faster, go, go, go. In my mind, I'm on the track team with Tonia Lowe and the other fearless, unstoppable girls, wearing a black tracksuit, with white stripes on the sleeves. I'm pumping my arms, pumping, pumping, faster, faster. If I were one of those badass striders in the pack, listening to girl rappers, *money money money,* blasting from the phone on Tonia's armband, maybe Bianca would be proud of me. She would cheer me on with a painted sign in school colors, and she would show up at the diner and warn me against high fructose corn syrup. I would be a thunderbolt, too speedy to be denied, too fast to be rejected.

I run toward the bus stop. There's one coming. I see its headlights and the driver wearing a hat. I force my legs to keep going. My lungs are on fire.

HEART ➔ LUNG ➔ HEART ➔ BODY ➔ LUNG

All of Mom's efforts turn into spirals and tornadoes. I should have kept her plum dress, should have kept it in her closet forever. I had one good, beautiful thing of hers, and now it's gone.

"Please, wait! Wait!" I wave at the driver. I huff and puff. I'm doing it, I'm going to catch this bus, and I'm going to get all the answers I need because I am motherless, fatherless—I'm Annie, I'm Madeline, I'm Mowgli fending for myself in the jungle—I deserve answers.

I catch the end of the line waiting to board, clutching my side. I'm going to die from this cramp. No one will care when I collapse. These bus passengers have had a hard day. They'll step over my body so they can get home in time for dinner.

We lumber forward. I touch the steel handrail. The cold shoots into my bones. I take a seat. The heater blows behind my legs. I fold my body forward and warm my hands. I stay this way, folded over my knees, and then, when I can feel my fingers again, I fish inside my bag for my phone and I start searching.

> *Penny loafers, designed by G. H. Bass in 1938, were originally called Weejuns. They became popular with students because of the leather band across the top with a cutout design. Although it wasn't Bass's intention, students started putting dimes in the cutout for the pay phone. Eventually, people decided that copper pennies looked better in the brown shoes, so that became the popular style, and that's how the shoes became known as penny loafers.*

It's dinnertime on Mom's birthday, and I'm sitting on the public bus googling the history of penny loafers because I'm going to be better than her. I plug in my earbuds. I find Broadway radio and press Play. When I say I'm going to do something, I'm going to do it whether I like it or not.

The bus is filled with tired adults in outdated puffer jackets who, after ten hours with angry bosses for minimum wage, are still going home to their children to feed them and bathe them. They'll quiz their kids on the eight-times table because it's the hardest. They'll do it for nothing more than raw macaroni necklaces and handprint paintings. They'll wear those rotting things and hang the ugly artwork on the fridge with alphabet magnets. That's what parents do. They go home, they hug their kids. They show up when they're expected, and they eat onion rings and fries.

But not mine.

I'm lost, she'd written in her notebook. *I give up. Shoot me.*

She isn't coming back for me. I don't have to turn eighteen for this waiting to end. We have never prayed or danced together. It's been over.

I've always known.

30

I'm here. It was easy to find, right across from the Cottonwood condos and the strip mall with the mini Carvel. There's nothing bad about the house, it's fine, it's tidy. It's just not the same.

I hold my arm up, find myself in the camera, and angle the little house in the background.

Click.

Happy Birthday, I type.

Send.

It's supposed to feel wrong for me to be here, so I've been told. *How could you go there? It's invasive! You should be arrested!* When you see people in expected places, it's okay. But when you see someone in an unexpected place, it's some kind of crime?

The car pulls up to the curb. I've been in that car. I've crouched on the floor in the back and have eaten cookies from the seat pocket.

My phone buzzes.

Where is that? I'm sorry I couldn't make it. We'll do it another time, promise. Can't you send me one of you smiling? For my birthday?

Through the open car window, I hear three full seconds of a dark, churning love song with the saddest voice I've ever heard, and then the engine cuts.

"Hello?" Mr. Bryant squints through the trees. "Who's there?"

It's me, your go-to girl. I step forward under the streetlamp.

"Rafi?" Mr. Bryant stiffens, crushing the grocery bag in his arm—one bag—single-guy food. When he eats his dinner he won't even use a plate. He'll stand over the sink with a fork and eat whatever it is right out of the pot so that he doesn't have to wash a dish or wipe the kitchen table. "What are you doing? You shouldn't be here."

"You came to Holy Family. Maybe *you* shouldn't have been there. That's my school. You don't even work there anymore," I say. If rules don't apply to everybody they shouldn't apply to anybody.

"I was invited to Senior Banquet, I told you that." He's talking very slowly now, as if I'm five, as if I have comprehension problems. But I understand everything. I'm not stupid. I got a B in his class, and I didn't even cheat. "You haven't been invited here, Rafi. How did you even find me?" He pauses. "Never mind. I don't need to know. Do your grandparents know where you are?" He reaches for his phone. "Don't make me call the police."

For dinner last year, the Bryants had lasagna and garlic bread, even salad. A hot, square meal. They listened to the radio while they ate: *top forty.* I heard it through the screen windows. I couldn't think of anything nicer than to listen to music during dinner with your family. He found the photo I'd taken on my roll. Why had he been so angry? The lighting was really pretty. It's always prettiest before dusk, the golden hour.

"I just want to talk. Please, Mr. Bryant." My voice sounds

small. "I just need five minutes to explain. Then I'll never bother you again, I swear it."

He glances at his house and then back at his car, planning an escape. From me. This is who I am to Mr. Bryant, a crazed Lifetime movie teenager who's forcing him to decide between fight or flight.

"Rafi, you need to leave me alone. This is serious. I told you a thousand times to back off. This has gone on far too long. Go home, and I won't tell anyone you were here, all right?" he says, walking up the driveway.

Back off, back off.

He presses his key fob. The car locks behind me. He learned from me. We learned from each other.

Last year, I had only wanted to see the Bryants' Christmas tree. It had looked so beautiful from the street with its white lights flickering and the angel twinkling on top. Inside the house, it was better than I'd imagined. There were handmade ornaments: snowflakes made of sparkly beads and wire, a popcorn garland, Styrofoam snowmen. The blanket from the sofa, so warm and cozy in my arms, smelled of maple syrup and oatmeal.

I took a glass pear off the shelf. I felt it, perfectly smooth and cool and heavy in my hands. It fit in my coat pocket. I wanted to set it on my bedroom windowsill to see if the sun would cast a rainbow through it.

"I never had a family like yours," I tell Mr. Bryant now, because I'm prepared. I found him this time. The banquet invitation list was right there in Mrs. Bardot's desk drawer. "My parents split up before I was even born. Then my mom left me when I was three." I can barely get through those words. I've never said it aloud before. *My mom left me.* "I thought you were perfect—you and Mrs. Bryant and your kids, even Boss Man."

That night, I walked around Mr. Bryant's living room while running my fingers over the smooth glass pear in my pocket. I looked at the family photos of birthdays and of Boss Man as a puppy. He was so tiny that he fit inside a slipper.

Now, there isn't a single light on inside his house. He didn't even get Boss Man. He should've at least gotten the dog. But he wouldn't take a pet from his kids, never, not Mr. Bryant. I took a video at Dabney Park when they were teaching Boss Man how to catch a Frisbee. I captured his first catch. He snatched the Frisbee in midair. Everybody cheered. Mr. Bryant picked Boss Man up and ran around with him over his head. He should have that video now, he could've saved that moment forever, but no. *Delete it. Delete it now.* Such a shame. It was Boss Man's very first catch.

"I couldn't stop watching you, all of you. I just . . . I didn't know families like yours were real. I took your pictures to have them close, as if you were my family. I just wanted to be near you all. It was never the way you thought," I say. "I didn't have romantic feelings. I wouldn't have touched you, it wasn't like that."

I remember how the floorboards in his house squeaked under my feet, step after step. I thought it was because the pear was so heavy, weighing me down, like when people fill their pockets with rocks before praying for forgiveness and walking into a lake. I felt like I was sinking. I had to take the pear out, had to rub my fingerprints off and leave it where I'd found it.

I took a picture of it instead, but the flash bounced back. It was too blurry for Mr. Bryant to decipher. He didn't know I'd been to his house more than once, didn't know I'd been inside. The flash of that bad photo saved me. I would have been expelled.

Mr. Bryant isn't lifting his phone. He turns instead. His expression is softer, because he cares about his students. Maybe he can understand three-year-old me whose mother couldn't stand being a parent anymore.

I'm thinking about the young mom from that old news story again, the one who suffocated her toddler and hid the body. While the toddler was "missing," the mom was photographed dancing on top of a bar. Her tattoo said "la dolce vita." I hate thinking about her and that baby, those grandparents, and that tattoo. It disgusts me to think about them. A chill crawls up my spine every time I do, but I think about them all the time. La dolce vita: that's what that woman wanted. The sweet life.

"I never wanted to cause you any trouble," I say.

"All right." Mr. Bryant's tone is an acknowledgment but not an acceptance.

It's my last chance to ask him, my time is ticking. "Do you still think love is real—I mean, that people can fall in love, and that it can last forever?" This is what I should have asked him a year ago, had I known it was the answer I needed.

He takes a deep breath. "I don't know."

"But you're a teacher." My voice cracks. "You're supposed to know every—"

"I'm not your teacher anymore." I feel him pulling away again, the way a cat bends its back and slips from your grasp when he's through with your affection. "I can't help you, Rafi."

My five minutes are over.

"I'm going inside now to have a peaceful dinner. I expect you to go home." He's walking away. The outline of his face against the streetlight is a portrait of Mr. Bryant alone. "Goodbye, Rafi," he says.

"Goodbye, Mr. Bryant."

I don't think I belong here.

31

Tomás Diaz, there you are. All I want is one photo, one lousy picture of you so that I can finish the Superlatives. Don't make a failure out of me, Tomás, please. I am going to do the things I promised to do if it kills me. I cannot stand it when you run and hide. I can't live this way. Why does everybody run away?

I see you by the water fountain talking to Summer Shah. Can you tell that Summer Shah is into you? She would sleep with you. Do you see how her body is facing yours and the way she's pushing her chest forward? She would roll over and beg for you. You don't even care, do you, even though she's cute? You're still not interested in anyone who isn't Laney Villanueva.

"Tomás!" I call.

I make eye contact. He pivots. I'm crushed. Stop avoiding me, Tomás. You and I are so much the same, you have no idea. We're both hoping for things that will never happen. Please, stop running away.

"Tomás! Wait up!"

He quickens his pace, leaving Summer Shah and me beside a poster of the HARMFUL EFFECTS OF SMOKING.

"I'm sorry. He's avoiding me. It's not you," I tell Summer

Shah. We read the list: ADDICTION, STROKE, WRINKLES, STAINED FINGERS, CANCER . . .

Summer Shah leaves, swinging her gym bag over her shoulder. Now it's just me and HEART DISEASE, UTERINE ULCERS, INFERTILITY, AND OSTEOPOROSIS.

I turn to find Nico Fiore standing at my locker. He doesn't have any reason to be in this hallway. His classes are in the east block and the new construction wing. He had to cross the courtyard from the senior hallway to be here. He's come here to see *me*. In my head, he's a movie boy who's ready to make a declaration. In three seconds he'll hold up a big radio playing our song or a banner that says, "Prom?"

This is what it feels like to be Laney, isn't it? To see the shape of Nico's shoulders backlit against the windows, to recognize the top of his head and the bend of his arm as he clasps the back of his neck. This is how it is to be Nico Fiore's girlfriend: lucky, pretty, lit up from the inside. I'm nearly skipping toward him, I can't help it, I'm practically hearing a love song in the background, I'm almost beside him. *Three . . . two . . . one . . .*

Closer, his face is twisted and pale. And then I remember. Laney is pregnant. This is no time for skipping.

"Hey, Rafi." There's pain in his eyes. "I was wondering if you could help me with something. It's important."

"Sure. Yes." *Anything. Everything. Always.*

"Do you think you can get me one of those official school envelopes from the office?" There's urgency in his voice I haven't heard before.

"Yes. No problem," I say. There's a box of fifty right under the counter. He can have them all as far as I'm concerned. But I will give him one envelope at a time to keep him coming back to me. "Can I ask what it's for?"

"I just . . . uh . . ." Nico lowers his head. "Laney and I, um, we're not so good right now." He hasn't showered or combed his hair. He's rolled the sleeves on his rumpled shirt, to hide a stain maybe, or a missing button. It might be yesterday's uniform shirt pulled from the hamper. If I press my palms flat against him, I can smooth the creases.

"A lot's happened." He pauses, weighing whether or not to say more.

Say more, Nico.

"I've been trying to talk to her, but she won't get back to me," he continues because *we're friends.* "She's not returning my texts or my calls. I put a note in her locker, but she threw it out. She didn't even open it."

I know. I know everything, I want to tell him. "I'm sorry," I say.

"I thought that maybe if I wrote her and put it in a school envelope, she'd have to at least look at it, right?" He exhales. "I don't know."

"Yes, she will. I'm sure of it."

Everything makes sense now—why I met Mr. Bryant, why I got in trouble last spring, and why Father Philip assigned me to work in the main office—it led me here, so that I could help Nico and Laney.

"I can put it in her homeroom teacher's mailbox, too. I mean, if you want. I think that'll help," I say.

Nico lifts his head. "You can?" There's a spark in his eyes— it's hope that I've given him.

"Of course."

"I don't know what else to do. She's never shut me out before. She usually tells me everything." He rubs his face. "Rafi . . ." Nico reaches into his pocket and pulls out a piece of paper that's been folded into fourths. He presses it into my palm. I close my fingers around it.

Three . . . two . . . one . . . Nico Fiore puts his arms around me and whispers over my shoulder. Our fourth touch and counting. His embrace is almost as I imagined it would be.

"Thank you," he says.

I'm the first to turn the copy machine on this morning. It takes a few minutes to warm up, the exact amount of time it takes for me to open the blinds, water the plants, pick paper out of the trash can and put it in the recycle bin, and turn on the computer consoles and monitors.

Beep.

It's ready. I press the button for one copy.

> *My beautiful Laney,*
> *I keep thinking about the day we met. I walked into Fernando's house. His brothers were play-ing music and horsing around, practicing a pyra-mid in the living room. It was pretty much chaos. His dad was putting food on the table, and his mom was yelling at Fernando to open windows. And there you were, sitting on a counter stool, eating grapes, wearing a baggy gray sweatshirt and shorts. Your ponytail hung all the way down your back. You were sitting so straight and graceful. Fernando said, "That's my cousin Laney. She dances, too, but like*

a respectable artist, not our type of bullshit. Laney, this is my boy Nico."

You were so pretty, so, so pretty. You lifted your hand and said hi, and that was it, that was all. You didn't even say my name. It killed me that you didn't say it, like an ax through my chest. You turned back to your grapes and kept eating. Damn, I wanted your attention so bad, I could've cried. I swore to myself, I swore that if I ever got you to look at me, to notice me somehow, I'd never take it for granted. If I ever got you to be with me, I'd take care of you till I died, and I meant it. I will. You just have to let me.

God, I miss you so much, Laney. I'm sorry for whatever I said that was stupid or insensitive or immature. If I did something that hurt you, I hate myself for it. You don't deserve it. I'd never do anything deliberately to hurt you, I hope you know that.

I want whatever you want. If you want to take care of things, I'll go with you. I'll hold your hand and make sure you're okay. If you want us to be a family, I'm here. I'll talk to my parents. I'll talk to your parents. I'm scared too. Of course I'm scared. But we can make it work. I'll do whatever you want.

I just want to be with you — I want it to be you and me no matter what. That won't ever change. I feel like it's the first day we met all over again.

Just look my way, Laney. Say it, just call my name because I'm dying inside. I'm here for you, for us. Please talk to me and tell me what you need. I love you so much and forever.

Your Nico

32

Laney's neighborhood is lined with thick trees that push the sidewalks up at their roots. The houses are small but charming, like storybook houses. It's strange riding my bike at night. I barely ride it during the day. I didn't even ride it much last summer. Bike riding is a happy person's activity. Was I unhappy then? I can't remember my feelings before autumn came.

Good thing I have gloves in my pockets. I can't wait for warmer weather, but I also hope it never comes. Laney has had her prom dress since last August. It's white. She saw it in a shop, knew it was the one, and just had to have it. I overheard her talking with Kendra Darling. I'm so happy the dress is white. White is classic and will look so good on her skin. She and Nico will be timeless in their photos. I can pose them on the staircase. He'll have his arms around her. She'll have her shoes in her hands because her feet will hurt from dancing so hard.

They'll probably stay out really late and go to the beach. Nico will give her his tuxedo jacket, and they'll walk up and down the shoreline like that. His tux will reach down almost to her knees, just as his windbreaker hung on her at the golf course. It will remind them of that night, and they'll think of me. They'll mention it then—me and MacGraw, the night sky, and the moonlight shining on the manicured greenway. Won't that be amazing? Nico and Laney talking about me on their prom night?

At home, while I'm scrolling through my photos from the dance, I'll feel a strange sensation because someone, *they,* are thinking of me. *What a year we've had,* they'll say. And what a night that was. *What a night, such a time, what a life.*

I made it here. Her house isn't as far as I thought, not bad at all. I needed the fresh air in my lungs anyway. She's up in her bedroom. I see her periwinkle walls through the cracked blinds. There's a dim light at the far end of the room. She's there, tucked in, ignoring Nico's texts. Or she's reading them over and over. Maybe she's writing and rewriting her replies, hovering over the Send button before deleting them.

Write: *I love you too, Nico.* Then press Send. One touch. That's all it will take, Laney, and he'll be here in ten minutes. Send it. Send it and be together, and then everything I'm imagining about prom night will come true. I wait, gripping my handlebars with gloved fingers.

He isn't here. Not in ten minutes, not in twelve or fifteen or twenty. Still not here.

Oh, Laney, how long are you going to make me wait?

She's watching a screen of halo purple. I know this video — the colors, the rhythm, it's on the tip of my mind — I'm reaching for it, I know what it is. I've watched it countless times. A flicker of orange. A beam of pale blue. A flash of white. I'm grasping to remember. Which video is it?

I want to say that it's her and him in Nico's bed. The blue of his sheets and the white of his walls. He climbs over her.

She turns onto her belly. He traces letters onto her back. But something about that isn't right. The lighting in Nico's room had held still. The camera had bobbled only at the end: white pillowcases, the ceiling, the dresser, the carpet. No. The purple and the orange and the movement of this video don't match up. That's not it.

I know it now—it's Laney's Ring Night performance to "This Year's Love." Laney is up in her bedroom watching herself be young and free and beautiful, and I know what she's thinking and feeling in her heart. I heard her say the words to Nico: *I'm a dancer.*

33

I'm late to American History. I don't know why it took so long for Father Philip and me to clean the birdcages today. They weren't as messy as last time. Last Wednesday there was so much more poop, and empty shells had been scattered all over the lobby floor.

We must've been engrossed in our conversation. Father Philip said I shouldn't be too broken up about Mom's birthday dinner. He's sure she's doing her best. Well, so am I. I'm glad I showed him the photos I've taken over the past couple of months. I wanted him to know that I've been productive. He was really pleased.

He liked the picture of eleventh graders Jason Shane and Ben O'Neal giving bunny ears during a football game. Father Philip looked at it and laughed. "That was a fun homecoming. Those two sure know how to work the booth. They really get the crowd pumping," he said. I think it was their idea to play song requests and read live messages from students and teachers. Jason and Ben are the life of the games, really. I'll write that in their caption. I'm pretty sure they'll win Cutest Couple next year, fair and square.

Father Philip was impressed with my favorite picture, too,

the one in the window seat near the cafeteria. I guess it's not an actual seat. It's just a radiator with plants on it, but students have made it a seat. I always imagine my parents sitting there together joking around—Bianca cross-legged, biting into a sandwich, and Carlo emptying a bag of chips directly into his mouth.

A few weeks ago, I couldn't believe it when I saw Laney and Nico sitting there in that exact way. I literally stood and stared for a good ten seconds. I was so stunned that I nearly forgot to take their picture. Thank goodness I finally did. It turned out great. The window seat looks like a greenhouse in the photo.

"Good one!" Father said when he saw it. "Nice kids, too."

I wonder if Father Philip would still think they were nice kids if he knew about Laney. I think he would. Sometimes these things happen. He expects a lot from students, but he knows that "we're only human." That's what he said to me last spring. *We all feel heavy emotions sometimes, and we all make mistakes. We're only human,* to put it exactly. But I know what his advice to Laney and Nico would ultimately be. As Laney said, we're Catholic.

My hands smell like parrot. I need to turn into this girls' room to wash up. Finally, this bathroom has been painted light pink, too, like the others. I thought they'd never get around to this wing. The old yellow walls were dirty and chipped.

Father Philip said that the parrots have lived at Holy Family since the eighties. They picked up random sayings that students used to yell in the hallway, and they still repeat the ones they learned back then. Cain says, "Sweep the leg, sweep the leg!" and Abel says, "You must chill, you must chill, you must chill!"

They haven't learned anything new since 1989. It's comforting, somehow, to know that my parents heard the parrots say the same old phrases when they were here.

When I turn the water off, I hear someone crying in one of the stalls. I bend down and peek beneath the doors as I dry my hands. There's a puffy quilted tote bag hanging from the door hook in the third stall. It's Laney. I pause and listen to her sniffling and unrolling toilet paper.

"Hello?" I walk closer. "Are you okay? Can I help you?"

The door unlatches. Laney Villanueva stands in front of me, shaking.

"Laney," I say. "Are you sick?"

"I don't know . . ." she says, clutching her stomach. "I don't know."

As she wobbles past me, I glance into the stall. My veins freeze. The toilet is bloody. Bright red. I remember bloated gummy bears disintegrating at the bottom of Nico's sink, fragile and translucent, boneless, no veins, no organs, no heartbeat.

"Did you get . . . are you having . . . do you need a pad?" I ask.

Laney walks toward the sink. A light pink wrapper falls from her grasp. Her hands tremble under the running faucet.

I remember red ink on my fingers, red on the counter and my shirt cuffs, on the white envelopes, and later, red on my chin when I saw my reflection. My red fingerprints were everywhere.

"Let me help you get to the nurse." I reach for her and give her a wet paper towel.

Laney places her hand on my shoulder. We hobble out of the

bathroom and around the corner. She holds herself against me, her arm against mine. Me and Laney, Laney and me. *Friends.*

"I'm just lightheaded, that's all," she whispers, pressing the paper towel against her forehead.

Her face is drained of color. She's so white, as if chiseled from chalk. I could scratch her into dust.

"It's okay," I say. "We're almost there."

She's grabbing me, sweating, although her fingers feel icy. Holy Family, do you see me holding Laney Villanueva up? I am her person to lean on.

"It's a good thing I found you," I say. "You're going to be fine."

We've made it. The nurse is reaching into the fridge, pulling out a bottle of dark amber medicine. There are two kids lying on vinyl loungers, fakers who are only here to cut class. Shame on them.

Laney sinks into the chair beside the nurse's desk. "Nico . . ." Laney says.

I hunch toward her. "I can get him for you."

"I don't know where he is," she says, holding herself around the belly. I know she's wishing for her cell phone, for that connection between her and him. But I'm all she has. I am her lifeline to Nico, the one person who can bring them together. "Maybe physics?" she asks.

He's in AP Euro, room 221, I know.

"I'll find him," I say.

She doubles over, pressing her hands flat against her stomach.

"I'll be fast," I say. "I promise."

I run through the hallway and out the door to cross the courtyard. Crocuses are determined around me, each bud straining to burst open. They'll never be as pretty as roses the color of pointe shoes, hearty and plush. *Plush.*

"Can I have Nico Fiore, please?" I'm panting, handing Mr. McNamara my own office pass from Father Philip. Mr. McNamara slips it onto his desk without a glance. Nico gauges my expression before grabbing his things and following me out.

Already, I'm running with Nico Fiore at my heels. "She's at the nurse."

"What happened?" he's asking. "Is she okay?"

"I don't know." We're rushing back through the garden. The crocuses seem to have opened within the past few seconds. How is that possible? They're absorbing the sun. How dare they bloom while Laney withers?

We reach her. Nico crouches at Laney's knees. "What happened?" he asks.

She doesn't answer. She only hugs her middle and cries into his neck. Laney's hair encircles them. I can't look away. I cannot look away from love.

"What's the problem here?" the nurse asks coldly. Fakers have sucked the compassion out of her.

Nico raises his head. "She won't say."

"She's lightheaded," I answer. "She's bleeding with cramps."

Nico looks at me. His face crumbles.

"All right, then," the nurse says.

"But—" I don't know anything about anything, but I know what a lot of blood looks like, and I know it shouldn't be happening to her.

"You can go," the nurse says to me. "Go on."

"I'm staying," Nico says, holding his girlfriend's hands.

Laney looks weak and afraid with her feet tucked beneath her chair on tiptoes. She should be dancing, not huddled over like this.

I remember third grade, going to the nurse with a bloody nose. The blood stopped after fifteen minutes, maybe ten, but I held that tissue on my face, kept on smashing my nose with it because I didn't want to go back to class. We'd been doing division, and I couldn't understand how the number on the outside of the "house" was related to the number on the inside. I stayed in the nurse's office until I knew my class was about to leave for music. I'm sorry I faked it. I'm sorry.

It's not her period, I want to say, but I can't. It's not my blood this time. "Can't I stay, too?" I ask. "I want to make sure she's all right."

"You can call her after school," the nurse snaps. "Get to class."

I walk slowly north toward the stairwell. From the roof, I'll be able to watch the parking lot and look out for Laney and Nico if they leave the building.

My hand is on the doorknob when I smell it: fresh paint. I want to weep before I even open the door. I want to sob for a loss so dark that I can't see the bottom.

There's nothing left in the stairwell. No one left. There's only a lifeless blank wall staring back at me. They've all been painted over—the couples of the past, who lived and breathed and loved at Holy Family, including Bianca Wickham and Carlo Tedoro—are gone. I will never find them. And I forgot to take a picture.

It's sunny and crisp and cruel on the roof. Every inch of infinity is bright blue. But something precious I can't explain has been lost. It won't be found again no matter how clear the sky.

34

My Laney,
I'll wait for you on the roof every day. Please
come.
Love,
Nico

Laney has been back for three weeks after two days out sick, but she still hasn't spoken to him. I know this sounds impossible, since there are over two thousand kids at Holy Family, but somehow the school is quieter and sadder. I still see them hanging out in the same circle, trying to act normal in public, but I don't know if they're warming up to each other or if they're just playing their roles to keep up appearances. They aren't touching or joking anymore. They're just . . . there.

So Nico and I are here, waiting for Laney on the roof, where we've been every day, just as he promised. Nico is sitting in the corner, listening to his music. I'm hidden behind the machines with my back against the brick wall and my feet tucked in.

It's cold today, colder than yesterday, colder than the day before. Early spring can be tricky this way. I should have brought my gym sweatshirt to put over my legs. Today is day *nine* of waiting on the roof for Laney. *Nine.* That's a lot of days in limbo. I'm actually reading up here, surprise, surprise. It's the only place I've ever been able to concentrate on a book. *Lord of the Flies:* what a downer this book is, and what an embarrassment of an essay Bianca wrote about it. She copied half the paper from the *Cliff's Notes* that were in her desk. The other half is gibberish, "fraught with symbols of good versus evil and asks the battles of which one we are at the core." Really, Bianca? What?

Nico's playlist covers the sound when I turn pages. The bad thing about his music is that it's so depressing—every song says *I'll die without you* in a different way.

He's lost weight. His uniform pants are looser. He might be using a tighter hole in his belt. And Laney, she looks fine by any normal standards, but there's a faraway look in her eyes, as if she isn't fully present. I'm certain that no one else sees what I see. Beauty hides so much pain.

I think Nico is doing homework. At least, he's trying to do some today. I can hear him on his laptop. Every few minutes, he's clicking away. Between paragraphs, he mumbles, "Come on, Laney," or "Where are you, Laney?"

There are hairline cracks in the concrete at my feet. I'm starting to pretend that the cracks are streets and waterways for a miniature town. The pebbles are houses; the broken pieces of asphalt are buildings. Millie would see it. She would see a water tower, and an outdoor marketplace, an amusement park with a Ferris wheel, and a church steeple.

I wonder what Millie is doing right now. She's probably

cleaning out her school desk in order to win a booklet of expired coupons. If I babysit for her again, *when* I babysit for her again, I'll ask her how Nico has been at home. Distracted? Short-tempered? Depressed? And what about her parents? How have they been acting lately? I'd like to find out if they know what happened.

The song on Nico's playlist is fading into the next. I know the voice. It's Elvis, the man who brought Laney and Nico together. It's clear to me now. This is the song, the one Nico sang at Gabby Hollis's party last year. Gabby pulled his name from the catcher's helmet, he stood at the front of the room, grabbed the mic, and serenaded his heart out. Laney, on the sofa with Tomás, looked up at Nico as he sang "I Can't Help Falling in Love with You" directly to her. And that was game over for Tomás Diaz. Nico made Laney notice him. In that instant, Laney Villanueva became Nico Fiore's girl.

Nico is singing softly for her now, probably remembering that very moment he won her heart. His voice is shaky and muffled. I lift my head, just the tiniest bit until I catch a glimpse of him with his face in his hands. "Please come," he says between verses. "Please come and call my name, just say it."

There's a push against the door. If it's Dorian and Metal with a joint, I might scream. The knob is turning. The door is creaking open. I duck low and hug my shins. Nico scrambles to his feet.

"You came," he says. His footsteps move toward her. The song, their song, worked. She's here. Laney's movement is cautious, unhurried. "God, Laney, I knew you would."

"Don't."

"I can't hug you?"

Silence.

"It's windy. Here, do you want my sweatshirt?"

"No."

"Are you sure?"

She isn't moving. No one is moving. *Say something.* Their feet shuffle.

"I've missed you so much."

Stillness.

"Can I at least give you this?"

One step forward. One step back. What did he give her?

Tell him you missed him, too. Say his name. Say it. Say everything.

"I'm so sorry, Laney. I'm so sorry you had to go through this. It's my fault."

"I don't blame you." Her voice is wooden, hollow.

"Then why wouldn't you talk to me? I left voicemails. I called your landline. I spoke to your parents. It's been weeks."

"I didn't want to talk. I still don't want to talk."

"Okay. We won't talk about it, then. We can just be together now and things can go back to the way they were."

The way they were—*Laney, singing her vowels, ahhh and ohhh. Nico, watching her from afar. Nico, smiling in a burgundy smoking jacket, Laney, clutching a stuffed puppy.* None of us can go back in time. Even I know that this hourglass is too heavy to flip.

"We can't do that. Don't you get it?" She stomps. "We can never go back to how we were."

Laney, resting her head on my counter. Nico, pushing her hair behind her ear.

"Then we'll be stronger."

"No. Everything's different now."

"I'm not different. I'm the same."

"But *I'm* not," Laney cries.

Him, gyrating his hips during karaoke. Her, spinning turn leaps across the stage.

"You're the same to *me*," Nico says.

"I'm telling you that I'm different! Why won't you listen to me?"

"I'm listening. I'm sorry. I am. Tell me, Laney. Tell me how you've changed, and I'll love you the new way."

"You *know* how I've changed! Do you really need me to say it? Is that what you want? You want me to tell you? I'll tell you," she yells. "One day I was auditioning for dance programs and highlighting my hair. And then the next day I was pregnant but I didn't want to be, so the baby died! That's how I've changed!"

"Oh, god, no. Don't do that to yourself. You didn't cause it. You didn't make it happen. Do you hear me? It wasn't your fault. It just wasn't healthy . . . it wasn't the right time, not yet . . . but everything's going to be okay now . . ."

"Stop it!"

"What?"

"You can't just hug me and think that's going to fix it. It doesn't work that way."

"I'm not trying to fix it." He sighs. "I'm just trying to be in this with you. Because I am. It happened to me too . . . it was part of me, too. We can go through this together, and we can be closer than we were before."

She's crying softly now.

"Can't you see that I'll love you more? I'll love you better."

"No!"

"No what? I don't know what you want."

"I just want to forget about it!"

"Laney, I—"

"I want to forget this year ever happened."

Nico, rushing down the hallway carrying pink roses in the air. Laney, laughing as they walk down the front steps. Nico, clutching his chest as he watches her arabesque to "This Year's Love."

"What about *us?*" Nico asks, breathing hard. "Are you saying you want to forget about *me?*"

Silence.

"Yes."

"Laney. No. Come on, don't," Nico begs. "Please don't do this."

"You need to let us go . . . just . . . please, let me go."

"I can't do that . . ."

"I'm sorry."

I press my forehead against my knees. The door opens heavily and then aches painfully back into place. She's running away, away, away.

I thought that the secret moments I witnessed—his fingertips across her back, their afternoon shadows on the roof—were the beginning of a love story. Laney and Nico had uncountable years ahead to be in love. How could I have been wrong?

"Fuuuck!" Nico screams into his hands.

She didn't say his name, not once, not a single time. She's already trying to forget. "Please don't break up with me, Laney. Please don't leave me," Nico repeats, again and again, as he smacks the brick wall. "Please don't leave me . . ."

He wants to break something, he wants to shatter something into sharp, vein-piercing shards, but there's nothing up here to break.

Only his heart.

And mine.

35

Nico slams the roof door shut. But nothing will stop me from getting to Laney, nothing. I climb down the rain gutter, skinning my knees against the brick, just as Laney and Nico did, back when it was romantic and funny. The second my feet hit the grass, I run all the way around the building and rush back inside.

"Laney!" I scream. The school bell rings, reverberating through my body.

She's hurrying through the hallway toward the side door. I can reach her with my track-team speed. I've listened to all the girl rap songs, memorized the one about not needing a man for a dollar. I'm fast, so fast, I'm going to win a medal.

I decipher one person in the sea of faces—he's watching Laney too, studying her as she hurries past him—Tomás Diaz. Yes, Tomás, Laney is shattered. This is what you've been hoping for. Laney and Nico have broken up. But you don't get it. She's further from you now than she has ever been. What Laney and Nico have shared is so painful that it's impenetrable. She will never, ever be yours.

I catch her by the arm. "Laney! You guys can't break up! You have to go back to him!" I yell at her because I cannot yell at my father from a thousand miles away, or my mother, whose five-dollar bills add up to nothing but uneaten onion rings that do not warm up just fine. How will it work for anyone if not for Laney Villanueva and Nico Fiore?

"Were you *spying* on us?" She pulls away. She doesn't understand that their love is the rarest of all.

"No. I . . . I overheard."

"You were on the roof?" She glares daggers at me. "How could you?"

"I only want you to be happy." Over sixteen years ago, the Cutest Couple broke up because of me. This time, I can bring them back together.

Laney steps back. "There is something seriously wrong with you."

"No," I say. "I care about you, that's all."

"Are you in love with me or something?" she scoffs at me.

"Homewrecker!" someone yells.

"It's not like that," I insist. "I love you *both*."

"Gross!" someone says.

"Threesome!" yells another.

I don't care what these people think. They're nobodies. Try to find them in the yearbook, it'll be nearly impossible, they don't matter.

Back off, back off.

"I mean"—I want to tell her that she and Nico are special to me and that I want to be special to them, but I don't want to cross the line—"I love you both because . . . we're friends."

"Friends?" Laney's voice is ice-cold. "We barely know you."

She's staring at me the way I stare at Greta Novak, as if I am the one who's annoying—as if I am the gnat.

"But you invited me to your party," I remind her.

"What party?" she asks.

What party? "At Fernando's!" I yell.

"That was a thank-you for Leadership Club," Laney says. "I invited everyone who donated clothes."

"That's . . . that's not true." She wanted me there, me specifically, exclamation point! We are friends! "But . . . I stamped your late passes, Laney." I point at my chest. "I gave you ninth-period study hall. I took your picture on Halloween, and in the window seat. I *made* you the Cutest Couple."

"What?" Her face is still pretty, so pretty, even when she's confused.

"I stole MacGraw for you."

She squints at me. "You shouldn't have done that."

"Nico wanted to drive her," I say. "He grabbed the keys."

"He grabbed the keys because you were acting like a lunatic. He thought you were on drugs," Laney says. "We stopped at the golf course to give you time to come off your high."

She's mistaken. The full moon lit up the night; it pulled at us. Our blood, like the tide, swelled as one.

"No," I insist. But I remember seeing that look in Nico's eyes when he took the keys. I'd seen it before, that first morning. What was that look? I was holding their late passes, and they were trying to pull them away. I push the image to the back of my mind. I don't want to know.

"We played EXO," I say. "It was the best night of our lives."

"*Our?*" Laney backs away. "You're delusional."

She's speaking to me the way Jenna did.

"Don't say that," I say. "I only wanted to be near you. I saw the way you and Nico looked at each other after your first time. You're supposed to last forever, like my parents should have. That's why I prayed at your audition. If you stay together, it'll make up for everything. You're supposed to *be the light!*"

She's not listening. She's escaping, zigzagging, through the crowd. Why does everybody leave? "I donated my heart to you!"

"Creep!" someone yells.

Others laugh.

"Weirdo!"

You're a stalker.

Back off, back off . . . too involved. You need help. You should talk to Father Philip.

"Don't run away from me. I found you, Laney Villanueva! I found you in the bathroom when you were bleeding!"

Laney whips around. Her ponytail swirls over her shoulders the way it does when she pirouettes, she's so lovely. I keep her yellow hair tie on my nightstand. "Shut up, Rafi, I swear to god, if you don't shut the hell up right now—"

"Nico loves you so much and forever," I plead. "Your skin makes him cry!"

Laney's black eyes are clear and wild. This is the look, the one on Nico's face that morning. I know what it means now.

Fear.

"What did you say?" she asks.

"Don't be embarrassed. Friends don't have secrets." I step closer.

"You're crazy!" she yells.

My heart stops.

"Don't call me that. That's a cruel thing to say, Laney." I grab her and pull her toward me. I can't bear that word from her lips. "I'm your *friend*."

"Get the fuck off me!" Laney shrieks, twisting violently. Her hair clings to my lip gloss.

"Listen to me! I'm trying to help you!" I dig my fingers into her flesh. "I'm a *really cool girl!*"

She wails, wrenching herself from my grip. She turns, and then bolts into the street.

In a flash, I see Nico's eyes and Nico's knuckles on the steering wheel, right before his Jeep slams against Laney's body, sending her flying across the pavement. Her tote bag bursts open. Notebooks, ballet slippers, clementines, index cards fly in every direction. She lands on the ground like a rag doll. Papers float gently down. At my feet, an envelope: *For Laney*. I pick it up and shove it into my pocket.

Jenna appears beside me, her jaw open. Screams and cries pierce the air around me. Nico's door swings open.

"Laney!"

"Oh my god!"

"Somebody help!"

"Call 911!"

"No! No, no, no, no!" Nico is upon her. "Please, please, please, no, please."

It's so beautiful. All he wanted was one hug. Now he's stroking her hair, her face, her arms that are red with scratches, he's touching her so lovingly, so delicately. Her limp, perfect body. Laney Villanueva is in Nico Fiore's arms where she belongs.

Trembling, Nico lifts his head, searching for help. He opens his mouth, soundless. His eyes meet mine. His tears are about to fall.

"You're welcome," I say.

"Oh fuck, oh fuck," Tomás says, holding his forehead with both hands. The afternoon sun shines behind him, carving his perfect silhouette. I lift my phone and take his picture.

I did it. I finished the yearbook! And I brought the Cutest Couple back together. Where is Father Philip? I want to tell him what I've done. Suddenly, I realize that I'm Wednesdays. Father Philip, licensed child and adolescent therapist, counsels Monica Reilly on Mondays, Aaron Page on Tuesdays, and me while we clean the birdcages on Wednesdays. There are such good people in the world. He's going to be so proud of me.

I turn my camera on myself. This time, I smile.

Click.

Send.

"Has everyone ordered a yearbook?" I ask. Faces turn to stare at me. I can really sell it now. "I laid out 3,107 photos. We're all frozen in time before everything goes wrong. Buy a yearbook! You'll see."

"Rafi . . ." Jenna's hand falls on my shoulder. "Take it easy. Someone called for help."

In the distance, sirens. They're coming. They're coming quickly. Wait. Give me this moment—let me look at them.

Nico cries over Laney, her motionless legs splayed on the asphalt, his shoulders shaking uncontrollably. The crowd multiplies. They want to see the love, the love, the love, that's pouring out of him and onto her. It's spreading through us all.

Look at what I've given them—ten extra minutes together, just like old times.

Everyone is here, including young Bianca and young Carlo, who have appeared, finally, so clearly in my mind. They're simply radiant among the crowd. "Mom and Dad," I whisper, "I fixed it!"

One Year Later

I've been doing well at Our Lady of Grace, so well. I'm fantastic. Greta Novak would be amazed by how many invitations I get. Not that I'm going to Tessa Rubin's barbecue at 3:00. No way. I have someplace much more important to be. Greta. Ha! I haven't thought of her in a long time.

I'm only three stops away. The subway smells like sour milk and Cheetos, but at least it's speeding along. I should stand and wait near the doors so I can hop right off. My adrenaline is pumping. I haven't felt this hyped since . . .

Two stops away.

Tessa Rubin doesn't even like me. I'm onto her. She only wants her barbecue in my yearbook feature: "Weekends." She's one of those who believes the old rumors, so screw her and her party. She and everyone else should get this straight once and for all—I wasn't "kicked out" of Holy Family. The assholes who scrawled YOU DID IT, DIE, and CREEP! across my locker were kicked out. I transferred.

One stop.

Jenna and Tomás Diaz said it was an accident, and security cameras don't lie. I'm done repeating it. Done. Accidents happen. It's so sad.

I didn't want to transfer. Father Philip didn't want me to, either. Holy Family was my home. I sold a record number of yearbooks. But Poppy said he should've put his foot down seventeen years ago, and I hated fighting with him about it. His wrinkles were getting deeper. And poor Gran, she couldn't hear her show over our arguing. I was turning into Bianca. I couldn't put them through that again. Giving in was the right thing to do. I accomplished something at Holy Family that means more to me than a diploma anyway. So, this is how it's done, Mom: a fresh start. Watch me. I'm thriving.

I'm here.

The theater is two blocks west, which is . . . that way. I'm tingling all over. There's nothing like spring in New York City. Can you feel it? The energy? The possibility?

There's the marquee. One more block. I waited so long for this day. Now that it's here, I can't believe it's real. Feel how fast my heart is beating.

The Desmond Auditorium. I made it. The line steps forward. I present my ticket to the usher. My hands are shaking. He scans the bar code. (EXCUSED)

I'm in.

Leaning forward on my lumpy seat, I scan each row, from the first to the last, from left to right. I'm sure he isn't here, but I can't help but look.

The lights are dimming. *I'm here. I'm here. I'm here.* A blue glow appears. It morphs into hazy violet, and then soft, pale pink. Scattered applause. The music begins. It's a string quartet, as if nothing at all has changed. Nothing has. No matter what uniform I wear, Bianca and Carlo, Laney and Nico, and I, are a Holy Family, whether our names are on a wall or not.

The curtain rises. One dancer strides across the stage, chin up. Two dancers now, then three, four . . .

I gasp.

There she is. In real life. Her body. Her movement. Her hair, black again, loose and wavy. That gorgeous line from her hand, down through her leg. Her face.

I'm found.

Every single day I searched high and low for an update, a photo, a comment, a location, anything. Poppy had said I'd have fewer distractions at Our Lady of Grace. He was right, even if it wasn't in the way he'd intended. I haven't been distracted from her at all. After a year without a trace, not even at her house, I finally found this, the Student Choreography Showcase. Oh, how I've missed her. Laney Villanueva.

I still recognize her triple pirouette and the extension of her arm as she unravels, so graceful. The new stiffness in her back and neck are not my fault. I'm sure no one else notices anyway. She'll probably recover with more time. That afternoon, I only tried to pull her close to make her hear me, to make her understand how much I cared, how much I'd done for her, but she refused to listen. She wouldn't stand still. It's hard to hold Laney Villanueva, remember—she's a dancer. And I understand now that sometimes, there's love behind letting go.

Her back and neck aren't the only differences I see in her. The joy is gone. She dances from a different place now—from a sadness so deep that her subtlest gestures bring a lump to my throat. She is so lucky, isn't she? She's more captivating than ever.

I hurry down the steps and toward the dressing room, squeezing past costumes on rolling racks and dancers who are stretching against the wall.

That's her. I recognize her back, of course I do, as she winds her hair into a bun. Her faded blue leotard dips into a low V. She's slick with sweat, her $S \ldots K \ldots I \ldots N$.

This is it, exactly as I imagined.

I step closer. "Laney?"

She turns carefully, keeping her neck still.

Our eyes lock. She freezes, stone white. She hasn't forgotten me. Now she never will.

I reach into my purse. "I have something for you."

Dear Laney,

I hope to do a lot of things in my lifetime. I'll row a boat on a glassy lake at sunrise. I'll sing on a TV talent contest and not get laughed at, hopefully. (I've always wanted to do that but was too embarrassed to tell you.) I'll travel through Europe with a bright orange backpack and a leather notebook that wraps with a string, and I'll tape my train tickets inside it. I'll have a job that helps people but doesn't break my soul. Maybe I'll move across the country and live beside a different ocean until it no longer feels as if the ocean is on the wrong side.

I'm sure that my life will be both beautiful and heartbreaking. But nothing will hold the same note of sadness that I feel right now as you push me away.

Every day I pray for you to meet me on the roof, but I'm afraid of what you'll say when you do come. I'm scared that you don't want this any-

more, that you're done with me, with us, with who we are and who we could be. I'm scared that I'll never be able to tell you all the things I want to say, so I'm writing them here.

If you want to move on, I'll have to accept that. But I want you to know that singing Elvis to you was the single greatest move I ever made. And, ten years from now, twenty years from now, fifty years from now, if I'm fortunate enough to be around, I'll still cherish everything that came after, even if you won't. Someday, I'll come across our old yearbook, and I'll see photos of us. We'll look so young, you and me, like babies to my aging eyes. A picture of us in the window seat, your gorgeous arabesque at senior banquet, you and me and our friends in our pajamas, with my pipe and your stuffed puppy, and us as Cutest Couple . . . wasn't that something? It'll be funny, in a way, to look at my young self with my hair sprayed white when I'm an old man with my hair actually white.

I'll see our faces and our smiles. It'll seem like no time at all has passed, even though there will have been decades of days and nights apart and millions of breaths taken without you. In an instant, I'll feel like we're together again. I'll remember the newness and the wonder of us.

Maybe I'll remember this pain. I know that I will, because right now I can't imagine it ever going away. I'll remember the sting of you slipping out of my arms and starting your life without me. It'll feel

*as if I'm losing you all over again. But mostly what
I'll remember is how lucky I was to have loved you,
Laney Villanueva . . . so much and forever.*
   Always,
   Your Nico

I must've read Nico's letter over a thousand times since the day it floated at my feet like a present. I'll keep my copy, but I won't need it. I like reciting it to myself by heart—not only the words, but also every pause and every pulse in between—every feeling. It reminds me, without a doubt, that I'm special to Laney Villanueva and Nico Fiore. I am somebody to them, the one who gives the gift of time. Even when they're old, it will still be me. I will still be the one who brings them back to those glorious days of last year's love. I am not crazy. I am Rafi Wickham. I am the best.